Something Lovely

by

Alan Weatherley

DREAMCATCHER PUBLISHING
Saint John • New Brunswick • Canada

DreamCatcher Publishing acknowledges the support of the New Brunswick Arts Council. We acknowledge the support of the Government of Canada through the Book Publishing Industry Development Program (BPIDP) for our publishing activities.

Canadian Cataloguing in Publication Data

Weatherley, Alan - 1928

Something Lovely

ISBN - 1-894372-27-1
1. Title.
PS8595.E165S64 2003   C813'.6   C2003-903642-1

Editor: Yvonne Wilson

Typesetter: Chas Goguen

Cover Design: Dawn Drew, INK Graphic Design Services Corp.

Printed and bound in Canada

DREAMCATCHER PUBLISHING INC.
1 Market Square
Suite 306 Dockside
Saint John, New Brunswick, Canada E2L 4Z6
www.dreamcatcher.nb.ca

For Bobbie, for her sustained interest in a story
she has known about for years, for her careful
checking of the manuscript and for her suggestions
about the ending - and, always, for her support.

Other Works by Alan Weatherley

Fiction:

The World That Is - DreamCatcher Publishing (2002)
Short stories in The Toronto Star short fiction contests, and in The
New Brunswick Reader

Non-Fiction:

Articles in The New Brunswick Reader

Scientific Books:

Australian Inland Waters and their Fauna: Eleven Studies, A.H.
Weatherley, Editor, 1967, Australian National University Press.

Growth and Ecology of Fish Populations, by A.H. Weatherley,
1972, Academic Press.

The Biology of Fish Growth, by A.H. Weatherley & H.S. Gill,
1987, Academic Press.

Acknowledgements

I wish to thank all those who read this novel in its manuscript form. *Something Lovely* is a work of fiction and it has not been possible to incorporate every suggestion or criticism received, but I am especially indebted to Mr Alexander Lilly (Test Pilot and former Vice President of Canadair), Commander Peter Savage (R.N. Fleet Air Arm), Mr Cam McNeil (former Flying Officer, R.C.A.F.) for their comments on the final manuscript with particular attention to its technical aspects. And my special thanks goes to Mr. Alex Henshaw (Chief Test Pilot of Spitfires during WW II) for his comments on a much earlier version of *Something Lovely*.

My sincere thanks, again, to Yvonne Wilson for her editorial efforts, especially in advising me to make major revisions of the initial version of this novel. It was hard work, but I think she was right. My thanks too to Elizabeth Margaris for her enthusiastic encouragement.

Success four flights Thursday morning against twentyone mile wind started from level with engine power alone average speed through air thirtyone miles longest 57 seconds inform press home Christmas.

Orevelle Wright

(The above telegram, sent to the Wright brothers' father, Bishop Wright, contained two transmission errors: the name should have been Orville and the longest flight lasted 59 seconds.)

Chapter 1

Over many years people have asked me what it was like to grow up in Sydney. I usually mention ocean beaches, Sydney Harbour, the benign climate, the frequency of high, clear and blue skies. Plus the fact that Sydney, even before 1920, was already a large, modern, 20th Century city, with new suburbs growing out in many directions from its core, the Harbour ferry terminal at Circular Quay.

Most Sydney people took the remarkable skies for granted, but after 1920 many more were looking up at them than in the past because now aeroplanes frequently roared and circled over the Harbour and nearly everyone understood that the Air Age had arrived in Australia.

My own initial excitement at these sounds and sightings was further kindled when my parents took me to see at close hand the shaking, bellowing biplanes at Mascot, Sydney's new airport. But what really turned me on was getting to know a builder of flying model aeroplanes when I was ten and he was seventeen.

Our house was high on a hill in a pleasant, sea-breezy suburb, and we had great views across the Harbour to the large buildings of the city centre. Charlie, my model-building hero, lived across the road.

From the first moment I had seen him at work, testing his models in the long, safe grass of an adjacent empty allotment, I was hooked. All it needed was my mother's "Charlie's out there flying his planes again," to send me wildly racing out to see.

"G'day, Rob," he would say in his quiet, unemphatic, friendly way. He tolerated me very well, this slim, handsome youth, who rapidly became my idol.

The models Charlie made were simple enough. Design and building of flying models was in its infancy and his planes' bodies consisted of stick-like, twin-booms of light wood, a "pusher" propeller at the rear end of each boom, the direction of rotation of each opposed to the other. The wing was in front of the propellers and the horizontal stabilizers were in front of the wing – the so-called "canard" configuration.

One thing troubled me about Charlie. When his planes were less than fully successful he destroyed them in what seemed to me wanton acts, because I – or several other kids who sometimes watched him – would have given almost anything to have a few such failures to play with. Later I realized he destroyed them because he wanted to leave no evidence of something botched.

*   *   *

My grandmother was a venerable country woman who came from Grafton, a town on the Clarence River in northern New South Wales. She had lived there until, in early middle age, her blacksmith husband had been told that her blood pressure was dangerously high and that she should move to the "cooler climate down south." My grandfather loved her deeply and unhesitatingly sold his modestly thriving blacksmith business so they could move to Sydney. Though cooler than Grafton in the winter, Sydney can have very hot summers. Anyway, my grandmother lived in essentially robust health to the age of eighty seven; I never knew what happened to her blood pressure. But her husband, a highly skilled country blacksmith, could find no job in a Sydney that no longer required his abilities. He was compelled to work at the only occupation he could get – wielding a heavy hammer at a forge in the repair shop of a coastal steamship company. He worked there into his old age, until he sickened and died of double pneumonia – a classic blacksmiths' condition brought on by a lifetime of exposure to the fumes from the forge. He was sixty eight when he died, and my grandmother outlived him – stoic about his death while always revering his memory – by nineteen healthy years.

My grandmother – "Nannie" to me – was widely respected in our neighbourhood for her quiet country manners, self-possession and dignity. She continued to occupy the small, pleasant house where she and my grandfather had lived – just sixty yards from my parents' home. I always loved her for her constant and empathic devotion to me in my childhood. That love – as I look back – was not very different from the love I felt for the sandstone cliffs, trees and sea of Sydney. They were reliable natural entities, ruggedly handsome, quiet, always there . . . as was my grandmother.

For months after I got to know Charlie, my grandmother had seen me dragging around in his wake, like a cattle pup at a drover's heel. I spent the evening before my eleventh birthday in her house and we played cards – euchre and five hundred; both of them games she had taught me. I slept that night as usual in the bedroom where my grandfather, whom I had also loved, died four years before. When I woke on my birthday – a clear, bright March morning – my grandmother's gift awaited me, perched in the middle of the dark oak dining room table. Its three-foot, tissue-covered wings were lacquered a brilliant red. It was like most of the flying model aircraft of the time, ungainly, lacking grace. But it was lovely. It was mine. And though of unadorned design, the finish of the whole plane was uniquely Charlie's – that of a master model builder.

My grandmother had, of course, commissioned Charlie to build this plane and, an hour later, as my joy ran not far below the level of hysteria, the builder himself arrived. "I'm supposed to show you the ropes," he announced quietly, but almost sternly. I was terrified and begged him to fly the plane for me. But Charlie was relentless, and off we went to the vacant allotment where, quietly but firmly, he instructed me . . .

By now, though I felt myself in a state of grace, I was far too excited to master the skill required for a simple hand launch. I kept awkwardly thrusting the plane down in shallow dives it could not recover from. Down, down it would go in the long dry grass. Then there was damage – a couple of holes punched in the red covering tissue by stiff dry grass stalks of late summer. I was mortified with shame and angry with Charlie at being – as I felt – *forced* to damage this shining perfect object. It seemed like more of his perverse ways with his own creatures.

I went on finding it impossible to launch the plane and, in my blend of rage and fear, excitement and frustration, coordination deserted me. Seeking to encourage me by demonstrating what the plane was capable of, Charlie himself eventually launched it on a couple of short flights that demonstrated its essential airworthiness. But soon I managed a crash in which the plane struck a concealed rock that damaged its starbord wing and ended further trials.

Charlie wanted to encourage me. He soon took me and the repaired aeroplane to the huge green open space of Centennial Park where, when the playing fields were not in use, scores of aeromodellers convened to flaunt and fly their wonders on Sunday mornings.

These folk ranged in age from fourteen to seventy – enthusiastic children all. Before seeing them I had thought Charlie unique, a plane builder of incredible skill. But here, among fifty of his peers, were several who were his equals, a few his clear superiors. I felt awash in riches. Almost crazy with delight.

Though Charlie would remain my favourite and idol, I realized that here were the ill-assorted members of a tribe . . . a family. Perhaps a family I could join. I felt a sort of love for them, even for those few who were tough-looking, rough-talking characters.

Everywhere rubber motors were being wound under tension on devices that resembled egg-beaters, twisted nearly to snapping point, then fitted to the twin-boom, "stick" fuselages of the planes they were to power. The planes, once launched, driven by their wound-up motors and aided by even the slightest of rising air currents, could rise to surprising heights, until their motors ran down and they glided to the ground.

These were early days in what would eventually become a boom in model aircraft building, and of course these models looked extremely crude in shape and form compared to full scale aircraft; in fact they more resembled the planes at the dawn of the Air Age, twenty years before. But to me, as I saw them against the bright sky, the ribs of their wings showing through their covering of translucent tissue, they seemed beautiful. I could even see the knots in the tightly wound rubber motors gradually slacken as they surrendered their stored power that these unlikely creatures – of which they were the black twisted hearts – might, for a short time, tread their uncertain pathways in the sky.

Chapter 2

When he'd got used to seeing me often, Charlie let me come into his garage to watch him at work. He had a bench under a window and in bins there were thin strips and sheets of light wood and special sharp knives and little saws he used to cut from the sheets the wing ribs and other forms he needed for building. There were little jars of liquid cement and sheets of special tissue paper for covering the planes, bottles of dope for tightening and strengthening the tissue, and paints for colouring it. I watched him work, marvelling as he carved and smoothed a propeller by hand from a block of light wood – wondering how I could ever achieve similar skill.

I began to guess he was probably not much of a scholar. He was of an age when he should be preparing to matriculate, but as far as I could tell, all his time after school went into crafting new model planes. I felt sure that within a few years he would be at work building real ones. If he did that, I wondered if I could someday join him.

He had a brother who was a lot older. He told me this brother – a sturdy, black- moustached man who wore glasses – was a lawyer. When I first saw the brother, and usually thereafter, he wore a well-cut suit, a hat, and carried a leather briefcase. He seemed pleasant enough, but I was wary about him. Because how could it be possible that Charlie could have a brother who was like this? What would *he* know or care about planes? No more than my own father, who was an accountant, who also wore a business suit and hat – even in the Sydney summer – and who, for recreation, played golf and sang in a male choir; and thought all aeroplanes were just "noisy bloody things".

But I needn't have worried about the brother, because a year or so after I first got to know him, and apparently without prompting from anyone, Charlie stopped building model planes, concentrating belatedly on his studies instead. And then, with his schoolwork over, he went into the hive of downtown Sydney to become a solicitor's clerk . . . wearing a suit.

So now Charlie was this man, this person who looked very serious and went off to business every day and had an adult-seeming social life. And I had been left behind . . .

* * *

Charlie had encouraged me in my dream of becoming a member of the model builders' club: "Start building something very simple, Bob. I can let you have a couple of plans and enough tools and materials. Don't get too fancy too soon. That's a mistake; you'll just get discouraged. When you're twelve I'll get you into the club."

But when I had built a few simple things, and was having many troubles getting them to fly decently, and was about to turn twelve, he was long out of it all, surfing and golfing in his leisure time. He forgot about his promise, and I lost the momentum I was beginning to get. And afterwards, Charlie's whole family moved to Melbourne and I never saw him again.

It had been my first experience of knowing someone who had appeared to love and be absorbed by his work, but who completely jettisoned his passion when faced with the requirements of making a living in the "real world". I pondered on what impelled people to do things like that. I decided it could not happen to me.

* * *

I attended a Presbyterian boys' school, where there was somewhat arbitrary discipline, achievement of excellence in rote learning and a powerful emphasis on organized sports (at which the school's teams excelled). I knew no one there who had any interest in aeromodelling.

As for making planes myself, I was certainly put off this by Charlie's departure. But I never discarded the dream of flight. At the school library I read the entry on the principles of aeronautics in the Encyclopaedia Britannica, and soon I began to travel by tram on Sunday afternoons to the Mitchell Library in the city, where I found several relevant volumes. These books could not be borrowed, so I returned on many Sundays to read them and make notes.

I read about the history of flight from the times when people jumped from buildings with crude wings strapped to their bodies – and sometimes to their arms. What seemed astonishing was that, having expended so much energy, ingenuity and time on their inventions, men seemed willing – almost eager – to risk their lives without some prior testing of those inventions.

But among all these historical readings a pattern of argument emerged. There was a line of men stretching back to ancient Greece – maybe even to the Egyptians – who dreamed of flight with an unquenchable enthusiasm. They had watched birds and bats and insects and had concluded human flight was realizable by the proper application of mechanics, if only the relationship between moving objects, and the properties of the air that must support them, could be finally made out.

Yet there was a second line – a line of unyielding sceptics, frequently scornful – who pointed to a history of rubbish heaps of fallen wood and fabric, blood, broken bones and death.

But the sentiments of the optimists were strong: "Humans will one day fly as birds fly, soaring at will among cloud castles, outstripping the birds for speed and grace, crossing dark oceans, unlimited by forests, mountains. We *will,* one day, fly!"

The sceptics' rebuttal was blunt. "Human self-deception and foolery are as old as the hills. If we were intended to fly, a generous God would have given us wings."

In the end it all came down to the 19th Century, when engineers became capable of building steam-powered locomotives and ships. And some engineers built small, light engines powered by steam, and later benzene, that could drive the experimental aircraft that they, or others, constructed – aircraft that, though tethered and unmanned, could, in a certain, circumscribed sense, fly.

Then, in some strange way, there appeared two clever American bicycle-makers. With nothing but a high school education behind them, these Wright brothers found the insight, the uncanny ingenuity, the drive to study bird flight, and to develop models and gliders and test them scientifically. Their study and work led at last to their building a heavier-than-air machine, an aeroplane manned by a human pilot, with more or less complete control of flight.

So they flew, modest but self-confident, their personal lives always essentially mysterious. And notoriously few of their fellow-Americans – members of a nation reputedly peopled by daring and ingenious mechanics – believed, for some time, that they had done so. This disbelief, however, affected more than the broad public, whose scientific ignorance was some excuse: only a few years before the Wrights, certain mathematicians had published "proofs" of the impossibility of human flight in a heavier-than-air machine.

When I had read until I was getting bored by it, I started watching the flight of birds, using my grandmother's battered, old-fashioned binoculars. Sydney is a maritime city and gulls soar over its waters at every time of the year. I knew the Wright brothers had carefully observed birds in the air and seemed to have gained much from this, but I can't have been a very perceptive observer, because I was unable to distinguish the types of wing and tail movements that resulted in bird aerobatics.

But one significant thing did result from my reading, thinking and observing: I turned again to trying to build flying models, and now sheets and strips of the ultralight wood – balsa – were becoming generally available. And whether it was simply the balsa, which was so easy and lovely to work with, or because I was now nearly fifteen, I began to succeed at levels that had previously eluded me. And the planes I built and flew were from my own designs, though these designs were different from what Charlie had built and from what I had been trying to imitate. For with easily cut balsa strips and parts, glueing them together with rapidly-drying acetone cement, it had become possible to fashion beautiful model planes with shaped, "box" fuselages – light and strong and covered with stretched, doped tissue and undercarriages made of piano wire or cane, with wheels of balsa or thin aluminum.

With growing experience in cutting and shaping balsa, and more patience and skill in finishing my creations, I turned out a line of planes. Some of them were very light and carried a great deal of elastic rubber to store power for long, floating flights at considerable altitude. But as my skill increased I constructed planes that were heavier, because their fuselages were covered by ultrathin balsa sheets that could be fashioned into perfectly streamlined shapes, smoothed and lacquered to a glossy finish. These planes, fitted with smaller, thinner wings, had no great endurance or altitudinal abilities – but, for short times, they could fly remarkably fast.

As far as performance was concerned I had been following the news of the amazing progress in air speed records, particularly as a result of the great series of international competitions for the Schneider Trophy, inaugurated in his name in 1912 by Jacques Schneider – originally an armaments manufacturer, balloonist and speedcar racer. The Schneider Trophy was won by Americans, Italians and, finally by the British Supermarine Company. Think of their final entry, a slim beauty of a seaplane, with a huge engine of more than two thousand horsepower that flew – in 1931 – at three hundred and forty miles per hour. And not long after at well over four hundred miles per hour. This sort of stuff set pulses and minds racing in all model-building kids.

*   *   *

As with all my deepest excitements it was not with my parents, nor with other kids that I shared them, but with my grandmother. And, as always with her, though she was an old woman with a mid-19th century childhood and limited schooling, she somehow managed to understand the way I saw the world, which was what most adults of much greater education, youth and working experience of the modern world failed to do.

Chapter 3

Like the majority of boys at my school, I rarely spoke to teachers unless spoken to. But at the beginning of my last year, following a problem in physics that had aerodynamics implications, I asked our physics master how you could become an aeronautical engineer. He was a haughty Englishman, a formidable disciplinarian, sarcastic but far from stupid, and he could be somewhat frightening, with his pale face, fierce, staring eyes, buck teeth and a deep scar on his left cheek which was reputedly the result of an explosion in a chemistry lab many years earlier. He gazed at me as though he had no idea of who I was, in fact with something like suspicion. Then, apparently deciding my question was innocent and serious, he replied.

"Not possible, really. Not in Australia. If you want to do anything like that you'll have to go abroad."

"Abroad?"

"Yes, to England, or perhaps America. Or, if you can speak German or Italian, there are good designers in those countries."

I had suspected this. But how to get abroad?

He hesitated, apparently to see how I was taking things. "Of course, first you could do an engineering degree here at Sydney University."

"Yes, Sir."

"But that would be a waste of time if you really want aeronautics. Are you keen, or just asking?"

"I . . . I think I may be keen, Sir."

"Then start working, boy! You need very good results. How are your physics and maths?"

"Lous – not too good, Sir."

"Then you'd better start to work. If you work hard enough to do really well in science and mathematics, there are a few scholarships to get you to places like Cambridge."

I thanked him, and went away.

I did begin to work much harder, and my marks did improve. The physics master showed no particular interest in me, and did not mention our brief conversation. I assumed he had forgotten it, or anyway was not concerned about the fate of one of the more nondescript of his pupils. But I did feel gratified because I was beginning to solve problems in physics that would formerly have eluded me. In fact, the entire subject of physics as a science, as a deep way of looking at the world and its natural phenomena, was now starting to force itself on me in ways I had never before imagined.

* * *

"You there, boy, come here." I was being called by my physics master from where he stood outside the half open door of the masters' commonroom. "Yes, Sir."

"You're working, boy. You got ninety eight per cent in that last test. That was a tough test, so your mark is very, very good. Are you really set on this aeronautics idea?"

"I think so, Sir. Yes, I – "

"Keep it up, boy, keep it up. You might manage Cambridge yet."

* * *

By the time I was eighteen – the age Charlie had been when I first saw him – I had made many model planes. I can't compare my skill to what Charlie's had been – a generational shift had occurred to separate the models I was making from those he had made. But my planes could certainly fly well, and I designed them all myself.

Like Charlie before me, I used to test-fly my planes over the grass-covered lot which had not yet been built on. And like Charlie, I often had younger boys watching me and firing questions at me. And like my grandmother, there was a woman, mother of one of the watching kids, who told me how enormously her son worshipped me and my "lovely" models, and would I please build one for him as a birthday surprise, and teach him how to fly it. She asked me how much it would cost, and when I named a price she objected.

"Look," she said, "I really don't know anything about these things, but even I can see how much work and care must go into making them. I'll be happy to pay you at least half as much again as what you're asking."

Well, I made it, and. perhaps spurred on by her praise, I put all my skill to work. If I do say so myself, it was a nice-looking object when it was finished.

I painted it bright red, in homage to Charlie. And again – as Charlie must have done – I transported it secretly to her house the night before the kid's birthday.

Just to round the thing off, as it were, I set it up ready to fly, on a dark, circular table in the living room where it would – we hoped – astonish and delight her son on his birthday morning.

* * *

Cambridge, when I arrived there in 1932 was still the enchanted home of the gilded youth of England. Spoiled rotten, many of them, to my colonial eyes, the feckless smug scions of a part of society that was, at that time, only a little diluted by the offspring of the middle class, or by American and other foreign students, and rough colonials such as I.

Never mind the beauties of the place – they are a given, not less now than then. But to survive there I needed friends. I found them mostly among some British scholarship types, a couple of Indians – merchants' sons from Calcutta, a Yank or two, a Kiwi, even two more ratbag Australians. Apart from that, one needed not to allow oneself to be patronized by the upper class Poms. This I managed, but it wasn't till I'd been there for six months that I was told by one of them – Peter Randall, the son of an earl, who happened to be a very friendly and open youth – that I had not only managed it, but how easily and undeservedly I had managed it.

"The point about you, Robert," he explained one evening at coffee following College dinner, "is that you really are such a bloody unreconstructed primitive."

"Meaning?"

"Oh, that your colonial childhood must have been so coarse-grained you don't even realize it when you've been patronized – so it's no use trying that on with you. Subtle digs are wasted on a rhinoceros like you, old boy. No fun for us. Besides, what do any of us really know of Australia, the Great South Land – former penal colony, home of platypus, wombat and ahh. . . bunyip? We can't *get* at you because we don't *know* you. You see –"

"*Know* me? Sounds a bit like something out of the Old Testament. Maybe it goes along with 'not sparing the rod' and other great stuff you Public School types get sentimental about."

"See, I told you," he roared. "You're an impervious brute, Robert." His loud laughter was turning heads our way.

"Jesus!" I said, reaching for the coffee pot.

* * *

The subject of Aeronautical Engineering had been introduced in Cambridge in 1919, just after The Great War. Professor Bennett Melvill Jones had been appointed as its head and remained till 1935. His place in the history of aviation design was secured by his demonstrations of the importance of streamlining in high performance aircraft, knowledge of which had been used by all the designers and builders of planes designed to break speed records since about 1925.

Of the two best of my instructors, one was a theoretician who had received prestigious awards for his research on the dynamics of wing forms and had been a co-designer of several commercially produced aeroplanes. He was also an ex-R.F.C. pilot from the War. He worked incessantly, though he had the glancing, easy, casual manner that was also a sine qua non of being a respected don at Cambridge. His manner was similar to that of many successful students there, who also worked hard, but spoke almost disdainfully of their efforts, doing their best to seem like leisured drifters.

"Ah, good morning, Mr Robert Bruce," he would drawl. "Now this fascinating squiggle," pointing to a diagram in an essay of mine, "may we take it as your prediction of the erratic course a plane might take if your estimates of the influence of a defect in the location of wings in relation to the aircraft's centre of mass can be assumed realistic?"

O.K.! A trifle sarcastic, and over-elaborate. But nice enough. For Dr Milland was a nice man. Smart, assured, but kind, helpful to a fault. I grew under his tutelage at a rate I would have considered inconceivable a year before.

The other teacher from whom I most benefited was a canny, sardonic Scot – Dr Andrew McIntosh. He had also been in the R.F.C. during the War, and he and Milland had known each other. With a slight difference. McIntosh, a product of Glasgow trade schools, had been an aircraft rigger, not a pilot. He had gone to Cambridge as a mature, ex-service student, where his native ability soon distinguished him. He was an ingenious practical man with seventeen patents to his name, three of which were reputed to have made him wealthy. We got along. He had relatives in Australia and, as with most Scots, liked Australians – or thought he did.

When it came to designing details of wing structure or arranging cockpit controls for maximum pilot efficiency, Andy McIntosh was a winner. I doubt he could have been a designer of whole aircraft, but he was very skilled in many aspects of aircraft construction.

"Not that way," he would rasp during practical classes. "An electric drill is not something to poke holes with like a bloody pigsticker. It's a precision instrument. Use it with care and love, like – " and here he would become cheerfully obscene.

* * *

In the course of their studies, engineering students were sent out to see factory work in progress. The aeronautical students visited factories of five of England's biggest aircraft companies – Avro, De Havilland, Hawker, Short Brothers and Vickers.

This was a highly useful experience – I mean, to see various kinds and sizes of planes being built in numbers. But I also saw that workers and their supervisors, except those who actually assembled planes, were divided up into groups, each of which was responsible for just a few of the many kinds of replicated components of wings, fuselages, undercarriages, and so on. Even in the drawing offices, all but the very senior designers and draftsmen were in little groups working on particular aspects of aircraft. The impression I took away was that most of these groups were only remotely connected to each other and to the general design concepts of the aircraft they were working on.

All that I saw made me appreciate the size and growing power of the aircraft industry and its subordination to the urge to meet what, even then, was being perceived as Britain's need for military aircraft.

Most people in the factories spoke in a crisp, informed way of the work they were engaged in and were generally helpful and tolerant of our far-from-expert enquiries. But I had to admit that it was the planes themselves – the simple fact of their huge *being* – that dwarfed, or made little of, those who had conceived or made them.

And that distressed me. If one or a few persons could conjure into existence things as complex and powerful as a huge flying boat, or other things that could exceed four hundred miles an hour in level flight, it seemed only reasonable that clear signs of their ability would show in their physical presence – in their faces, in their words. But the men I met were solid, pipe-smoking, apparently unpretentious engineers who manifested little of the intellectual brilliance to have managed these feats.

Were they, then, members of a sort of guild or secret society of geniuses, among whom it was tacitly agreed to affect no more than an ordinary – even banal – mode of appearance and speech, the reward of their reticence being to dodge the cloying attention of adoring masses and the jealousies of the less gifted?

Yes, I thought, it must be something like that. Because some of the men I met were chief designers for their companies. Somewhere in their innermost hearts and minds there had to be forces, dreams, a sense of creating – an ongoing vision of grandeur.

All that had to be there, whether in the drafting office of a designer, or even out in the middle of a factory floor among the half-built wings and fuselages. There had to be a bond of tremendous power between physically unimpressive men and the huge, portentous artifacts that were their creatures.

My questions, that I never put, were: how did such men ever get the will to prevail, and how could I ever manage to acquire that will?

And when I returned to Cambridge after these visits, always the questions remained. For I knew – all appearances to the contrary – that I must have met some great men, in whom the artless creativity of Charlie, as it had been, but boosted by orders of magnitude, must exist and even on occasion show itself. Sometimes those men must have looked up from their plans and specifications, to stare reflectively, wonderingly, at what they had made, or to dream of what they hoped to make. Then, if only to a few friends or workmates, their faces must have shone for a moment as they took up tools and pencils to rough out ideas that would end in becoming the gleaming leviathans that were the children of their hearts.

And then I would remember that Charlie himself had always remained cool and detached and technical in behaviour and manner, so perhaps I would never catch more than momentary glimpses of what I was hoping one day to witness.

*   *   *

You might think it natural that people who design and build planes would also wish to fly them – in fact, that flying would be the more primal urge. Yet even the history of the Wright brothers suggests that getting their aircraft built so that it *could* fly was more important to them than being the pilots. Orville Wright hardly flew at all after Wilbur died from typhoid. And Reginald Mitchell, who designed the Spitfire, was not a pilot – though late in his life he was trying to become one.

Of course, in the public mind, it's the fliers who are the heroes.

Anyway, to me, in the early days, there was never any doubt – to make was to triumph. That doesn't mean I would not want to fly what I had made, but that – like the Wrights – I would be happiest to know I had made something that people *could* fly. And one thing was now certain to me: I didn't want to specialize in any one area of aircraft production – whether in design of fuselages, wings, engines, or in the details of their construction. I wanted to do it all. I wanted, desperately, to *make aeroplanes*.

Meanwhile, on the assumption that at least several years of engineering studies hung before me, I continued trying to drift energetically.

*   *   *

But despite what I've said, I soon grew to believe that I must become a pilot. After all, I would surely be better at design if I could appreciate at first hand what pilots experienced and had to contend with.

In addition, it did seem that it might be great fun.

But oddly, even unaccountable as it now seems, up to that time I had never been up in a plane.

By great good luck, there was a Cambridge University Air Squadron which I joined and was startled to find that Dr Milland was one of the Squadron instructors.

I began – as so many others in the flying clubs around Britain – in a de Havilland Gypsy Moth. This tiny biplane, powered by a sixty horsepower engine, looked ridiculously fragile, but because it weighed only half a ton, with a correspondingly low wing loading, it was extremely difficult to crash it – which was a major reason for its enormous popularity.

Dr Milland and I climbed into our cockpits in a Moth with dual controls. I did not feel in any sense heroic. I adjusted and fastened my seat belt with the feeling of performing a special rite for the first time. As we taxied slowly towards our takeoff starting point, everything in Dr Milland's hands, I was sweating badly.

We paused, the engine ticking over, the propeller turning very slowly.

Then a sudden rushing noise from the small engine and a live quivering throughout the plane's whole fabric-covered structure – a feeling as of a stirring animal – and we began to move.

And there came the long-anticipated thrust in the small of the back, the gathering of speed as the ground whipped past and the last rush as we finally cast off the earth. And then we climbed.

We climbed!

And we were there, sitting in the sky. I felt I could touch the air, caress it. It was the element I had been born to love. I thought it loved me. I wanted to tell it that I felt the same.

*   *   *

To my disappointment, I had only a limited natural flair for flying, being slower than average in my initial progress. Milland was an excellent instructor, calm, patient, humourous when he needed to be. I learned, but not quickly. I think Dr Milland was as surprised as I was at this, but if he felt disappointment he kindly concealed it. After my umpteenth appalling landing approach, I finally gritted my teeth, somehow forced myself to see what I was doing wrong, and then – quite suddenly – things began to come together.

Dr Milland's slightly grave expression – to which I had become accustomed – was replaced by encouraging smiles.

"You know, Bruce," he said, as he climbed slowly out of the instructor's cockpit after my first really decent landing, " I have to confess I was beginning to get a bit anxious that perhaps you just weren't pilot material at all and that, although these little planes are considered very safe, you might finally manage to wipe off our undercarriage in one of your landings. But I think you've broken through whatever it was that was the trouble, because you're coming right along now. "

I grinned at him. "I think it's the way I am," I said. "Not a very quick starter. But if I get rolling I can usually make progress. Anyway, thanks for putting up with me."

Soon I was soloing, getting on well, and feeling that one day I would be able to call myself a competent pilot.

Chapter 4

Well into my first year at Cambridge and things were going along. I was making more than satisfactory progress in my studies and felt I would soon be doing even better. I was on excellent terms with my instructors. But I was also aware of how much I still had to learn of engineering in both theory and practice. This I found very hard to deal with, because I realized I was living in a period of turbulent and brilliant mechanical creativity, when planes of startlingly new form and performance kept appearing from one year to the next. I was fearful this period would somehow be past before I could make my own contribution – whatever, and however modest, it might prove to be.

Engineering students were sometimes offered chances to work in the aircraft factories at low wages in their university vacation periods, opportunities that were supposed to afford valuable experience in the post-graduation job search. But most senior students complained that, in the factories, they had been given only dull, repetitive work in the assembly lines, and rarely even got near any state-of-the-art, cutting edge projects. Such information increased my impatience and uneasiness.

* * *

I needed other activities to relieve me from the daily routines. Flying practice was my main escape. I loved flying and was making good progress now, but it was not cheap, and I could not fly as often as I wanted. Moreover, sessions of flying practice could cut deeply into one's time.

I needed to improve the social side of life, but still felt unsure among the English – regardless of the remarks of Peter Randall that might have given me some measure of assurance. But even if I did manage to achieve a social life, I knew it would make large calls on my time that could all-too-easily write finis to academic performance – the evidence was all around. There were a lot of very rich young men at Cambridge who felt no stint about spending time and money on lavish celebrations, and whose studies, in the main, took a nosedive . . . something my meagre resources would not allow me to get away with.

But I did go to a New Year ball. I was not crazy about it and, when another such occasion came up a few weeks later, I decided to skip it. But a couple of my friends – concerned I was getting too isolated – insisted I accompany them. So I did go to that ball – which was the first of two big things that happened to me within a few weeks of each other.

* * *

So we arrived at the ball, I, who was alone, accompanying my two friends – an Australian and an American, with their girls.

Most of the girls and young women attending the ball were either from the non-academic community of Cambridge (Cambridge University did not admit women until after WW II), or from London, where women had been University students from about 1830. I knew none of them. But at this second ball I noticed Peter Randall, and "Pete", as everyone called him – old Etonian, stroke of the Cambridge Eight, heir to an earldom, but lacking any air of superiority – was of an uninhibited, cheerful and convivial disposition, and the very obvious focus of a lively crowd. I took in at a glance that Pete's group included several very good-looking, fashionably-dressed girls. I tried to avoid staring but Pete spotted me and soon trotted over.

"Ah, Robert, I know you're dedicated to your studies to a most grotesque extent, but here you are. Good show. Excellent! But I notice you seem to be lacking a female – bit of a vital necessity at a do like this, don't you think?"

Before I could move or speak he grabbed my shoulder with his big, top-oarsman's hand, and dragged me – in a very friendly way – in the direction of his group.

"There's a lass here who's made the same asinine mistake you have, old man. Let me introduce you. She'll be speechless with awe when you start to drivel on about aeronautics and wallabies and other esoterica."

His hand stopped me as easily as it had dragged me. "Here you are then, young Robert, meet Janice Whitcombe."

I stared. I didn't mean to, but I did. And she looked directly at me. Our gazes locked for a second, but I could not redirect my stare, knowing it would reveal my self-consciousness. It can't have been more than another second or two, though, before we were both managing to inspect each other with rapid glances.

Janice was a tall, slim and very beautiful girl – these were the first things I noticed. She had dark-blonde hair that flowed just to her shoulders. Her face was high-cheekboned, rather lean and modelled, her blue eyes of a conspicuous clarity. She smiled widely and said, "I hope you don't think you're being dragooned by Pete. He's in one of his 'masterful' moods this evening."

I laughed and at the same time realized I had better get my act together. I was at Cambridge, I was a Colonial. But I had been taught to write and speak and I certainly did not dislike girls – and surely this was the time to bite the bullet.

"Well," I said, "I'm here, or at least I came here, as the odd person in a party of five. And the main reason for being by myself is that – " Here I paused for a while, not knowing how to finish.

Janice Whitcombe quickly said, "Yes, well I'm alone because I really didn't think I would come, and when people sort of dragged me along at the last moment I couldn't find anyone to come with."

Pete Randall patted me on the back with his right hand and Janice on the back with his left. "Listen," he said, "the two of you are going to love each other so much you'll probably get married tomorrow morning. Now come and join our crowd, and Robert, bring over your friends with you. We're aiming to be the noisiest and worst-behaved bunch here tonight."

Janice and I looked at each other. She smiled. "I doubt it's worth arguing with him," she said, as Pete moved off, calling out jollities to others.

"He's really a pretty good bloke," I said. "At least, he always goes out of his way to try and see foreigners he meets aren't completely overlooked."

Janice looked at me quickly. "Oh, yes, Pete really is the soul of hospitality. But have you yourself felt particularly isolated at Cambridge?"

"Well, not a lot. But it's just that, to me, this is still a sort of foreign country where they do things differently, and you can sometimes be made to feel that you come from the edge of the world – I mean if the world was flat and people still thought you could fall off."

She laughed a little.

"As an Australian – which Pete told me you are, though I can hardly detect it in your accent – I wouldn't have thought it too much of a problem, surely? Of course, I know there's this class thing we have here that – "

"I don't worry much about that," I said, as we finally squeezed our way past people to find a couple of recently vacated seats near the edge of the dance floor. "As Pete kindly pointed out to me one day, I grew up in a place where class distinctions – at least those based on manner of speech and dress and so forth – scarcely exist, so I really lack the antennae to let me know where and when I might be patronized. So anything like that would be wasted on me."

Janice laughed. It was the kind of female laugh I like – open, musical, not at all restrained.

"Where do you come from?" I asked.

"I live in London nowadays."

"Nowadays?"

"Yes, because I'm at university there."

"Doing . . . ?"

"Oh, an Arts degree."

"I see. In what?"

"English at the moment, but one day I want to do art history. And you?"

"Engineering. Though I have only limited interest in civil or electrical or mechanical engineering. I want to work with aircraft and this seemed the way to go. There wasn't much future for it in Australia."

We stopped talking about these things that were just filling the blank space between us and I said, "So how come you know Pete and are coming to a dance at Cambridge?"

"As to Pete, we sort of grew up together. The Randalls have what is rather comically called a 'country seat' – meaning it's a great big place near Eastbourne where his family spend their summer holidays. Pete's father – who's Lord Randall, though he's a very open, unpretentious person who insists absolutely everybody call him 'Jack' – bought the place in the early 1920s. My family happens to live nearby. I might have met him anyway, because the Randalls are a convivial lot and entertain frequently, but the fact of it is that my mother is a second cousin to Lady Randall and so we used to see them a great deal. Anyway, Pete asks me to come up to Cambridge to functions like this and I usually come if I have the time – and someone to come with. This time, I'll stay overnight with my aunt, who lives in Cambridge."

This, I felt, was a bit rich for my blood. So I suddenly stood up. "I'm no great dancer," I said, "but you can just hear above all this racket that there's a band playing. So . . . shall we?"

She stood up even as I was speaking, clearly pleased to get at it.

I took her by the hand and waist as we moved out into the growing throng. I had not lied about my dancing, but she moved with an effortless lightness and precision, and so responsively to my uncertain leading, that it all seemed easy and natural.

For a while I gazed over her shoulder; I dared not stare at her. But I could feel her slim, strong body and her hand which had tightened in my own. As we swayed to the rhythm I noticed the clean smell of her hair when it brushed my face. No, I had never been a dancer, but I felt we could go on for hours.

As the music stopped and we drew apart, our hands remained together for a moment and I looked at her face which was slightly flushed, her lips parted and her eyes shining.

I guessed she was a year or two younger than I, and again I had difficulty in not staring. I had only ever been out with girls in a casual way, and had not experienced anything like what was going through my head now. She was so beautiful, almost haughty-looking, poised, but seemed actually quite open. Several men asked her to dance and she did, but then she always came back to me.

We danced the evening away. We didn't talk much. That could come later. But as it moved towards midnight I took her hand as we sat awaiting the band's final numbers.

"I don't want to be too blunt about this, Janice," I said. "But I'm not going to just shake hands at the end of the evening and hope we'll see each other one day at some other ball. You have to tell me how to find you in London, and I'll be down first chance I get."

She looked at me, then, steadily. And she did not appear to be what I might have expected – startled, or reluctant, or anyway needing more coaxing. All she said was, "Yes. Yes, I'd like that very much." And held my hand hard. And smiled. And smiled.

* * *

Two days later I was back at the usual routine of studies and lab classes and workshop practice, but the following Saturday I took a train to London to see Janice Whitcombe.

We met for lunch outside the Reading Room of the British Museum where she had been studying that morning, and ate fish and chips and some kind of sweet pudding, and drank very poor coffee. The food was stodgy, over-filling, but the day was cold and we were young and healthy and equal to the task of metabolizing such stuff.

Janice wore a red beret and scarf, a long, oatmeal-coloured, fitted pullover and a short, dark skirt, plus the sort of long, black woolen stockings that young British women affected in cold weather in those days. She looked splendid in the cold, hard light of day; her skin glowed, her eyes were clear.

We nattered away over the bland lunch, which seemed almost delicious, and downed many cups of coffee. We sat for three hours as we poured ourselves out for each other. It wasn't frenzied over-excited stuff; it just felt right to be talking with her, and to be listening. As far as I could gauge, she felt the same. As the short afternoon grew dark, waitresses were looking impatiently in our direction, and it was time to go.

We decided to see an early-evening film. I cannot recall what it was, but I know I reached for her hand in the dark and found it waiting for me.

I was very excited by her beauty, and by her vivaciousness and wit and quick intelligence. But I was also stirred at a deeper level by a quality I could not put a name to. And I felt I had already known her for a long, long time.

*   *   *

In the weeks that followed I kept my mind on my work to the extent possible, but I did manage to meet Janice in London a few times. As I had nobody to stay with there and hadn't the money for overnight accommodation, I caught early morning trains to London, and returned as late as possible the same day. Most of our time together was spent over lunches and wandering around the city with Janice as the guide, and ending with another film. And we talked about our childhood years – which, as we were both so young, really meant the recent past.

Janice had already invited me to come down into the Eastbourne countryside to visit her family's home and stay for a few days as soon as the university vacation period gave us a little time. She was very serious about her studies, and because of her interest in art history was knowledgeable about London's galleries and museums, which she proceeded to drag me to. I say "drag" because I had not formerly paid attention to art. Now – stimulated by her enthusiasm – I discovered what seemed like a new set of eyes I had never used before. And it was very easy to become interested in painting and sculpture.

When I asked her whether she had thought of being a painter, she answered that she had some ability but judged it less than enough to become a functioning artist.

"Anyway," she said, "I've always been interested in history, and since painting isn't just confined to the present, art history seems to be something I should be considering. But I won't get into that until I've finished this first degree."

It was clear she was ambitious but not self-important. I found her playful and funny, and without the tension, the anxiety, I felt in myself. Perhaps the difference was related to our fields. She had already shown me that art could be profound and absorbing, also that its history would continue to accrete forever, the past, present and future being different from each other but none less or more "significant" than the others. But in aviation, though its history was fascinating enough, it was the knowledge and artifacts of the present – or those being planned for the near future – that were always the more important. And aviation in 1933 was heavy with a potential unmatched since the very earliest days of aeroplane design and building. Everyone in the field felt like a surfer trying to catch and ride the biggest wave that had come along since the Wrights.

*   *   *

And then, one day, I said, "Look, Janice, it's about time we got out to see some aeroplanes. I saw in The Times this week that there's an air show at Hendon today. What about us having a look?"

So it was a Saturday, very late in the spring of 1933, after seeing some aerobatics displays by the R.A.F., that we walked into a lecture room at Hendon for the second of four consecutive one-hour talks on "Aircraft of the Future". This talk was the inflated twaddle of the sort you could find in the popular mechanics magazines of those days, replete with garish coloured lantern slides of "Artists' Impressions of the Aeroplanes of Tomorrow", delivered with fatuous smoothness by a junior executive type – a sort of "front office" representative of one of the larger aircraft companies – who wore a double-breasted suit and a guards' tie. We heard only the last few minutes, followed by a sprinkle of naive questions, and I was getting ready to leave, unhappy about having exposed Janice to such boring twaddle about things I had conveyed to her as my ruling obsession, when the next speaker began.

His appearance contrasted starkly with that of the shiny article who had preceded him, which, in itself, held out a fragment of promise. So I waited to see. However, after two minutes of his muttered apologies for his inexperience and ineptitude, I was again about to urge that we leave when, abruptly clearing his throat, the speaker shifted gears and got down to business. And the business, in total contrast to his predecessor's whole approach, and his own weak beginning, rivetted me to my seat. I'm not sure what it did to Janice because, for a while, I was concerned just to make sure I missed nothing.

Off he galloped. Not only did he know aeronautics inside out, he had the power to focus his audience's interest, so that at least the essence of his expertness actually came through to this collection of uninformed adults and restless kids. Within a minute, nearly everyone was quiet, held by the swift pass of his arm as it gestured towards the screen on which clear and beautiful plans of aircraft – past, present and future – were flashed up. The presentation was simple, concise, logical – in a word, elegant. He told of the history of aircraft, and kids stood up so as not to miss a thing. Parents gasped, chuckled, grew silent again – but were all attention – as the successes and flops were described in brilliant style. On he forged. The Great War, the Schneider Trophy Air Races, all the breakthroughs in plane design. Simple but beguiling expositions on the construction of fuselages, engines, wings.

His talk was over too soon, people clapping furiously. Flushed, embarrassed, clearly not used to such appreciation, he answered some questions – one or two surprisingly acute ones, others silly – with good humour, politeness and clarity.

And that was that, it seemed, for Philip Gibbs White, private plane builder of Kent.

I made Janice and myself endure one more awful talk – which was the last – just to be sure of meeting him before he left. At the end, I introduced myself and Janice, offered my compliments. He had a cheerful manner and when I said I was studying aeronautical engineering, with hopes of being a designer, he lit right up, asked me some questions and replied to mine in detail. I said, "I was really struck by what you were saying about optimal design principles for speed and performance. Are you working on this yourself?"

He looked at me for a moment, perhaps gauging the seriousness of the question. Then he said, "As a matter of fact . . . Robert? You said your name was Robert, Robert Bruce? . . . Yes. Building something that will, I sincerely hope, be able to include those things. I was by myself, at first, but now a friend's joined me. We're building a plane together."

It was a bit confusing. I had heard of amateurs who had built light planes in their backyards, and even flown them. But we had been talking of high performance planes. All my recent experience had led to one conclusion – that it took a designer, several engineers, and a team of technicians, all funded by big company money, to produce anything worth talking about in modern aviation. Gibbs White ("Call me G.W. Everyone does, for some reason. Like some Yank business tycoon, what!") looked almost apologetic and said, "Yes, well, it may appear odd, but alone I can please myself, do things the way I want. Just bumble along. See where it takes me." And then his expression took on a slightly challenging, even defiant look. I must have appeared interested, even if somewhat doubtful, because a little later, as we had a cup of tea, he said, "Look, you seem pretty keen. There's an Easter weekend coming up. Why not take a train down to Ham Street? It's close to Romney Marsh and I've got a few acres near there and a shed where we're doing what we're doing. Come down and have a look. Might amuse you and be a bit of a foil to all the stuff you must be buried under in your studies; I know what that can be like. We can put you up. Plenty of room. Come, if you're at all interested. You could even lend us a hand while you're there if you wanted to. Very welcome."

I thought I could sense in his tones a hint of loneliness. But indeed I did feel interested. I accepted his invitation, but for a time not at Easter but in May. We shook hands. His was the hard, roughened hand of a manual worker, and his grip was powerful.

* * *

As we made our way back to the centre of London where we would eat and see our film before I caught a late train to Cambridge, Janice said, "I have the idea that you were very impressed by Mr Gibbs White. I mean, you must have been, if you're going down to see him at work."

"Yes," I said. "It's true. I mean, if he's really doing what he says, it'll be like nothing I've ever seen before. I have very good lecturers and I've seen how people operate in the aircraft factories. But . . . how can I put it? A guy like this, who's not only designed a plane but is making it with his own hands – well, let me tell you, that's very rare these days. If he's any good at it, I might learn a lot. If he's not any good, there's another sort of lesson to be learned." I didn't say what the lesson would be in that case, because I wasn't quite sure.

"Anyway," I said, "on the offchance that he isn't fooling, I do think I should waste a couple of days."

I looked at Janice a bit slyly and said, "After all, he sure knows his aviation *history*."

Chapter 5

G.W.'s instructions had been clear. "There's this funny little bus – thing's on its last legs – that runs cross-country from Ham Street. You get off at Milson's Lane, about eight miles. The driver will tell you. If you can catch the 10 a.m. you'll be there before 10:30. Then it's just a hike along the lane for a couple of hundred yards."

The bus was small and old and red. It smelled musty inside and also of the burning engine oil that was the source of its trailing smoke plume. But it had got me where I was going, or nearly.

At Milson's Lane I got out and the bus lumbered on its slow malodorous way as I started up the hedgerowed lane carrying a Gladstone bag that held a change of clothes. The bag had belonged to my long dead grandfather, who carried his lunch to work in it for twenty years. It was a nondescript, battered article that I valued because it had been his. In those days I never went anywhere for more than a day without it. It was my talisman from Oz. Inside it there was a stained and faded label that proclaimed it had been made in England – in fact, in Kent, by Morgan Bros.

Two hundred yards and, just as G.W. had said, a house-sized wooden building showed through a break in the hedgerow. It was new, of solid construction, and lacked paint. Beyond stretched a very large, smooth field – a greensward without trees, shrubs, thickets, ditches, or even depressions.

I knocked on the first door I saw. No answer, but I could hear hammering inside. The hammering continued through several more knocks, and the buzz of an electric drill joined it. I tried the door. It was unlocked and I came into a plain, unpainted room lined with shelves piled high with books and papers. There was an old swivel chair behind a battered oak desk, and to one side was a once-elegant armchair covered with faded and worn tapestry. That was all. An inner door was open and I looked through it into the rest of the building which was about sixty feet by forty.

Gibbs White was there, drill in hand, wearing a stained overall. He saw me right away, waved, and called a greeting, "Ah, Robert Bruce. Our Aussie. At last!" On the other side of the building, the hammering ceased.

G.W. parked his drill and stepped forward briskly, hand outstretched. He seemed to be smiling, but because his teeth were gripping his pipe it was hard to be sure.

"Very good to see you, Robert. Hope you had a good trip down? Well . . . only hope our poor arrangements will suit you. You're not too fussy I trust. May I call you Bob . . . or do you prefer Robert? Bob, then? Capital! Well, come in, old boy, come in. There's some sort of tea in the pot though I'll not warrant it was made in the recent past. And – Good Lord, I'm forgetting – meet my friend Jim Grant."

Grant, a slender, dust-coated man with sharp bright features in a narrow face came over with a grin to shake hands.

We sat on upturned boxes in the workshop and G.W. poured tea from a huge black kettle.

I sipped tentatively at my tea which was in a big chipped enamel mug. The tea was stewed and tasted of iron.

We sat there in a moment of silence, perhaps nobody quite sure how to begin. I looked quickly from G.W. to Jim Grant and back again.

James Grant was someone you could imagine at a workbench doing some quiet, solitary thing that called for concentration, meticulous care – a skilled and reliable man, perhaps not very inventive, but indispensable. As it turned out, my instant impression was spot on.

G.W. was something else. I had, of course, already got a look at him at Hendon. But now, in this large untidy shed in the rural countryside, I wondered what I would have felt if this were our first meeting. He pulled off his overall to reveal an old tweed jacket with unmatched baggy pants. On factory visits organized for engineering undergraduates I had met some designers and executives of three big aircraft companies. G.W. certainly looked nothing like any of those neatly dressed persons – or even the clean-overalled workers out on the factory floor. I had to wonder if his apparel and demeanour could be taken as any indicator of his ability, but then I remembered the fluency, the expertness of his talk at Hendon.

And then, too, as he puffed his pipe to life, something cut across the generally seedy appearance, something in the concentration of the blunt features, the eyes, something too, in his precise, rapid, economical movements. And some other thing . . . I was not quite sure. Some impression of ruthlessness? Not quite. Perhaps of unbudgeability. Something . . .

He was ruddy-complexioned, had fading red hair and a short gingerish moustache. Skin creased as from living outdoors and squinting in strong light framed bright blue eyes – his single arresting facial feature. He was of sturdy build and medium height. The pipe he smoked was, I soon saw, of the kind that requires continual rekindlings with many matches, many knockings out of dottles, cleanings with a pen knife, and refillings – and that is used to point at and tap things with.

When I met him he was thirty seven. He looked strong and active but also much older – fifty or more. It may have been partly due to his worn and neglected clothes. As he leaned back nursing his tea, and crossed one leg over the other, I saw he had on battered but good quality shoes instead of work boots like James Grant's.

After the long pause, G.W. finally spoke again. "Well, Bob . . . here we are. Actually, you've arrived at a good moment. I'm about to take a little run over to Barnsworth. There's an Air Ministry testing station there. Perhaps you've heard of it?"

I nodded. "Heard of it, yes. That's about all."

"Right."

I sensed that he was becoming more his relaxed self now, brisker in manner by the second.

"Well, we have use of their wind tunnel and a few other facilities to test a couple of our ideas. That's, of course, whenever the Air Ministry types don't need them, or think they do. Anyway, just swill down that nasty stuff in your mug and we can cut along immediately. James won't come. He's right in the middle of something."

James Grant nodded. "Sweating away at some stressed skin

tests of metal for covering wings and fuselages. D'you know what I mean?"

"Yes," I said. "But I've had no practical . . ."

"Time enough for all that later," G.W. cut in. "We must be away to Barnsworth now." He solemnly inspected an old watch he had removed from his waistcoat pocket.

"Our turn at the tunnel is from noon to twelve fifteen. We have to go at once. It's fifteen miles away and the time's about twenty five to twelve."

He threw his overall into a corner, downed his tea to the dregs and took a worn soft hat from a peg.

"Dump your bag here, Bob. We'll pick it up this evening."

The day was cold and clear, and soon we were shooting smoothly through the sparkling air in a souped-up Vauxhall tourer. As he drove, G.W. spoke grittily around his pipe that was somehow alight in the tearing breeze, telling me where we were in the countryside, pointing to notable buildings as we slid by them.

After fifteen minutes we turned off into a short side road, wheeled past an armed, uniformed R.A.F. sentry, at whom G.W. directed a casual salute, and stopped at a long grey wooden building.

"Here we are, then," said G.W. and I felt a guiding hand at my shoulder.

Some of the men in the building were in R.A.F. uniforms and as we walked rapidly down a whitewashed passage a few pipes bobbed G.W.'s way in greeting, accompanied by grunts whose sentiment I could not make out. Then we were in the large room that housed the wind tunnel.

G.W. took a meticulously constructed wooden model from a bag he was carrying – I was not sure just what it represented – and secured it in the wind tunnel's viewing chamber. He patiently adjusted it, then closed the chamber and set the speed and direction of air flow. By this time about ten minutes had passed, and already four other men had gathered behind us and were talking restlessly among themselves. G.W., as if by way of punctuating their talk and emphasizing that his time was not yet up, brought out his watch and examined it with slow deliberation, but the gesture seemed lost on them.

I joined him in staring at the model in the tunnel. He said little but, as coloured threads distributed over the surface of the model either trailed smoothly or wobbled in the airstream, he glanced at me, eyes bright and young in the weathered face.

"Well, there, then . . . What do you think?"

G.W. aimed his pipe stem towards a spot on the model where the coloured threads danced erratically.

"See that there? I don't know about that at all. This is where the published drag data seem to break down. I wouldn't have thought of turbulence . . . there. Why?" He leaned towards the model, to peer intently through the glass wall. "Well, let's just watch it. Something may occur to us . . ."

I did as requested, though my thoughts were hardly of mint quality.

I now realized that the model was a quarter-scale facsimile of part of a fuselage, with wing root and streamlined fairing. The coloured threads kept jiggling where wing met fuselage, but still I felt remote from it all, unable to engage . . .

G.W. eventually stirred beside me, sighed, and switched off the air stream.

"Yes, well, I suppose we'll just have to brood about that for a bit." He inspected his old gold-cased watch yet again and said reluctantly, "Time's up. Have to let these other beggars have their turn I expect."

In a minute or two he had removed the model from the wind tunnel, received muttered acknowledgements and some almost surly looks from the "Air Ministry types", and was leading me quickly back along the corridor. We burst out into the cool brilliant day, G.W. laughing suddenly. "They'd like to see the back of me, most of that bunch would. And soon they will. They've a programme of their own that's supposed to call for full time use of the tunnel, and then all favours to civilians such as yours truly will be suspended. *Cancelled* is what they mean! They reckon I'm crazy to be trying to do what I'm doing – and maybe they're right." He laughed again loudly, rather self-consciously I thought. He stowed the bagged model in the back seat of the Vauxhall, cranked the starting handle and sprang into the driver's seat.

"And now, Bob," he called above the engine as he revved it, "a spot of lunch, I should imagine."

Gibbs White drove the Vauxhall along narrow roads through the slightly warming air of early afternoon, pointing out more landmarks as we dashed along. He drove with spectacular flair and sureness . . . and very fast. In a few miles we reached an old inn, and he pulled to a stop. He bounced out and led the way through a rustic doorway to be greeted familiarly by the publican and a few patrons. Following brief introductions, we collected mugs of ale and moved to a table by a window where we were soon biting into thick cheese sandwiches and G.W. was talking again.

"Now, tell me, Bob, what started you on all this nonsense, anyway? I mean, you were explaining at Hendon why you came here, all this ruddy way, to do things with planes. But, Lord! Australia must be a good big place. Lots of air and light and open space. Seems a confounded shame if there aren't quite a few local chaps in a place like that all hell-bent on the sort of things fellows like us are doing here. I mean, building their own kites, what! And if there aren't, well, tell me why that is."

He was looking at me with great directness and it came to me that he wasn't simply making conversation but genuinely wished to be enlightened. I cast about for a reply, finding one that had the merit of some truth, though only a part of the whole.

"Sport," I said. "Australians are crazy about sport. Not always so crazy about other things . . ."

"Oh, sport," said G.W. "I can see that, of course. Very partial to sport myself. Played rugby not all that long ago. Cricket, too. Still manage to watch a bit now and then. Lords in summer. And in Australia . . . sort of a giant Riviera, I suppose. Be a first-rate environment for sports. But people – I mean countries – need quite a few other things, too.

"But you know it's interesting," he went on, "there are Australians right here in England – Edgar Percival to name one – who are oustandingly successful plane designers. The Percival Gull is his.

Did you know that?"

I confessed that I did not.

"So, anyway," he looked hard at me, "it's fine you're here. We can certainly use another good head on *this* job." I felt uncomfortable. I was surely just a temporary visitor. How could he expect much of me? We drove back to the workshop in the lemon light of late afternoon, G.W. still explaining the landscape, pointing with his pipe. Later we drank more of the stewed tea, while Grant was told about the wind tunnel tests. A long discussion of the results ensued, to which, to my surprise, I was able to contribute a little.

Around five o'clock, G.W. said, "Well, Bob, stick your bag in the Vaux and we'll bowl off home now." He explained, while we drove the few miles to his home, that he "got left a little bit by the Old Man, got a penny or two from patents of my own and" – here he gave a short barking laugh – "even earned salary in the honest toil of an actual job in an aircraft factory. Once. Feels like a long time ago. And . . . here's the house! Not bad. No palace. All I can afford. It was my father's place."

He pointed to a cottage coming up on our right. "And I must pay James a bit. Not much. But I absolutely mustn't lose that chap. Unthinkable. Besides he's a friend I persuaded to come and work with me. I owe him a huge lot more than I imagine I'll ever be able to pay him. Anyway, though we may borrow and scrounge, we've not quite got to the point of pinching things – yet. But it all does take most of what would otherwise let me live with all the comforts a type like me could ever want."

Home was an old stone cottage which sat in a large area of long-untended grass, shrubs and trees which, in summer, would nevertheless be a green and leafy refuge. We pulled up on a circular gravel drive before the front door.

My quarters consisted of a summer house built by G.W.'s father as a place to read and practice the flute. It was just a wooden box, measuring some twenty feet by twelve, with a large window and a door, but there was some simple old furniture and two antique electric heaters that G.W. correctly predicted I'd need at night. The place was clean, and it looked out on the wild garden.

G.W. showed me around the house. In a room he sardonically referred to as "The Study", he kept untidy piles of books on assorted engineering topics. On a shelf were the classics of the early literature of aeronautics – works by Cayley, Lilienthal, the Wrights, Canute, Maxim, all of them. The room looked out on the garden, and two walls were plastered with photographs and plans of aircraft past and present. On a third wall, at right angles to the windows, was a large blackboard mazed with calculations and sketches, many half-erased. Slide rules and notebooks lay on benches. A black-painted electric calculating machine loomed solidly on a small low table in a corner.

In addition to the room G.W. occupied, which had a bed, chest of drawers, small desk and chair, there were three other bedrooms, largely empty of furniture. In his room, on a chest, there was a photograph of a woman in a silver frame, but it was too far from the door for me to make out her features.

The spacious living room had a large stone fireplace with the cold remains of a recent fire in it. There were three Morris chairs with leather cushions, a low table with a whiskey decanter and some glasses. Threadbare Persian rugs decorated the floor and one wall was occupied by shelves that bore an eclectic collection of books and magazines. In a bay window stood a little hexagonal oak table with a blue pottery vase of local spring wildflowers. The room looked out to a little stream. With a bit of money and effort, house and grounds could have been made charming.

The kitchen was large, fairly well-equipped, again with a big fireplace that was much used in the winter G.W. said. The huge, worn pine table and five chairs suggested he spent a lot of time in the kitchen. In fact, as soon as the housekeeper had brewed us some coffee – which unlike the workshop tea was excellent – he planted himself at the table, gesturing me to a seat. He drank the coffee slowly, appreciatively, not as he had drunk tea. Tea, I saw, was to punctuate the day's work rather than to savour.

The housekeeper-cook, a pleasant local woman of about sixty, a widow who occupied a room behind the kitchen, soon put a savoury and substantial meal before us.

We ate hungrily – myself especially – and G.W. kept offering more. Then, as the evening grew dark, we lingered over an after-dinner scotch, saying little. Soon I felt very sleepy and G.W. saw this.

"Wander off whenever you feel like it, Bob. Lots to do tomorrow."

At ten I said goodnight, went through the chill, moist air to the summer house, turned on the radiators for ten minutes to dry the air a bit, then pulled an old clean-smelling quilt around me and drifted to a deep sleep.

Chapter 6

We ate bacon, scrambled eggs, toast and marmalade for breakfast, washed down with coffee while G.W. scanned the morning paper delivered from a nearby village. He continued reading, sprawled on a couch with his pipe going, for ten minutes more. This, I was to find, was how he started his days – a way to gather himself for what would follow.

Halfway to the workshop G.W. pulled the Vauxhall off the road and braked.

"You drive of course?"

"Yes."

"Have a try, then. Same side of the road Down Under, isn't it?"

Surprised and pleased I drove the remainder of the way. The Vauxhall behaved more responsively than the one or two of its type I had ridden in before and I remarked on this. G.W. gave a short laugh.

"Well, this bus has been modified a bit. We had a couple of ideas and thought it might be fun to try them out and James did most of the work because he likes to tinker. Learned to be handy building boats as a Thames shipwright."

When we reached the workshop G.W. showed me what they had done.

He pointed to where the front axle would have been. "We built these things – not sure what you'd call them . . . sort of 'wishbones', one for each wheel. And they pivot on a shaft, so when the wheel encounters a bump the wishbones compress these heavy coil springs and each wheel can be displaced independently and the shock is damped."

"And what's this for?" I asked pointing towards a thick metal bar.

"Ah, yes, that. That's to damp down lateral front end sway in a car. It's been tried by a few auto makers. I think they'll be calling it a torsion bar.

"These are not essentially new things," he went on. "I mean we haven't invented them. But there are few, if any, production model cars that have them as yet. We've simply made our own versions of things others have invented, because we wouldn't have had them in any car we could buy. Just as fun, you understand, and to see how well they'll work."

He pointed at some other things. "We've also tried to improve the petrol pump. And we've rebored the engine block to accept larger pistons, which certainly bucks up performance, what? And see, here, we took out the carburettor and replaced it with a fuel injection system."

"But, my God," I said, "fuel injection – in a car?" All I knew about fuel injection was that it was used in diesel engines, but not in car engines that ran on benzene. G.W. replied he was not sure that it had significantly boosted the car's performance, except in its acceleration at certain speeds. "But here," he said as we kneeled down and looked at the car's wheels, " is the one thing we did that really has made a great difference. I'm not talking about performance but about safety." They had replaced the original drum brakes with discs that he assured me had reduced the possibility of brake failure from overheating and also improved stopping power. "The real trick was to produce these calipers that press the break pads against the disc hard enough that they'll really grip. Well, they seem to be holding up."

I began to feel a cheerful glow. These modifications were not mere installations of parts cannibalized from other vehicles. Each had been contrived to serve a specific, thought-out purpose. Some of them might work better than had been expected, others worse. But it was clear to me that G.W. and Grant must be colossal mechanics.

What, though, would it take to do the thing G.W. wanted to do? Because I knew well enough it was going to need more than pretty demonstrations of superior bench skills.

Perhaps these two "backyarders" could indeed make a plane – and damned nearly anything else – as a technical exercise. But what about the overall achievement – conception, design, the pioneering constructional challenges?

*   *   *

In the workshop, below the roof, windows ran in a continuous high band around the four walls to provide good natural light, whatever the position of the sun. There were overhead lamps to boost the daylight if needed, lamps that were strong enough to work by at night. A workbench, continuous except for doorways, ran along all walls. I could see two lathes, three mechanical saws, two drill presses, electric hand drills, metal shears, implements for shaping metal and wood, jigs, gauges and forms. Hammers, screwdrivers, chisels, and other tools I could not name lay around.

There were models, too, some of them free-standing, one on a table. Here and there were plans, sketches, sheets of calculations. G.W.'s gesture took in all the models and the plans.

"Here we have it," he said. "The Beast. Or rather, bits and pieces of The Beast."

We contemplated the table-top model, which was of a half-scale, metal wing section. He passed his hands lightly over the smooth surface.

"Now this – a very thin section. Low-drag profile. But big problems . . . See: with such a thin section in a fully cantilevered wing there's the question of how d'you get enough spar strength? Of course you could get it with tapering I-sections. But then there's going to be a weight problem. And, then, for us, with our facilities, constructing a tapered spar would be very, very difficult. And I couldn't afford what it would cost to have it built by others."

He put his pipe between his teeth and stared hard at the model for about ten seconds. Then he moved abruptly to a tail assembly mockup.

"Same thing here," he grunted. "Thinness and strength. Thinness and strength. We need the metallurgists to come up with something special for us. How we do!"

He turned to his right and pointed to several rectangular frames to which test patches of thin shiny metal sheet were attached in various fashions.

"This aluminum – really duralumin – skin, flush rivetted, we're trying different thicknesses. We want it as thin and light as it can be and still be strong enough, what! Did I hear you tell James you knew something about this?"

"A very little," I nodded uncertainly.

"More troubles with this stuff, anyway. These are all very well, but what one would really like is remarkably simple. Just a totally seamless surface, yes? But we can't seamlessly weld stuff this thin."

We drifted to other models, and moved eventually into the office to sit while G.W. repacked his pipe.

He looked over at me, smoke drifting up lazily from his pipe. He leaned back.

"What's your family's opinion of what you're doing, Bob – all these crazy things? Do they really know why you're here in Britain, why you came all this way? I mean, do they actually understand?"

"They know . . . sort of. I think they think I may be a bit touched." I laughed nervously, "They haven't quite said so."

"Ah –" He smiled. "But are they . . . sympathetic?"

"In a way," I said. "I suppose so. But I think they're more tolerant than they would be if I weren't paying my own way."

"Your scholarship pays for everything, then?"

"Yes . . . or I certainly couldn't be in England."

He nodded, seeming to reflect. "Yes. Well, there's lots of folks find us types hard to fathom." He sighed lightly and smiled as if to himself. Then he sat up, looked at me, and changed the subject.

*   *   *

Later, as he shaped a fuselage former from wood, that would become a template for one to be rendered in thick sheet metal, G.W. told me how he had begun to study engineering at Cambridge in 1914, then joined the army engineers in 1917 and saw action for a year, fortunately escaping wounds. Later, his interest caught by planes, he managed a transfer to the Royal Flying Corps, did basic pilot training and returned to France in 1918. It was getting close to the war's end, but in time for just a few weeks of aerial action – which he also survived unscathed.

After the War he did not resume formal training as an engineer, even though aeronautical engineering had begun to be offered at Cambridge. But he had become fascinated by planes and impatient to take part in building them, and in the early 1920s he began work in both construction and design with one of the big manufacturers, which, he said, "Let me learn a lot. But then I felt I just wanted to break away from the mainstream and try some things of my own."

During the time he had worked for others he had become enthused by the international races for seaplanes, instituted by Jacques Schneider, the French arms magnate. But the Schneider Trophy Races – really just attempts at air speed records – became a closed shop for a few designers and construction companies that had big private or government backing. A British Trophy team prepared a plane that, in 1929, set a record of 328 mph. But after that British contenders were too underfunded to enter again until Lady Houston – widow of a wealthy shipping magnate – donated enough money to enable the British to put forward the Supermarine S.6B. Its prodigious Rolls Royce engine propelled it at 340 mph to win the trophy outright. Later, its engine boosted to 2,500 hp, it was flown at 407 m.p.h. But, by then, that kind of enterprise no longer interested G.W.

"I'm not sure where all this really took us," he said. " The Schneider races and other speed trials like them mean so little. They're essentially jingo exercises, and we can never say what a whole raft of other chaps might have managed, if they could only have scraped up even a fraction of the funds and facilities the Schneider teams had."

"But surely the planes they made for the Schneiders advanced aviation –?"

"Oh, I don't want to underpraise the work of Reginald Mitchell of Supermarine, or of the American or Italian teams. They all of them made great planes – but for a very specific purpose: to go fast! But other chaps might have managed anything they did, and perhaps done even more, had they ever been given a crack at it."

"So what let Mitchell and the others get their crack?"

"Oh, ability, of course. Plus persistence in seeking backers. Plus luck – being there when backers appeared, or at a time when someone understood and appreciated what they were trying to do."

He paused, I think anticipating what my question might be leading to.

"So, how do I imagine we'll ever get our crack? That's what you're thinking, what?"

I nodded.

"Well, we are very small and lonely, if you like; but though we can't build quickly we don't have to meet anyone else's deadlines, and by building with our own hands we can work our way around certain outmoded construction practices the big companies seem to find it hard to avoid. And we won't make too many asinine mistakes caused by poor liaison between designers and workers. And lastly, please understand the plane I want to build will not just be fast, but will handle well in ordinary flight and be a rugged aircraft, not just specially rigged for a speed attempt."

He became more concentrated, his eyes drilling at me.

"Look! I'll tell you what's really wanted for anyone trying to build a new sort of aeroplane. A Super Brain. That's what. I mean some chap that can take the overview. Absorb it all. Every blasted thing. Analyse all the needs."

He was running ahead in his mind now. There was the feeling of a powerful engine revving. The words came fast.

"There was a fellow once, mathematician called Babbage. Lived a hundred and twenty years ago. Very smart chap. He thought the smartest thing of all would be to have mechanical calculators that'd let you handle the toughest computations fast. So he designed one. Only it was never built. Too big for the engineers of the time. Pity. Because mathematicians now think it would probably have worked, if only a way could have been found to drive it.

"Anyway, had he built it, we might have had super calculators a century back. Wonder what that would have done for us?

"Well, we'll have a Babbage sort of thing a few years from now, they say, but it'll be electric rather than mechanical. Then we'll be able to manage the sums we can never manage now – not because we're too stupid to do them but because they take so long."

He drew on his pipe and blew a long smoke plume as he looked through a window at the few visible clouds.

"See . . . we need all this terrible mishmash of facts – all these wretched viscosity data, drag coefficients, stalling speeds, angles of attack – we need all of them in our tiny skulls at once, we – "

"But it's there," I broke in, "in books and papers –"

"Of course, Bob. But we need it in our heads – all of the time, so that in our thinking we'll be able to get immediately at everything that ought to be stored in an organized way. Now if a blessed machine could only do some of *that* for us . . . you see?"

"I suppose so – "

"No doubt of it, old boy. None. None at all." He puffed at his pipe. "For now, though, our wretched brains must carry it all . . . somehow." He looked at me, grinning self-consciously at his own outpouring.

"Anyway, back to the start . . . I want something the Schneider contestants never did manage, because they had to build seaplanes, since that was what old Jacques wanted. And you can have the fastest seaplane, but its design is inherently limited. I want a plane that'll come pretty close to defining, in shape and form and performance and general handling, the bounds to which we can hope to push plane design . . . ever. At least while keeping our machine still something that looks, flies and handles like a plane and not some blessed rocket or projectile. What we've already talked about – this 'optimal design' idea, what?"

I looked at him. "You think you can make a plane that'll fly much faster than the Schneider planes?"

"Faster?" His eyes flashed. He sat up straight, waved his pipe at me. "Faster, yes! And higher, and be able to barrel roll at top speed at fifty feet altitude, climb at five thousand feet a minute, dive faster than sound can travel. All of it."

"What about the Air Force? Do they want it?"

"Do the Air Force want it?" Again his eyes shone. Then he waved a finger as in judgement. "Those types just think of plane design as a function of Air Ministry specifications. Specs are their God. They'd learn more in ten months if they'd attend to design basics than in ten years by their present sodding system. Here's a bet!" He leaned forward eagerly. "I'll bet Supermarine's Reginald Mitchell himself will build planes for them before long. And the planes he'll build will not be anywhere near as fast as his own blessed S.6B that he won the Schneider with."

"But why not?"

"Simple. He'll have to bend his mind to specs, R.A.F. sodding warplane specs."

"I don't see . . ."

"Why? Because that's the way it goes. It nearly always takes about ten years or more to translate speed records into comparable service aircraft performances. Only the Air Force and the Dear Lord know why!"

"So will you want to make a plane so good the Air Force will eventually . . ?"

"Bob, not to mince matters: to blazes with the Air Force!" He pulled testily on his pipe, the corners of his mouth turned down. Then his ruddy face gradually cleared and his eyes sparkled and he smiled, winningly.

"For now, old boy, I just want to make something lovely. Something really lovely that people like you and I can fly!"

Chapter 7

We drove back to G.W.'s cottage that evening in milder weather than the day before, the landscape looking freshly green with a touch of gold from the last of the sun. Far above us came the full roar of a very large aeroplane, and a giant Handley Page H.P. 42 passenger biplane passed over – the kind with which Imperial Airways were pioneering European and Eastern airline routes. It would be carrying up to thirty eight wealthy passengers in its sumptuous cabin, and for a moment I imagined myself in a nice window seat as it nosed its way over The Channel towards Paris in the clear evening. What a way to go! I thought. Ships, trains, no matter how luxurious, would soon be categorized as slow surface monsters, while these great birds soared their stately – if ungainly-looking – ways above.

But I knew already that G.W., imperturbable at the wheel, couldn't care less about the Handley Page. He was no aeronautical technologist, but a follower of Daedelus, of Wilbur and Orville Wright – a man with a simple dream. And I understood the force of his possession, and it was a new experience, even though my own dreams seemed fervid enough.

And as I thought of it a little more I began to think that, to G.W., the building of his plane had become a way to pit his imagination and spirit against the indifferent vastness of the sky. It was how he was determined to define himself – to what end, for what satisfactions, to assuage what itch, I could not at that time properly understand. Some people might think his absorption crazed, but I had already sensed that he, like no other, might have the key to unlock in me powers many are born with but few manage to exercise.

And it came to me – for all their differences in age, personality, education and the circumstances of their lives – how the G.W. of now, and the Charlie of my childhood might have sat talking happily together over cups of G.W.'s black, bitter tea.

Chapter 8

After my few days with G.W. I came back to Cambridge. But my mind was on fire. What I had seen and heard and thought had not been something I could ponder and set aside in my stream of memories, perhaps to profit from later in my life. I knew I had to make my mind up about its importance, which might otherwise elude me forever.

I immediately sought the opinions of Drs Milland and McIntosh about my visit and its effects on me, but Milland had barely heard of G.W., McIntosh not at all. I wanted to tell them everything, but a hollow place seemed to open up inside me into which everything drained that I needed to say, and for a while that place kept my feelings from being expressed. But now that I was back at their lectures and labs, I knew neither of those estimable men possessed – or perhaps even knew about – whatever it was that drove G.W.

I had come twelve thousand miles from my homeland and understood how any sort of future I could imagine for myself might be marred, even destroyed, by an attitude that people perceived as frivolity – an unfocussed attitude – towards my studies. To abandon Cambridge, and with it my scholarship, could seem pure recklessness. And yet . . .

*   *   *

I telephoned Janice and said, "Unless you are absolutely tied up with something else, please come up here and stay overnight with your aunt. I've got something I need to talk about that just won't wait."

"It's got something to do with your visit to Mr Gibbs White, hasn't it?" she said, getting the point at once.

"In a word, yes. But don't let's go into it now. I need to see you."

She waited a long moment. "Robert, I doubt I'm the one you should be talking to. Your teachers – "

"I've tried to speak to them and plan to speak to them again, but I want to see you first, because . . . it may be important for both of us, if what I think is –"

"All right, then. I think I understand. I'll see you at the weekend."

She came, and we strolled "The Backs" – those famous fields running behind university buildings that were tenderly green at that time of the year – as I tried to tell her what was on my mind.

I knew she could be talked to, that she was level-headed, would make an effort to understand, and "I spilled my guts" to her as Australians would say, as she listened quietly, her hand in mine. Her listening, her quietness, her female presence, calmed me; it was not the same as trying to say things to a man.

"I think I've got to go there, to G.W. – if he'll let me."

"Well, I understand what you're saying, but really, aren't you being just sort of swept off your feet? I mean, I'm sure he's a charismatic person, but he'll still be there after you've finished at Cambridge and you could go to him then, and take so much more experience and knowledge with you?"

"No," I said. "No, and for this reason: he is currently doing something that he'll finish long before I get through here."

"But there'll be other – "

"No. That's just it. What he's doing, right now, if it succeeds will be years ahead of its time. And you know, he thinks so big! There may never be anything to surpass it."

"But really, Robert, dear, can that be? I'm not an engineer, but anyone can see that progress in the things engineers do never seems to stop. I mean, how could they?"

I stopped walking, faced her. "My dear, you're *not* an engineer, and this guy is a marvellous engineer. See, he understands the principles of optimality. If you use certain kinds of building materials that are the best there are, and a design that is just as perfect as practice and theory can make it, you can approach a limit beyond which it's very difficult to do things better. I guess I have faith in him, and faith that he'll open my eyes in ways other designers and builders can't. I suppose it's what I've got instead of religion."

She laughed. "It's what you've got *as* religion."

I kissed her then, for a moment, and realized how unusual it probably was that we'd seen quite a lot of each other, and yet, with the mutual attraction palpable, this was our first kiss. But though she was a cheerful and open person, never withdrawn or taciturn as far as I knew her, she was also serious and self-contained. So the kiss happening so "late" was not that remarkable – though its nature and feeling were . . .

*   *   *

It was very hard to explain myself to Drs Milland and McIntosh. Whatever I said – or could think of saying – ran directly against the received wisdom of how one acquired an engineering education. Dr Milland looked worried and vaguely hurt. He may have been seething inside, but it was not his style to show much anger, disappointment or resentment. He was just too urbane a gentlemen to make more than good natured-seeming objections.

McIntosh, the blunt Scot, was different. He looked me fiercely up and down from under his bristling eyebrows and shook a thick forefinger at me.

"See here, laddie, this isn't the eighteenth century. Thousands of good men have slaved over the generations to make it possible for the likes of you – and me, for that matter – to study engineering as a learned profession, instead of being just a bloody blacksmith or an amateur clock-maker. You want a touch of gratitude and a sense of reality about you, my son! And here you are, you know, a bloody colonial who ought to be as pleased as Punch there's a process that can magic-carpet you across the waters so you can enjoy the advantages your own country couldn't provide. You . . ." He was very angry, words stuck in his throat. His pointing finger was wagging under my nose.

I struggled to reply.

"Please try to understand. I am enormously grateful to be here.

And I've already learned from you and Dr Milland things I'd probably never even have heard about otherwise. But . . . but at this point I just have to get the feeling I'm helping to make something.

"I've seen what happens on the factory floor and it just seems very remote to me. There are people working on all sorts of different tasks at once that don't seem to have any relation to each other. Of course, they are supervised and the work all comes together at the end, or there wouldn't be any planes made. But what G.W. – uh, Mr Gibbs White – is doing really lets you see what he's striving for. I mean, he explains every step and everything seems so clear – even when mistakes are made. And this plane of his, it's new. It's not just one more copy of all the other planes on a factory floor. And it's . . . sort of growing into something before your eyes. Something that may be really tremendous!

"If I go to work with him it'll be because I can never expect to get a chance to see plane design and construction in just this way again.

"Later on, I'll want to come back here, more than anything. And I'll need to. I know that.

"And I'm sorry that – "

He cut me off with an abrupt gesture. "Save it laddie. Save it. Look, the factory visits ought to have told you what a colossal enterprise building modern aeroplanes has to be, even when there's big money and every kind of technical help and expertise known to man to get the job done. Well. . . I mean, how can you think one man, working by himself can really build a plane at a professional level – a plane that'll seriously compare with the best these big places can manage. Why, there isn't one example I can think of in the modern world."

"The Wrights?" I said.

His hand swept my words aside. " You can't think back to people like the Wrights. It just isn't . . . And look! You can have no certainty that Gibbs White can actually achieve anything like what he thinks he wants. There's simply not going to be any checks and balances in whatever he may be doing."

"I can't argue with you about that," I said, "though what I've seen of the way he's working and what he's told me make me think he may do pretty well.

"And" I said, after a slight pause, "what if you, Dr McIntosh, had known the Wright brothers when they were building? You couldn't have been absolutely sure they'd succeed, could you?"

He stared at me, waiting.

"But, I'll bet you'd have seen they were onto something pretty wonderful, and if you'd had a chance to hang around and help a bit and see how it would turn out . . . well, would you have refused?"

His eyes had looked hurt, and then sad, but now I saw a gleam of something else. Understanding? I wasn't sure. Anyway, he put out his hand at last.

"Good luck, son," he said. "I hope to God things do work out for you somehow because, in my opinion, you've got it. You're one of the few who could *really* succeed in this profession, when we can expect so few of you to be more than ordinary. I truly hope this Gibbs White turns out to be even ten percent of what you think he is."

Well, it had been a bad few minutes – and it was very hard not to feel rash and hasty and much too young. But I also knew I was dealing with something basic and primal and true. I knew in my bones, as one knows that a fresh breeze from the sea is good, that I must go.

I wrote to G.W. I told him I wanted to quit Cambridge for a time, that I didn't want to argue about it any more with anyone, including him. I wrote, "It's clear to me, if to no one else, that to work with you on building your aeroplane would be the one experience I shouldn't miss. One way or another I can get a formal education in aeronautics. But you are doing now the sort of thing I know I want to do later. If you have any use at all for my help, I'll work like hell for you, but please don't try to stop me because you think it would be harmful to my 'career'. Just decide it on whether or not I can be of help."

G.W. sent me a telegram: *Don't jeopardize future. Could not accept responsibility. Come down talk next weekend.*

* * *

I came all right, with the three bags that contained all I had, except for two boxes of books that arrived the following week.

Later, on many occasions, G.W. told me he could scarcely believe he had allowed my "child-like wheedling" to overcome all his own sound judgement and sense of responsibility.

* * *

By leaving Cambridge I had, of course, abandoned my scholarship, a move viewed with sour disfavour by those who administered it. And certainly it did look like a crazy move. With no more than a hundred pounds in the bank, I had no idea how I would survive my time with G.W. I suppose I had vague hopes of getting part-time employment as a farm labourer or something. My actions must have looked preposterous, with the stubbornness of callow youth their sole excuse.

But even if he didn't intend to, G.W. sorted things out for me, by saying, as we drove away from the station, that I could count on food and lodging at his cottage for as long as we were working together – "assuming you don't mind sleeping in the summer house", and that he could also scrape together about fifty pounds a year that I could use for clothing, train travel and the like.

So as far as I was concerned this meant that all immediate problems were solved and I could concentrate on learning the job.

Chapter 9

G.W. gave me no immediate schedule of work as summer loomed. All he wanted at first was my assistance in certain tasks, and for me to familiarize myself with various aspects of construction and the tools required so I could be of real use to him.

For a few days I just watched. But by the end of a week I was joining in. And somehow there was little prompting. I think G.W. quickly assured himself that I could be reasonably competent in a workshop, and as I began to see what was wanted I simply found that I was doing it.

But, whenever the chance came, I watched as carefully as I could to see how G.W. and James Grant performed.

Grant wasn't an especially quick worker, but immensely sure. To everything he brought an understated beauty of execution and perfection of finish. For G.W., the workshop was where he could actualize his ideas and designs. Like Grant, he worked carefully and accurately where high engineering tolerances were needed, but declined to devote time to imparting a finish beyond that required for the job. He worked much faster than Grant.

The main thing with both men was versatility. Grant could fashion things in any sort of material – wood, plastic, aluminum, steel, glass. G.W.'s strength was his improvisational virtuosity – the way he could use ordinary tools, materials and even preformed parts, in new ways to produce unexpected results. He could always and everywhere grasp the manifold possibilities of the shapes of things – and the shapes *in* things.

G.W. could draw his ideas with a pencil – and like lightning. I'm sure he would have scoffed at being described as a gifted draftsman, yet the swift, expressive sketches of mechanisms and structures that he slashed out in frenzied seconds when the juices were flowing showed powerful artistry. Now, in place of people with his gift, industrial designers have computers and virtual reality.

G.W. kept no complete model, however crude or simplified, of the aeroplane-to-be, which surprised me. He was surprised at my surprise.

"Model? We've got models all over the bloody shop, Bob. What d'you want?"

"Yes, but I mean of the whole thing."

"Bless you. You'll never see one, old son. Here's a model – on paper." He pushed plans and sketches my way, pointing with his pipe. "Those things are a model."

I frowned. "Well –"

"Look. How long's a model of clay, or wood, or metal, painted a nice silver, going to take us to make? And when it's done what in hell do we do with it? We work with drawings, and otherwise our models are bits and pieces, Bob, bits and pieces. We can make them to quarter scale, even half scale. We can load them, or tunnel-test them, and have a good notion of how they'd behave if they were at full scale. Though you know, of course, that arguing about scaling transformations – how the full scale product will behave compared to how the scaled down model will behave – can be very tricky. And as you know, big structures are always weaker pound for pound than small ones are if they're of the same shape and made the same way and of the same materials.

"That great Handley Page I saw you gawking at – it's fairly weak. Oh, you could make a big plane that's *pretty* strong. One day they'll make them a lot stronger. But they'll need some special features that'll have to be properly thought out, not just be sort of overscale box-kites like those blighters!"

I nodded, "I see, and . . ."

But he cut in on me. "But on the other hand, our own plane, though it'll be small and strong, mustn't be *ridiculously* small. Got to be big enough for a chap your size to get into comfortably, and cushion the buffeting of actual flight. And, because we've no magic motors that some of these 'popular mechanics' magazines tell us are just around the corner, we have to assume the engine we use will be no smaller than those beasts that Reginald Mitchell used for the Schneider trials.

Big, big boilers. So. You take a large fellow like you as a pilot and a huge great engine – the smallest most compact huge great engine you can get! – and then you just wrap the best air-frame you can make as tightly around both pilot and engine as either can stand – while still trying for total streamlining. See?"

I saw.

"Point is," went on G.W., now in full flow, "you simply can't think about a plane as something you make and then just tuck a person and an engine into as afterthoughts. It's all a system. Somehow, you must get – borrow, steal, make, whatever! – a bunch of components. But . . . accommodation . . . mutual accommodation of part to part, purpose to function . . . *compromise,* d'you see? That's the ticket.

"A plane's a product of complex engineering. It's never going to be an absolutely pure product like a statue, or a painting, because, even if it looks a whole, each of its parts has its own being, its own size limits and tolerances. It simply has to be a compromise, the whole thing. That's why it's so damnably hard to get it right."

He puffed momentarily at his pipe to bring it aglow again. "However, our task is in a way simpler than that of the poor beggar who designs Handley Pages."

"Why?" I asked. "What do you mean?"

"Well, at least we haven't to worry about space for chefs in kitchens and waiters serving gourmet meals and cabin stewards. All that nonsense they advertise."

"Oh, yeah . . ." I felt myself frowning then, and said, "but getting back to the original point, after all the tests are put together and you've designed it all on paper, do you mean you'll then go straight to building the final thing?"

He nodded. "What else?"

"Oh . . ."

He chuckled then. "I see. You really still want that nice big model. Something to take snapshots of to send back to Sydney. Maybe see in a museum one day. Right?"

I nodded, feeling stupid. "I suppose I thought we'd have been sure to need to . . ."

"Of course," he said, smiling. "You're still thinking about

building a model you can hold in your hands. But see, Bob, I can't waste the time, which also means waste the money, on any side issues like that. We'll get our plane just one time. And it has to fly – and fly in the way we want!"

I stared. "But can you really do that?"

He looked at me levelly. "Son . . . I've got to."

Chapter 10

I accompanied G.W. on his next provisioning trip to the village of Timley, ten miles away. There were two closer places, but Timley had the best range of goods and services. I had written Janice a brief note, giving as my return address G.W.'s mail box at the Timley post office. A letter from her was waiting for me.

From there we drove to the market and G.W. said, "I'll just trot in here, Bob, and pick up some meat and vegetables and a few eggs – oh, and some butter and bread. Come and see the market if you like, but" – he smiled – "I see you have a letter you may want to just sit here and read, what?"

I thanked him and opened the letter, as soon as he had disappeared into the market.

"I hope things are still *going well"* it read. *"I also hope you continue to feel you were right to leave Cambridge. The more I think of that decision, the huger, the more portentous, it seems to have been. Of course, I know you're very fortunate to have this opportunity – I understand that. You're also fortunate to know your own mind. When I finish my degree here, I'll try to think about becoming an art historian – as I've said. But, of course, there aren't a lot of opportunities in this field, so it may be difficult to find an opening. And who knows if I will have the necessary analytical and writing skills?*

Well, I hope we can see each other sometimes, but anyway you know that my family's place is at Arlington, which isn't far from Eastbourne. I'll be there late in May. Could you come for a visit? Our place is fairly large and my parents are used to me and my brother asking our friends to stay."

She sent her love.

* * *

G.W. was back soon, loading bags and boxes into the back seat. He climbed behind the wheel and glanced in my direction and smiled.

"I noticed your letter hadn't got an overseas postmark, so I'm wondering if you've heard from that very nice lass who was with you at Hendon."

I nodded, knowing my face was reddening, but smiling.

"She seemed like an exceptional girl. If you ever want her to come down and visit, have a glance at what we're doing – there's no problem. She could stay in a room at my housekeeper's sister's house for a day or two. It's only five minutes walk from the cottage."

"Thanks very much," I said. "I might just ask her if you're sure that –"

"As I say, no problem. A girl like that is not easy to find."

*　*　*

That evening I sat in G.W.'s parlour, writing a reply to Janice.

Yes, I acted on a hunch, if you like. It was just too strong for me to ignore. Of course, I believe it was the right thing and it still feels right. I do think this man has special abilities that aren't the same as other people's. But I admit there's always the possibility I have made a fool of myself, though I don't for a moment believe that I have.

One way or another let's get together as soon and as often as we can. I'd love to come to see you at your parents' place.

There was more, but that was the gist of it. James Grant had to visit one of the smaller villages next day and he posted it for me.

Later I sat thinking it was starting to feel it could be as important to me that I not lose track of Janice as it was that I work with G.W. . . .

Chapter 11

In the following three months I found some skills to let me share significantly in the construction work during the coming winter. At G.W.'s insistence I also resumed flying practice under his tutelage so that I could further my training as a pilot and obtain a licence. Again, my solo flying was in a De Havilland Moth. But much of the time I flew accompanied by G.W., with him commenting on my every move and gradually teaching me how to control the aircraft in steep banks, dives and other manoeuvres, even loops.

"At your present stage of experience, Bob, you're still pretty raw as a pilot," G.W. said, "but your cockpit drill is painstaking and you're careful in preparing to take off. Those, above all, are things I want in a test pilot. But you have a long way to go.

"You told me you're not an instinctive flier, well, I wouldn't worry about that; you're showing a lot of feeling for the basic manoeuvres. So if you really don't have a natural instinct for flying, practice will get you there."

All this flying was near Ashford and between flights G.W., would light his pipe and ask me endless questions to force me to think about problems I might meet at the vastly greater speeds we were anticipating. He said he was satisfied with my basic progress, but kept on pointing our that my greatest challenges would occur when – and if – he decided I could eventually share in flying the machine we were going to produce.

He said, "The best I can say is that by the time we reach testing – if we ever do! – you'll be as familiar with what we've built as anyone can be, and that when you do fly – if you do – at first you'll have to keep speeds as low as are safe and be very modest about all aerobatics till you've thoroughly got the feel of the thing."

We seemed unable to obtain planes of greater performance in which we could perfect our manoeuvres at high speeds. There simply were not very many fast aircraft available to most civilian pilots in those days.

But G.W. re-emphasised Dr Milland's earlier criticisms of some of my landings. It was frustrating that this earlier fault – which I thought I had overcome – had returned. I supposed that whatever did not come naturally might be overcome – even perfected – by hard work, but also might be the first thing to recur with loss of practice.

"For Christ's sake, old boy," G.W. would shout, "show some bloody precision – and delicacy! You can dump this little bus down like you just did and it's so light it'll just bounce up again. But, compared to this one, ours will be like a falling brick if you try to put it down like that. I mean, count on about five times the wing-loading and three times the landing speed. Forget that and it could be your coffin." A bit later he said, "Well, I said you were *mostly* careful . . ." But he never nagged.

He did, however, as my landings finally became uniformly smooth and reliable, make me execute landing approaches at speeds far above normal for the Moth so that I would have some feeling for what it would be like in a modern high-speed aeroplane.

In the workshop our discussions grew more detailed and specific.

"We need a cockpit cover. Only thing we could adapt would be one of those stupid affairs that Progress Aircraft Supplies would make to order for us. But their stuff would be like sort of birdcages covered by perspex. Be an insult to 'optimal design' to use such horrors. In fact, our cockpit – and cover – must fit the pilot like a glove. A pretty loose and comfy glove, of course. Let's do some measurements, now – on ourselves. You be the long of it; I'll be the short."

We worked out in detail a cockpit rig based on body measurements and the movements we would have to make during flying. It took days to determine the right seat angle and placement in relation to the joy stick, rudder bar and the other controls and instruments. We could have made the seat more adjustable, but at the cost of space and added weight. We settled for the near vertical angle G.W. preferred. As he said, "Prerogative of the aged. You're a kid. You can put up with a bit of discomfort better than an old man." We were careful, too, about hip and shoulder space and angles of view for the pilot. As usual, compromise was the watchword.

But with the cockpit cover G.W. decided there must be no compromise, that the major part of it must be a single streamlined piece (a teardrop shape), made of clear perspex and without joins or marks. And in deciding on its dimensions he said, "Let's just work out how big our heads are, how much we simply must move them round in, say, a two hour flight if we aren't to get welded spines. Then we can make wooden moulds, and heat sheets of half-inch-thick perspex and press them into the moulds. Yes. That'll be the ticket."

Our greatest problem was the super-thin wing. G.W. had worked out a wing loading of about thirty pounds per square foot that wasn't to be exceeded. If he used the most powerful engines available – which would also be the heaviest – the resultant loading would be the highest tolerable if the plane was to manoeuvre and handle well at high altitude.

"What we need," he declared one morning, as we drank our horrid tea, "is a super-metal for wing spars. That's why I'm off tomorrow to see metallurgists in Birmingham. Be away a day or two. You and James can get on with the wing root model for further testing."

When he returned from Birmingham he was in low spirits. "The metallurgists say 'no can do' – for quite a few years. Titanium is going to be 'it' one day. Then we'll have titanium alloys strong as steel and much lighter. But 'one day' mark you. Not now. And how the devil am I going to make a job of this bloody aeroplane if I can't get a good metal? I feel just like that poor Babbage beggar: know what's wanted and how it ought to be made, but not how to get it."

For a couple of days he was morose, uncommunicative. Then one morning after breakfast he fronted up to us. His voice sounded jaunty again, eyes gleaming in defiance.

"Look, we just have to get on with things. We'll go the route of another kind of wing spar, use box sections like this", he sketched what he meant, "fitting together, but with bigger sections where the spar meets the fuselage and smaller ones near the wingtips where not as much strength is needed, and the whole series welded together. Then we'll have a spar on the cantilever principle that will be light and strong, with limited vertical movement and good lateral stability. I hope . . ."

Grant nodded, but I said, "I thought you needed a quite rigid wing."

"Since the metals to give it to me aren't available, this is the best I can think of, Bob – if we're to obtain lightness and strength. Got a better idea?" He looked at me, head on one side.

"But," I pursued, feeling slightly emboldened, "you want to push design to the limit."

"Of course. But in the end I have to face facts. What we do will never really be the last word. You know about asymptotes? Yes . . . well, at some point a law of diminishing returns operates when you contemplate further improvement of a design that's already OK. You get towards a limit of result versus effort, and eventually you have to be content."

So if he was falling a bit short of his construction ideals I saw that he was realist enough to absorb this and just battle on.

He drew up a plan for the wing spar, we discussed it, and we built it. A week of cutting, fitting and finishing and we had two model spars – the one we would use in tests and a spare. The spar model would be tested for strength based on known stress factors for high performance flight at various wing loadings. The spars would also be installed in scale models of whole wings with the relative dimensions of cord and thickness that had already been planned and tested for aerodynamic performance of wing models in the Barnsworth wind tunnel. Effects of air turbulence at critical speeds on super-thin and slightly flexible wings had also to be examined.

"They might just wobble like a butterfly in a breeze," said G.W., with a sort of grim laugh. "While we're about this," he said, "let's make a tail assembly mockup to scale. Test the lot over a few days. Might be our last chance, even. The R.A.F. types are getting quite sticky over our time in the tunnel."

"Can't you pay them a bit more?" I asked.

"I don't pay them a farthing. Money's not the question. They neither want nor need it. They don't even have the business apparatus to accept payments. They're supposed to help civilian inventors when their own need of facilities isn't excessive. Air Ministry official policy that is, in theory."

"So what's wrong?"

"Oh, dog-in-manger attitude. *They* are the professionals of His Majesty's Royal Air Force and the Air Ministry. Damned sure no self-trained, amateur could have ideas worth spitting on. So – go away and lose yourself, you tiresome little man!"

I laughed, but behind his own smile G.W. looked troubled. "They'll stop us soon. They'll say, 'Terribly sorry, Mr. Gibbs White, but we've a fearful lot of pressing work coming up.' And that will be that." He nodded his head. "We have about two months, I reckon."

"What then?"

"We'll just have to hope we can utilize our maths and our ingenuity, and hold our weak nerves together while we make an aeroplane, what!"

He nodded again. "Two months."

* * *

It wasn't that long. We had worked for nearly four weeks on wing and tail models in preparation for a week of testing. G.W. phoned Barnsworth to arrange ahead for use of the wind tunnels and other facilities. He spoke for ten minutes. Grant and I were outside in the workshop and could hear no details of speech at first, but his voice gradually got louder. Grant put down his tools and moved to the open office door where I joined him. There was a long silence as G.W. listened. Then he said "Right!" crisply and distinctly, and hung up. He rose and came to the door, roughly packing tobacco into his pipe.

"That's it, then."

"Just like that?"

"Indeed. We can test these things for a day – Tuesday next. Then . . . finish. That was Wing Commander Henderson that runs the show. Very polite chap. Not at all like most of the chaps we meet there. Very ignorant chap, too. Much worse than most of the chaps we meet there." He lit his pipe carefully, drawing on it, looking at the bowl as it glowed to life.

"He . . . let me down . . . very civilly. Seems they have a vast schedule for months ahead. Top priority stuff." He gave a short laugh. "Testing new issue tail assembly spares for those famous Hart biplanes they acquired recently."

"Can you go somewhere else?" I asked.

"Nowhere near enough, Bob. We'll just have to do all we can with these last tests and then guess our way along from there."

Suddenly he looked at us, his face cleared, and he smiled.

"Don't look so glum. We know enough to manage. Be a real *tour de force* to get it off the drawing board, to the workshop floor, into the air, what?"

Grant and I glanced fleetingly at each other, then back at G.W. When I looked at him I began to feel buoyant again. He could make you believe.

A bit later I wondered just how much of the buoyant feeling was really justified.

Chapter 12

One morning G.W. drove off in the Vauxhall to stay with his sister in Salisbury for a few days and then to "potter around Dartmoor to get a bit of exercise and do some quiet thinking." At this same time he sent me to Glasgow to discuss engines with a friend in the engineering department at the university. I arrived by train on a fine day early in August and went to see Dr. David Robertson, an aeronautics lecturer whom G.W. had known since student days. Robertson was an aircraft engine specialist and I was supposed to get his views on the relative merits of the basic engine types we might use. I felt flattered by G.W.'s entrusting me with this task, and hoped his confidence in me would be justified.

Dr. Robertson greeted me with courtesy and affability in his narrow office, its windows open to the morning sunlight. He referred to G.W. as "Philip" which told me their friendship was real.

I told him of successes and the reasons for recent holdups. I said I did not doubt the plane would eventually be built and flown.

He nodded. "Yes, Philip has something quite special about him.. The fellow's brilliant, but the real point is that he won't be beaten. If determination can do it he'll probably be getting what he wants. And considering the odds against him that's quite a prediction for a sceptical professional like me to be making, because making planes has become a sophisticated game – and a damnably expensive one." I remembered what Dr McIntosh had said.

A woman came in with cups of tea and Robertson pushed one towards me; it was a bit better than GW.'s bitter black brews – but not too much.

"But you want to talk of engines, Robert. What can I possibly tell you? Philip himself knows engines."

"He says you know about them in a comparative way that's second to none."

Robertson smiled. "I think he gives me too much credit."

"Main thing is, Dr. Robertson, that while G.W. knows a lot about in-line, liquid-cooled engines, he isn't confident he knows enough about large radials."

Robertson nodded, his head slightly on one side.

"And if we were to use one of those, for example, then the airframe in front of the pilot –"

"Would have to be quite different than if you were to use an in-line engine." Robertson nodded. "Of course. To say nothing of the aeroplane's centre of balance and general streamlining. Yes. Well, let me put it like this: for liquid cooled, in-line engines you probably have to stop at Rolls Royce. They're the permanent winners of the Schneider trophy, and that pretty well guarantees the quality of their engines. Of course, some believe that Napier engines of even greater power will soon become available. But Philip knows all about these things."

I agreed.

"Yes. Well, the Americans seem at present to be going mostly with radials, and in Britain we also have good radials in every kind of military aircraft. On the other hand, they haven't been much seen in recent speed record attempts. And as the new generation of engines in British fighter planes comes into being I think all of them will be in-line. However, the Americans believe radials are extremely reliable."

"But the streamlining?"

"Quite. Always a problem with radials if great speed is the requirement. The radial may be a bit lighter, so you save there. But any weight saving will probably be offset by the extra air resistance that results from the big frontal area."

"I understand that," I said, "but as in-line engines gradually become more powerful and bigger, will the larger air intakes they'll need tend to offset their present advantages in the form of a better streamline shape and less frontal area?"

Robertson nodded encouragingly and said, "Very likely."

As he was saying little, I began to feel I was saying too much. But I hurried on . "And so, you risk ending up, in the case of a very powerful engine, with an intake scoop of such size that you may lose more and more of the advantage of the small frontal area."

He nodded. "Yes, though in-line engines have only just been getting big enough for this to be a real bother."

He fumbled in a folder. "I can give you some data on this sort of thing, obtained by a student of mine last year. And here are performance graphs from an American team in Baltimore that compare frontal resistance of several in-line and radial configurations at a range of air speeds. You can see where the curves of performance-change with each type of engine start to converge.

"My own present guess – from what you've shown me of the sort of plane you're building – is that you'll need to go with some kind of in-line engine . . . which is probably what Philip has already almost decided. Yes?"

He handed across some documents that I began to examine.

"Whatever! You and Philip may still need to do some front end mockups and some hard thinking. He's very good at that kind of thing, of course . . ."

I agreed. Looking at him I found him staring at me. I flushed. He smiled quickly.

"Philip's given me the idea you may soon be good at that kind of thing, too. If so, he can be pleased. He needs a sound man to help him."

"But," I said, "I really know so little. See, I came from Australia recently, and now I've left Cambridge . . ."

"Philip wrote me a little about you, Robert," said Robertson. "I think I can tell you he feels these things – in your particular case – may not be so much of a problem. At least for this job. And since I have lots of respect for the man's ability and judgement, I assume he knows what he's talking about. Does that at all reassure you?"

I nodded. "It helps . . ."

"Mind you," added Robertson, "if your eventual aim is a whole career in aeronautics, my advice would simply have to be a complete formal training in the end – when all this caper is over."

He pulled out more papers and passed them across to me. "What about propellers? They'll be critical to performance. Here are some details of constant speed, variable pitch ones – things that are only just starting to become really effective, but that you may find useful."

*   *   *

As summer drew nearer I received a note from Janice, reminding me of her invitation to come to her family's home near Hankham in Sussex, a few miles from Eastbourne. Janice herself, her examinations now over, was still in London, spending two weeks studying paintings in the London galleries before going home for the summer. She suggested I come to Hankham, and stay for a week, because there would be plenty of people to meet and things to do.

I wanted to accept her offer – felt, in fact, desperate to do so. But I was not sure about how to broach it with G.W. Eventually I mentioned that I would like to slip across to this place near Eastbourne to see Janice for a day, perhaps two, if that would be OK.

G.W. looked at me as if startled. "Couple of days? Don't be daft old boy; it's thirty or forty miles. I know you Australians drive a couple of hundred miles, shoot a kangaroo for lunch, and get back again in time for tea, and all that. But in England it'll take you a day in total just to get there and back. For Heaven's sake, Bob, accept this pretty girl's invite, and stay for a week at least."

I think I looked askance. I was delighted in one way, but in another way had hoped he would at least pull a long face and tell me how much I had helped so far and how he had been counting on me in the next few months. I said, "Are you quite sure I won't be leaving you short-handed?"

"No chance," he said. "See, I don't have to punch a time clock twice a day. If I want a day off to watch some village cricket – or go up to London to see rugby, I darned well take it. We only come this way once, old son; might as well enjoy ourselves along the way."

"Well then, I think I will go to see Janice, soon."

"Good. And by the way, Bob, you can get to where you're going pretty easily. The railway runs from Ashford right through Ham Street, hits the coast near Hastings and then runs near the water right down to Eastbourne. Quite a pleasant little train trip. Not an express, mind."

* * *

On a fine morning two weeks later Janice picked me at up Eastbourne in her family's car and we sped off to her home. After about fifteen minutes we turned down a small rustic side road lined by big trees, and a large red brick house swung into view seventy yards beyond an open pair of iron gates. "There it is, then, the ancestral pile, so to speak."

As we drew up at the end of a gravel drive, she pulled on the parking brake, flung her arms round me and we kissed frantically. "I've missed you," she said in a choked voice, but smiling widely.

"Likewise."

And so, at last, we began the attenuated task of knowing each other a bit better.

Janice's mother, Elaine Whitcombe, a very pretty woman in her mid-forties, was shorter than Janice, who otherwise resembled her. Janice's brother, Richard, a few years her senior, and a tall, good-looking man, bore no great likeness to his mother or sister. Janice later told me that he resembled their father.

Mrs Whitcombe did everything to welcome me and put me at ease. I knew, though, I was going to experience a kind of life at her home that was new to me. To begin with, the Whitcombe family had been living in this part of England for several hundred years and, as I realized, must in the past have been substantial landowners. Janice explained that any real wealth the family had possessed was long gone and her father, Hugh Whitcombe, actually earned most of the family's income. Mr Whitcombe had a profession which I, as an Australian, could not have imagined possible. Following his initial education in the classics, he had studied the history of art – hence Janice's own interest in this subject – and then earned degrees in architecture. At the time of my visit he was away in northern England pursuing his professional architectural vocation of ecclesiology – advising on the restoration, repair and maintenance of church buildings. He had had, as Janice explained, great admiration for the design and construction of churches from his boyhood, so he had deliberately gained an education that suited him to the work he had taken up. His skills were much in demand.

"Of course," said Janice, "you have to realize that Father is not at all involved in the practice of religion. In fact, though he makes no show of it, he's an atheist."

I must have looked surprised, because she laughed and said, "It's the buildings that he loves, and what they tell about history. And the thought that, in the case of cathedrals, people often continued to work on their construction over several generations – sometimes several lifetimes; sometimes even for centuries. As he says, there's never going to be a time when things of this order of craft and design and beauty are going to be built again."

We spent the day with Janice showing me round the park-like grounds of the family home and at four in the afternoon we went into a large sunroom with views of a small wood backed by a low hill. It was a beautiful and restful domestic environment and I felt envious of the casual and private comfort it represented. Janice's mother was there and she poured tea and offered cake. She spoke mostly in terms of welcome and of "How nice it is to meet a new friend of Janice's – and someone from such a faraway place." She questioned me about Australia, but excused herself to answer a telephone that rang in the library next door.

After a minute I said to Janice, "You know, what you said about your father is very interesting, and not just because he has a career few Australians could ever conceive of, but because – to an Australian only recently arrived in Britain – he seems to be part of a sort of pattern."

"In what way?"

"Well," I said, "your father's work would sound so completely unusual in Australia that it would probably seem something for a bit of an eccentric to be doing – I mean as a profession. And you've met G.W. and he's certainly an unusual type. And you haven't met Dr Milland – one of my lecturers. Well, he's not exactly eccentric, but he has a combination of speech and manner many Australians would think very affected – even though he isn't like that at all. And even Pete Randall, who's going to be an earl and all that stuff, is *not* puffed up, but really a good and helpful bloke – which means he's playing against type, so to speak."

Janice nodded. "Yes, well what do you make of it?"

"Well," I said slowly, trying to pick my words, "something like this: Australians believe they're a classless society, and even many of the kids who went to a private school would support that view. And it's true, in the sense that most of us talk with the same accent and figures of speech, even though some have better grammar than others. But in some ways it's not so much a classless society as a uniform one – in which the 'tall poppies' get cut down. Eccentrics can be criticized and sneered at."

"So you're saying that Britain is, in some ways, more tolerant?"

"Maybe," I said. "I don't know, really. I'm just kicking ideas around, trying to understand."

Her mother came back then, and asked me things about Sydney. Then she said, "You must forgive me if I seem to be quizzing you so much. But several more friends of Janice and Richard are coming tomorrow and I might not have another chance to talk to you."

This made me feel a bit jumpy. I had assumed – unrealistically I now saw – that I would have unrestricted time with Janice for a week. But now – and in the rage of activities that began the next day – I saw this was not to be.

* * *

The Whitcombe home included grounds that featured not only large lawns, trees and garden areas, but also two tennis courts and a large field of cropped grass that served as a cricket arena.

"Mean to say your family actually plays cricket at home?" I said.

"Only in the summer, of course, and when we have a number of guests. And Pete Randall's family, and various relations and friends and people from the villages around here will turn up. Sometimes people will have to field for both sides to make up numbers, but we muddle through. Besides, some of these people are extremely good players. One of them who will be playing – Nicholas Cartwright – has played for England as a spin bowler. And my brother plays for

Sussex from time to time. Anyway, you're a guest and you'll have to play this week."

"Good God," I said. "In this sort of company I'll just record the score."

"No you don't," said Janice. "Everyone – that's every man – plays. We have some very good women cricketers hereabouts, too. Some of them may play. No exceptions, unless you're sick or a cripple – or over eighty. Besides, everyone knows that all Australians are terrific cricketers."

"Who's this 'everyone'?"

"You too 'mate', you've got to play," she laughed. "You too."

* * *

I had a funny feeling over the next few days, as I met and mingled as best I was able with the four other young people who'd come to stay, that this bloody game of cricket could be absurdly important to me in the social milieu of this society.

When the day dawned there were more than two dozen young men most of them from other households and families or from nearby villages or farms. Also included, to my personal satisfaction, were Pete Randall and his two brothers – all tall, athletic-looking young men.

Pete clapped me on the back and babbled on cheerfully, unstoppably, as was his wont. But his presence made me feel easier.

The game itself was fun, though taken more light-heartedly than it would have been in Sydney.

Late in the afternoon, Whitcombe's team needed about sixty runs to win and my turn to bat had come. I'd been sent in at eight wickets down. Some wanted me to come in much earlier, but I pleaded lack of practice, limited competence and no experience of English cricket pitches.

I began to feel I was right about my inability, as I missed several balls by wide margins and could have been out in the first over I received. But we still needed that sixty and I thought it was now or never. I told myself to forget technical batting and just trust my eyesight

– which was acute in those days – and throw the bat at everything within reach.

The one thing I could still do was hit hard. So I ignored defence, struck out at everything as if there was no tomorrow, was lucky, and managed to score a pretty quick fifty.

With the game won, Richard draped his arm over my shoulders and said, "You were right, Robert, by God. You were in lousy form. But even if you mostly swung like a baseball batter, you still hit the damn ball enough to destroy them. Great fun!"

And Pete Randall, who had bowled some fast – often inaccurate, but sometimes very awkward deliveries at me – laughed in his loud and cheerful way and said, "An engineer's innings, old man. Not pretty but loads of brute force. Seriously, you ought to get yourself in practice, because if you did you'd be a star in university cricket circles in no time. A couple of the bowlers you beat up today are considered very good. I mean, Nic Cartwright's a bowler of great distinction who's played well in internationals."

I laughed and said, "Well, I had a lot of luck today."

"Sure," said Pete, "but not enough to explain how you scored over fifty."

* * *

All this was nice, but to myself I made no secret that I had come to the Whitcombes not to meet the rest of her family and their friends and relations but to put myself on a more intimate footing with Janice herself.

I could not say whether this had happened. If it had, it was not because I now knew her better – there was too great a screen of company around her, and notably what looked like admiring male company, many young men she seemed to know well and who appeared to be on excellent terms with her.

Her mother hosted a rather splendid dance one evening, and I danced with Janice. But it wasn't like it had been that first time. Every man present danced with her, and every man looked very interested in her, and in fact I danced with her less than almost anyone.

Perhaps I was doing all right with her family and friends, but . . . As she drove me back to the Eastbourne railway station two days later, she was quiet, hardly looking in my direction. As the train drew in I said, "When will I see you again?"

She looked at me. There was regret in her eyes. "It wasn't very satisfactory, was it? I shouldn't have asked you under these conditions. Perhaps we can do better soon." She kissed me briefly as I got on board the train.

Chapter 13

Next morning, after G.W., James and I had been at work two hours, we stood for a few minutes as the teapot passed from hand to hand. G.W. put his pipe down, pulled out his pocket knife to clean it, put the knife down, picked up the dead pipe and pointed it vaguely in our direction, put the pipe down again and said, "What's the date? November the something . . . ?"

I knew he knew the date; he was never absent-minded. He was just not sure how to start.

"The second of," said James.

"The second of November. Right. Well, as of tomorrow we have to start putting this aeroplane together."

This got our attention.

From his hesitancy we had been expecting some problem. Not this.

I had always supposed we were already making the plane, that the whole object would, as it were, eventually just stand before us. I felt suddenly unsure, far from ready for what was now being told us. It was as if I were being ordered to pick up a gun which I had formerly only weighed in my hands, while examining its mechanisms, and thinking about firing one day. Now I had to aim it and fire it and hit a bullseye. And do it again. And again. And again.

James slowly drank some of his tea, then said, "We haven't started the undercarriage design. In fact, we've barely discussed it. We've made no final decision on the engine. And the duralumin stressed skin tests aren't finished."

"I know," said G.W. "But we have to bite the bullet, notwithstanding. We've got a lot of the hard parts done. Many of the really hard parts. We'll start immediately now to make what can be made. James, you'll be building most of the fuselage. We'll help you physically wherever you need it. But just get started, what? Meantime,

Bob and I will nut out the undercarriage details, and exact wing and engine placements. Oh, and following what Bob brought back with him from Edinburgh, I've decided on the engine. It'll be from Rolls Royce."

Grant and I stared. Unconvinced. A bit stunned.

"Look," G.W. said, "not to put too fine a point on it, my cash situation just won't carry us much beyond next spring."

"Is it possible to get government grants or commercial contracts?" I asked.

G.W. looked at me in a way that made me feel I was somehow missing the point. At last he answered. "Not impossible, Bob. No. But probably not feasible for such as myself. With grants or contracts we'd have to specify every nut and bolt in advance, put in quarterly reports, have committees here to view our 'efficiency' and 'progress'. Things like that. They'd want to order our whole strategy.

"As for industry and commerce – if they liked what they saw we might get some sort of contract and even have a publicity bonanza. Or they might want to keep very mum about things and shape the machine to Air Ministry specs . . . Or even to some other purpose. Can't tell. But either way, the world might tumble in on us. I don't want that. Anyway not yet."

He spoke firmly, without hesitancy. He was, after all, an individual, a private plane maker. We were his assistants, his employees, though I knew none of us thought in that vein most of the time. And if I could readily visualize the glamour, and possibly the fun, of having the world tumble in on us I could also see that, in rejecting the committee, the team, the panel of experts, G.W. was being instinctively correct in believing that even if experts could disclose weaknesses in his project, they would be unable to augment his single-minded drive and the wholeness of his vision.

We drank more tea, speaking now mainly of readying the workshop, of logistics and supplies, the use of machinery and, finally, of rough schedules for the completion of the major parts of the plane. Eventually G.W. stood up between us and put a hard hand on the shoulder of each.

"Let's close up now and have a bite," he said. "I know a little place – used to be part of an abbey. They serve a good pint and the cold beef and ham are pretty fair. We can go there for lunch."

We drove ten miles to an attractive rustic pub on the edge of a village. It was too cool in the garden, so we sat inside at a window and ate a leisurely lunch.

G.W. talked a bit of his first tries at plane design which had been exclusively theoretical, since he had neither the practical experience nor the physical plant needed to build. For two years he had steeped himself in aeronautical lore, studied the classics of the field and peered minutely at available plans of aircraft of every shape and size and vintage. He had somehow contrived to make intellectual progress by such means, augmented only by talks with aeronautical engineer friends and the few plane designers he managed to meet. In the end, he had the essential plan of his aircraft – either on paper or in his head. If realizable, he would have in his hands an aeroplane whose design embodied every particle of advanced aeronautical thinking that ran to just two ends – maximum performance and handling.

I told him how models had begun for me in Sydney with Charlie. I told him how I had nearly given up until my fearsome physics master had challenged me to work harder so that I might have a chance to come to Britain.

G.W looked at me reflectively. "I hope to God you will still feel you've done the right thing after all this is over," he said. "There's no guarantee that what you may learn from what we do on this plane will make it one jot easier for you to get work later. In fact, as far as one can see you'll almost certainly have to go back and complete your degree before any reputable aircraft firm will consider you. You may find any experience you get working here will be discounted, even if it helps you in the way you personally look at plane design."

"Yes, I know." But, of course, I knew nothing . . .

The afternoon ended in reverie without much talk, but for the three of us there was the rising realization that once the work began we would at last find ourselves caught in the trap that allowed no backward step, no hesitating, only the one-way surge, the burning concentration of our work-time as we were propelled towards the target. No more leisure. And no more mistakes either.

As we drove homewards I felt a pleasant light-headedness, only partly a result of the ales I had drunk.

That evening was fine and after dinner G.W. and I stamped round in the cooling air of the garden in our heavy coats, looking up at the stars. I told him the southern constellations looked grander, richer, an impression probably enhanced by the dry clear Australian skies.

"Like to see that one day," he said absently. "Anyway . . . despite my by now well-known concerns about how you may be damaging your future, and my contribution to that, do you still feel sure you want to see this thing through?

"Of course. I –"

By the little movement of his glowing pipe I think he smiled in the dark. Then he pointed up. I could see the shape of his extended arm, because it hid some stars.

"One of those things up there is mine," he said dryly. "Has to be. Without it, I'll be the idiot of the age."

I wanted to say something. Something seemed called for. But too many years of living and experience lay between us. I ended up by keeping silent.

I thought that later on, years on, when all this narrow absurd, obsessive, beautiful apprenticeship was long past, perhaps I would be able to approach G.W. and say the things to him that ought to be said – praise, criticism – and talk to him of the strangeness of it all . . . He would understand it all himself, then, and would tolerate my questions, because a man would be talking to him, not just an ignorant, if enthusiastic, child. Perhaps my own understanding of people would have improved, my experience of the world of creative work. Then, maybe, I could ask him questions of the "What, really, are you? Why are you? Will you?" variety.

Chapter 14

Then we shifted gears and were working with unparalleled speed and concentration.

James Grant erected a scaffolding of steel pipes to support the monocoque fuselage he was to build. Soon he was working with smooth precision using shears, strips and sheets of metal, presses and a rivet gun, pausing repeatedly to stare at pads covered by calculations that converted G.W.'s plans to full-scale measurements. It was the most basic possible sort of aircraft production. There were no pre-formed parts (except for those James had already cut using wood or metal templates), no stamped-out components – nothing ready-made except nuts, bolts and rivets. James Grant was putting together a plane's body from raw metal. If he wanted moulds or forms, he made them. As jigs or clamps were needed they were conveyed to the structure, which grew and took shape before our eyes.

G.W. and I concentrated on the undercarriage construction. G.W. mistrusted narrow track undercarriages of the sort that would be later utilized in fighter aircraft by both Mitchell and Messerschmitt. The wheel struts of the narrow track undercarriages were close to the fuselage and therefore easy to anchor securely, but provided poor lateral stability in landings. So we built a wide-straddling assembly, with wheels as far apart as wing section and strength would allow.

After two weeks we looked up from our own labours to stare in wonder at James' progress. A light, yet rigid structure of slender, dully-gleaming, metal stringers, was appearing, that gave the rear body and cockpit regions of the fuselage a delicately traced elegance. Cross-bracings were few. The fuselage had the cleanness of the monocoque design, its strength in the slim oval sectional elements that were cut from sheet metal and through which the longitudinal stringers passed. A very thin, duralumin metal skin would eventually impose further tautness and rigidity on this skeleton. This sort of construction, which was already catching on among aircraft builders, had been made possible because of the discovery that duralumin – an alloy of 95% aluminum, 4% copper and less than 1% of magnesium and manganese – could be rolled into very thin sheets whose strength far exceeded that of aluminum alone. Stretched tightly over a fuselage or wing structure, rivetted in place, these sheets could impose great strength on an aircraft with very little more weight than if the sheets had been pure aluminum.

Years later, I happened to see time-lapse cine-film of the changes in form that occur in animals during development – particularly in vertebrates. The extraordinary "writhings", the self-directed struggle-to-become of these creatures . . . only time-lapse could show it. We could have filmed the development and growth of the aeroplane by time-lapse, shooting a few frames each day. I believe it would have born an eerie resemblance to the development of some great animal. G.W was already calling the aeroplane "The Beast"; in the light of the film, that name has seemed uncannily prescient.

One day James paused in his fuselage work, to take a break by constructing a seamless, streamlined, cockpit cover. He first shaped a heavy wooden mould and sanded it to a perfectly smooth finish. Heat-softened clear perspex was then pushed into the mould by means of curved wooden blocks with attached handles. It was hard, hot work, and G.W. and I assisted. After the perspex was cool, James trimmed the canopy with saw and file to a precise fit over the cockpit, then burnished it to a gleaming finish. The parts of the canopy through which the pilot would see ahead and to either side without distortion would be replaced by pieces of shatter-proof glass cut by a firm in London. The glass directly in front of the pilot would be an inch thick. The main part of the canopy could be slid smoothly backwards or forwards on metal tracks and secured by a ratchet.

The front end of the fuselage would, of course, house the engine. Problems abounded here, because the engine bearer had to be both very strong and not too heavy.

* * *

One day, as we hoisted and manhandled the wing into the position it would occupy in the finished plane, but before bolting it into place, we got our first overall impression of the creature we were making. We stood there muttering, staring, pleased . . . somewhat bemused.

*   *   *

Early one December morning we sat for ten minutes gulping hot tea. Near us, an old oil-fired space heater roared away and there was a second, more centrally located one that gave a limited amount of pervasive warmth to the whole workshop. But even though we wore heavy work clothes, conditions were not very comfortable and we bellowed our disgust when anyone left the outside doors open for a moment longer than necessary.

G.W. was now functioning in a way I had not previously seen. I could never picture him leading a large group – he was too intensely concerned with the details of plans and action. He sometimes took tools out of people's hands to do jobs himself rather than wasting time explaining. But now I could see that, with small groups, he might always lead effectively by example, by the directness of his actions, the speed and certainty of his performance. And we – we would follow him by the hour, the minute.

But our days were not hard days, because filled with the wonder and the love of our work. And Grant and I grew to understand that we were seeing G.W. living his life as he wanted to live it. It was not so much that he worked, but that he made things. And he cared not a jot for anyone else's views of what *he* was doing.

Those days – except when we ate our lunches of bread and cheese, hard-boiled eggs and apples, washed down with bottled ale or cider – were a patchwork of varied tasks, starts and restarts, and disappointments. But the wonderful shape that we were making held us in its spell.

For me, it was a time of bliss.. . . perhaps of grace.

As we finished our tea, I followed up on the few remarks G.W. had made about the German plane designers to ask what he thought about the prospects for a European war.

"Coming. Five years. Six. Nineteen forty at the latest. When Hitler's strong enough he'll not have much trouble getting Germany armed and ready. And there simply doesn't seem to be the unity in the rest of Europe that could stop it happening.

"Of course, a person could argue that we should be taking part in making warplanes. But then, I'm an independent plane maker. Not important. Just me and a couple of friends. It's the big commercial manufacturers who should research warplane design. And some are doing that. Anyway, my contribution would be a drop in the bucket."

"Not if this aircraft does what you want it to," said Grant.

"And," G.W. resumed, "we've no credibility in the outside world. No one would pay heed to our efforts at this point in time."

"They might do, soon," I said.

"Perhaps," he conceded. "Yes, perhaps. But even if I went to work for some big show I'm unconvinced I'd be able to do anything of real value – for anyone. The Air Ministry simply insists on inflicting its specs on everybody. They'd do a lot more good if . . . but I've said it before.

"And as for me joining one of the big companies, I really don't think I could manage to insinuate myself into the system. My best course is probably just to chug ahead with what I'm doing, hope we can make a good aeroplane, and get our ideas noticed because people like what they see."

We were silent, then he said, "Thing is, really, I don't think any independent designer can hope for much success persuading the brass hats and bureaucrats to break their pernicious habit of just writing out specs, instead of occasionally looking out of their windows – to see what's actually flying by."

I looked at the windows as he spoke – I suppose I was thinking instinctively of a bright blue day when we might at last be trying to fly, but all I could see was steady rain dropping out of a dirty grey sky.

*   *   *

I had not seen Janice since I had stayed at her home, and the few letters we had exchanged were tentative affairs on both sides. And we were both hard at work – she getting ready for examinations – so I was very surprised when a letter arrived.

"Dear Robert,

I have been doing nothing much but work, and I assume it's the same for you, but is there any possibility you'll have to come up to London on business, because it would be good to see you and have lunch or dinner. I know things were not right when you visited, but it would be nice to see you again and I'd like to tell you a few things.

Love,

Janice

Love? Was that a polite informal salutation she would offer any friend, or . . . ? Well, I had no idea.

I sent a reply at once. I said I could probably manage a day off, but why didn't she come down and see us at work: "You might find it interesting as you've had no experience of this sort of thing." I added that I was anxious to see her, but that "while I have some idea of what your work and interests are like, you've never seen what I do." I told her G.W.'s housekeeper had a sister with whom she could stay.

I also signed it "Love."

Her letter came in two days to say when she would be coming.

* * *

She arrived in Timley in the bus that had delivered her from where she had left the train at Ashford. She looked as beautiful as ever and managed a great smile as we embraced, though I thought I could sense a certain tension.

"Incredible to see you," I said. "Hope to God your studies won't suffer too much at this time of the year, and that you won't be too bored by our performance here."

"I don't think that's likely," she said. "And as for coming now, I just had to get away from what I've been doing at this very humdrum time of the year."

"What surprises me is that . . . well. . . that you've come to me. Here. I thought the pre-Christmas festive season – you know, parties and balls and all, would be just starting and there'd be a horde of chaps who – "

"Other chaps, more attractive and available than you, you mean?"

"Something like that."

"Don't be a fool, Robert. There isn't any horde of chaps, because I'm just not that interested in most of them in the way you mean – even if they were interested in me."

I took her hand in my right hand, and her suitcase in my left hand, and guided her to the Vauxhall.

"It's only three o'clock," I said. "Would you like to whiz over to our workshop and see what's going on before we have dinner?"

"Wonderful," she said.

I thought she was a bit shocked at how fast the Vauxhall went and I eased up a bit, but we were soon there.

G.W. greeted her with a smile and an unreservedly hearty embrace. "Delighted to see you, my dear. Just step in here out of the cold. Mind you it's not that much warmer. Keep your topcoat on."

It was interesting to see. G.W., whom I might have thought would be a bit withdrawn, was outgoing, charming, explaining everything in simple, clear terms. Then I remembered how brilliant he had been that first day at Hendon. I saw that it would not be me doing the explaining while G.W. worked away in a corner, and that it would immediately be clear to Janice that this was his show.

In minutes they were bending over as he held a lamp near the floor to show her some construction detail of the fuselage that James was at work on. He showed her various tools and how they worked, pulled out plans and sketches. I saw her eyes light up at the sketches as she recognized them not as "plans" but more as personal works of art. I saw him wave his hands in complicated patterns as he illustrated the movements of ailerons and tail surfaces and the sweeping flight of aircraft. I could see she was absorbed, and she asked many questions. I thought, as objectively as I could, that his words and actions would have intrigued me too, if I had not already known what they signified.

There was little left for me to say as he finished, inspected his old watch and said, "My God! It's a quarter to six. You must be bored stiff by now and absolutely famished, Janice. Let Bob and me get out of these work togs and we'll race home and see what the housekeeper's got us for dinner."

I was feeling a bit diminished, for though I knew he had put on a virtuoso performance for her, and was grateful, I knew I could not possibly have matched it. But she looked at me with shining eyes and said, as G.W. went into his office to hang up his overall, "This is wonderful, Robert. How lucky you are to be working with such a man. If a person like this wants you to work with him, he must think a lot of you."

*   *   *

G.W.'s housekeeper/cook outdid herself that evening and we had a splendid dinner. We talked a lot over the meal and afterwards. I had not seen G.W. so animated. He was clearly responding to Janice's presence and approved of her. To my amazement, he also drew her out concerning her studies and ambitions and showed that he knew more about the history of art than I could have imagined. I began to get a new picture of him, realizing that whatever the intensity of his focus on our present task, he was also a man of wide culture.

At a little after ten o'clock I drove Janice through the half-mile of darkness to the cottage where his housekeeper's sister lived. All she said was, "I'm so glad I came, Robert. What you're doing is completely fascinating. I really learned a lot. And G.W. seems like the kind of mentor a person dreams about. He is certainly a bright man."

When I got back, G.W. was smoking his last pipe and reading a newspaper. He looked up quickly as I came in.

"That's a great lass, old man. You're a lucky young devil. Treat her well."

*   *   *

Janice was to catch a return train from Ashford the next afternoon, but she came into the workshop again in the morning, when

G.W. gave her a ten-minute – but masterly – description of aerodynamic principles and flight of aircraft. At the end, she said, "That was wonderful. I never thought I'd suddenly start to understand about aeroplanes – not in a hundred years. And you made things so clear."

G.W. beamed, looking a bit embarrassed. "I probably go on too much about these things, but it's been a pleasure meeting you, my dear. You must come again when we start to fly The Beast. That should be quite fun."

As I drove her to Ashford, she said, "It looks as if we are both going to be very busy for a while now. I suppose it means we – "

"Won't be seeing each other?"

"Well, not for a time."

"I want to tell you something, Janice. It's important. It's about what I feel for you. I –"

"I don't want to talk about what I'm sure you're about to say, Robert. I feel a lot for you. But I'm not very old, and you are not much older. We're trying to do a lot with our lives, but at the moment I think we should keep things as they are."

"All very well for you, my love," I said. " But with the way you look – and are – I'll always find it hard to believe there's not a battalion of guys out there who would want to express what I'm – "

She gently put her fingers against my lips.

A few minutes later we were looking for a seat for her on the crowded train. Then she suddenly turned and we kissed. And she smiled again as she got to her seat.

"It was a great visit. Write soon, I'll be back for the test flights."

Chapter 15

The wing remained our concern . . . always the wing. Loading tests told of more than enough strength in the leaf spring spars. And now we built a leading edge covered by a heavier duralumin than the rest of the wing, thus boxing it in to form a D-section of great strength. This increased the wing's rigidity and allowed us to stick to the thin airfoil profile that favoured high speeds.

*   *   *

One Wednesday near the end of February, a dark densely wet February in 1934, the engine was delivered in an enclosed van – a conspicuously neat and genteel-looking van elegantly enamelled in black. Besides the van's driver there were two cleanly uniformed mechanics and a brawny youth whose job was simply to lift things.

Five minutes before the van's arrival a large black limousine had drawn up smoothly outside the workshop; from it had emerged a slim man wearing a long black topcoat and a bowler hat. When he entered, he removed the hat to reveal light brown hair swept back meticulously from a high, narrow forehead. Under his topcoat, which he also removed, he wore a well-cut, double-breasted dark suit. His black shoes shone. He rubbed his hands together as he approached our space heater and looked around with gleaming eyes in a face whose expression did not quite manage to conceal a mixture of wonderment and scepticism. Smiling, and cheerfully deferential to G.W., he nevertheless continued to eye us keenly.

G.W. introduced him as "Mr Wharton, Rolls Royce Engine Works Deputy Superintendent."

Mr. Wharton was, I felt, probably inclined to view G.W. as a wealthy crank, Grant and me as his hangers-on of unspecifiable rank and relationship. With the tiniest elevation of his brows he somehow contrived to convey a hint, not so much of doubt as perhaps of patronage. It was nothing you could be sure about . . .

"And so, Mr. Gibbs White, you expect to install the motor (he actually called it 'the motor') rather soon? That will certainly be interesting. As you all –" here, he smoothly included Grant and me with a flick of his eyes – "are doubtless aware, this type of motor has never been fitted till now into a privately built aeroplane. I only hope – The Firm only hopes – it will do justice to your machine." He looked at us again, one by one, and he gave vent to a little chuckle, which may have been to cover some uncertainty.

Then he began really to look at the plane and his expression changed. He moved towards it.

"Yes. Yes . . . That does look like something very . . . very interesting indeed, Mr. Gibbs White. Quite remarkable in fact!"

Mr. Wharton, ignoring his fine suit, dodged agilely under the plane's nose to peer up past the engine bearers.

"Good Lord!" he said, "you people can certainly handle metal." Now he looked round at all of us. "If I'm any judge whatever, this is going to be an amazing aircraft."

He turned suddenly to G.W. "How," he asked, almost brusquely, "have you managed to do this astonishing thing? I mean – all of you, here, isolated? And, forgive my curiosity, what are you going to do with it? Something to stagger us all, I feel sure!"

G.W. smiled. "Well, we're going to play around for a few months. Beginning in May, we hope to try to just fly the bugs out of the Beast, what?"

"Well, Rolls Royce get precious few orders from groups anywhere near as small ... and as gifted . . . as this one obviously is. But we're very jealous of our products. We want to be very sure our motors only go into aircraft of real merit. But we can get really excited if our engines are going to power things we believe are of outstanding quality."

Wharton was now bubbling over with good fellowship. We pressed on him and his helpers mugs of our terrible tea. The helpers looked doubtfully at theirs and contented themselves with a couple of reluctant sips. But Mr. Wharton downed his tea with as much relish as if it was a tumbler of well-aged Scotch.

* * *

Three days later after we had carefully checked the uncrated "motor", and given it extensive bench tests, G.W. helped Grant and me work a gantry to lift it to the aeroplane's engine bearers.

Now our bird had a heart. Someday, as G.W., and possibly I, piloted it, it would have a brain. Could that brain infuse this hybrid of design and power with an adequate spirit?

* * *

Finally, my year had turned. The days of early spring were here, like a film of polish on the land that the warming sun would soon buff to the high shine of summer.

We matched our efforts to the unfolding year – arduous at first, more and more they became matters of detail, fitting, finishing. All winter we had worked in our den like medieval artisans, fairly warm, active but constrained, stopping our ears against the dulling drip of rain, our eyes straining against the grey light, never looking far ahead. Yet I seem to have been aware of coming objects and events whose precise form was masked, rather than revealed, by some great light.

And now we were opening the workshop doors whenever it was warmer, and even when they were shut we would scan the high, dirty windows hoping for a glimpse of white cloud or blue sky or the green flash of opening leaves in one of the nearby apple trees.

The workshop itself changed by the day. Now we were busy with small tools only – drills, metal shears, rivet guns, screwdrivers, burnishing pads. All the massive things – lathes, presses, moulds – were pushed back against the wall. And soon, though we pursued no conscious plan, these heavier items somehow drained away into a single corner.

The workshop had now turned into a little hangar. To the curious few who had looked in on us before, it had seemed filled by a confusing tangle of objects used in the activities of three crazed hobbyists. In earlier days, the meaning of what we were constructing would have been unclear for many observers simply because of its technical setting. "Something is being built – fascinating!" – was the common reaction of those who had seen our labours during the cold months, when the tools and techniques had seemed more interesting than what we were using them to build. And us? We could almost be disregarded, less the authors of some vague enterprise, the builders of some weird, spidery structure (an aeroplane? not really!), than the eccentric slaves of the workshop – scruffily colourful machine minders. But now, the local people, those who knew us because our plumbing needed fixing or because they delivered paraffin for our heaters, all began to assume an attitude of growing wonder. And, as the word got round, a local constable rode in on his bicycle to ask us politely if we needed any help with possible security problems.

So our local fame soon spread; when we entered a pub for an occasional drink the grins and muttered greetings now had something else in them – was it a sort of amused respect? No one teased us. Everyone was properly courteous in greetings. But I remembered the English tolerance of eccentrics. G.W. didn't give a damn, but I was young enough to be self-conscious.

Now, however, it would no longer do for us to be considered just harmless loonies. A charming jumble of equipment no longer veiled our efforts. Now we *had* something – something stark and pure, its primal presence not to be disregarded by anyone who saw it. Very soon, as the word spread and The World got wind of it, we would be expected to do things with it!

* * *

1934 was the spring against which I have measured each spring since. As we began to open the doors wide every day there would be an intoxicating flood of light. Spring and beginnings. We had beginnings, then. All the beginnings of time were ours.

It still rained, and there were sharp wet English winds that could knife you with their cold. There were storms. Yet all the bad weather was absorbed by the fine, by what I can only describe as the source of life and being that was coming . . . coming raging at us in its light and beauty.

The beginning of the month of May. A Thursday. G.W. pulled on worn white overalls. Grant put on his dust coat, grey as usual. I wore an old blue boiler suit. We drank our morning tea in G.W.'s office. We talked neutrally. Grant told us some cricket scores and began to kid me about Australia's poor chances in coming Test Matches. G.W. would normally have joined in amusedly. He had been a good cricketer and knew more about the game than either of us.

On this day he spoke little and held his pipe tightly in his teeth. Suddenly he put his hard, roughened hands squarely on his desk, waited till Grant stopped speaking, and said quietly, "Let's get the nose out so we'll have more room."

It could have seemed a strange idea but Grant and I understood what he was feeling. Together we pushed the plane towards the door, the tail held clear of the floor by a dolly. We got the nose out and there we left it, peeping from the hangar doors, like a creature long laid up over a winter hibernation that senses the warming spring sun and sniffs warily at new growth and damp earth.

All day we worked at servicing the engine, completing wiring, adjusting the small padded seat to the angle that fitted G.W. better than it fitted me. We sat in the cockpit by turns, installing instruments, endlessly pulling, pushing, caressing the controls, making corrections. How did the position of the stick feel after ten minutes in the seat? After two hours? Was the cockpit cover big enough to permit free head movements, as we had hoped? Just. Would it slide freely at all times? It stuck on the fifty-third push. We fixed it. Would we be able to get at the engine readily enough for later inspection or work, as intended? Yes.

We braced the fuselage well clear of the ground in a contoured and padded cradle. Would the undercarriage retract and let down without a hitch a hundred times in succession? No. Failure after fifteen trials. We found a crimped hydraulic line, relocated it, and had no further problems.

Every evening our timidly spring-sniffing creature returned to its den.

Every following morning we worked on the things we had left, plus a list of new things.

By now G.W. was using some of his rapidly dwindling funds to pay a retired constable to sleep at the workshop each night. I was glad of this, having long been uneasy of his casualness about security.

*   *   *

And flying practice recommenced. But not merely as more of the same exercises as before. Now, in a dual control Tiger Moth, G.W. started to teach me aerobatics.

"Bob," he said, "you're a fairly decent flier now in all the straightforward stuff. But to fly as any sort of test pilot you'll have to know just about everything of the nuts and bolts of stunt flying. You may never use any of it, and in actual test flights – most of them – you'll have formal, circumscribed steps to carry out. That's the only way we can really find out how a plane handles. But if you do get into some sort of difficulties, you have to know how to get out of them. That calls for an instinctive sort of control you have to acquire." He smiled. "Some of this will be fun. A lot will be hard work. Buckle up. Make sure your seat harness straps are as tight as you can possibly make 'em. I mean this. If you get upside down, it's disconcerting to suddenly sort of slump into them and realize they're all that's stopping you from plunging towards the ground, what? If they're tight from the 'word go' you'll feel pretty safe. Oh, and make sure your parachute is on properly."

We climbed to about three thousand feet and began systematically with barrel rolls at moderate speed. For the barrel rolls G.W. told me to pull back on the stick so the nose went well above the horizon, then push the stick all the way to one side. We ended up as we were supposed to, doing a simple rotation in which there was enough centrifugal force to hold us "down" – that is, with our backsides still in contact with the seats while the plane was upside down. Barrel rolls like this could be continued in a series if you wanted to do that. A snap roll was harder; pull the stick back to raise the nose and kick the rudder full right. Hold the control deflections as you spin upside down through the roll and, at about about forty-five degrees, before returning to level flight, relax the back pressure on the stick and kick the rudder sharp left. Later we faced the challenge of slow rolls that require aileron control to get you into a vertical bank, then use of the rudder bar to stop the nose falling away. Then, disregarding the strong pressure of the restraining straps, that really are now holding you in, you push forward on the stick to prevent the nose from dipping. And you must then reverse the rudder deflection to continue holding up the nose. If this sounds tough to do, it is. You need, when learning it, to have the aerodynamics of it firmly in your mind, but later, as you get used to it, you just feel your way along as you would if you were riding a horse, or driving a car at high speed, or playing tennis.

Loops were not as hard as they looked. Lower the nose (stick forwards) and speed up, then pull the stick back, opening the throttle as you climb vertically, then relax the back pressure on the stick as you go upside down over the top of the loop, and descend carefully to level flight. If I flew steadily upside down, I could, of course, feel the harness beginning to bite into my shoulders.

Gradually, step by step, G.W. took me through every manoeuvre. The things that absorbed me most of all were stunts like tail slides and other things that could lead me into the spins all test pilots fear because of the great difficulty of getting out of them once they really take hold.

*   *   *

I began to sense I was in the hands of a master. G.W.'s understanding of every aerodynamic aspect of a plane's handling allowed him to explain in detail exactly why one thing followed from another, and the consequences of every kind of error. And he would never let me off the hook.

"Not bad, Bob, not too bad. But a long way from showing that you really see why you're doing it even this well," he said after I did a "hammerhead", or stall, turn, and flattened out again. "And, son, you've got to get it right! Otherwise . . ." He made a thumbs down gesture.

Well, as I had told Dr Milland long before, things didn't always come easy to me, but they came. And once I knew just how to do them, and could perform them well, they stuck. At the end of it all, I suppose I could call myself a soundly trained pilot.

* * *

But one thing continued to haunt us; everything we were doing was in the wrong sort of aeroplane. We needed a plane with an enclosed cockpit and capable of much greater speed.

At last we got one. A friend of G.W.'s, a man who had met him when they had been engineering students together, had been hearing of both G.W.'s plane building and of the lessons he was giving me. This man, Gus Holden, realising that we needed a faster, more advanced aircraft, telephoned G.W. one evening and offered to fly his plane down to Ashford and let us use it for several days. The plane was a Percival Gull – an aircraft with room for two in its enclosed cockpit, and of greatly more advanced design and performance than the Tiger Moth we had been stuck with.

G.W. was almost speechless with gratitude, and a few days later we went to meet the plane.

The pilot-owner, now an automotive engineer, stepped out of the Gull's cabin and shook hands warmly with G.W. and said, "I have to get back to Sheffield in four days, Philip, but till then she's yours."

"I'm not sure how I'll ever manage to repay you, Gus, but what you're doing for us will make all the difference." He introduced me. "Here's the young chap who's going to share it all with me."

G.W. wanted to take Gus Holden home with him, but he politely refused. "I've already arranged to stop with my niece and her husband. They live very near here; at Aldington, in fact. They are both artists. I don't know him that well but the girl is my sister's kid and she's very sweet. Haven't seen her for a couple of years, so I welcome the opportunity."

"I can run you to Aldington in the Vaux – and bring you back when you have to return," said G.W.

"Not needed, thanks; she'll pick me up herself later in the

evening. But after I show you a couple of things in the Gull, I do want to have a look at your project – word of it's starting to get out, you know."

An hour or so later we took him to see the plane. He was almost silent as he inspected it. Then he said," You know, there are quite a few rumours about this among those who used to know you, Philip, before you came down here to live like a hermit. It's been said you're doing something out of the ordinary. But this . . . my God! this looks like something that . . .well, I hardly know what to say." He looked at us all, then; at me and James Grant as well as at G.W.

"Let me just say that if a few days of the Gull will help you reach your goal it'll be my pleasure and privilege to have helped you in a tiny way."

*   *   *

The Gull was a revelation. Comfortable, superbly engineered, of elegant design and rugged construction, its engine delivered enough power to make it twice as fast as the Tiger Moth. Everything we had done to the point of tiresomeness in the Moth we did again – and many, many times, in the Gull – with a quietness, a smoothness, that were the results of advanced aeronautical engineering and beautiful finish that imbued all our manoeuvres with a new sense of delight.

As for speed – absolute speed – we knew we were still far short of what we hoped our own aeroplane would deliver. We did the best we could to get nearer to that speed by putting the Gull in a series of long shallow dives that gradually built up to something getting close to that speed labelled critical for this model, at which we then practiced many of our major aerobatics.

So at last we were approaching a semblance of what it would be like.

*   *   *

There was one thing, though. Even though I felt enormous satisfaction from learning so much so quickly and from knowing I was now reaching a point of skill much beyond that of the "ordinary" amateur pilot, I realized this was not the kind of flying that was, in itself, what I liked best.

What I liked best was "bird" flight. The great effortless soaring, wonderful smooth-banked turns, the sense of buffeting by the passing air, the deep dives, the great climbs towards the clouds, through the clouds, out into the glare of blue. Birds did not – could not – loop or barrel roll, or stall and recover. These tricks, though thrilling, remarkable, sometimes very dangerous, were artificial – the outcomes of our physics and our engineering. But there was a deep, joyous dignity in bird flight. That was the flight I sought. Not the flight of the engineless glider. Engine power was needed to do what I sought – to fly faster or higher, swoop down and pull up again without an updraft. And birds, though they could glide, had power too – that of their wings – to give them the sovereign control they displayed.

I thought about it a lot at that time: the power of flight. What we were doing was perhaps the only step towards it that our wingless species would ever be able to take. And I thought too that it was very strange that ours was the only one that could actually envy birds.

Anyway, it seemed to me that the air was my true domain.

Chapter 16

Someone else who had heard of what G.W. was doing turned up a bit later in the form of a shambling bear of a man with a soft deep voice and the weather-beaten look of a sailor or a farmer. He rolled as he walked and, as he rolled into the workshop through the door we had left open, G.W. stopped work and they shook hands warmly. I realized by the easy familiarity with which they greeted each other that this was another old friend of his.

"I want you chaps to meet Bill Parker," said G.W., turning to James Grant and me, "a former comrade-in-arms I shared some real adventures with in the war. And what's more, the blighter builds planes."

Parker was hardly in athletic physical condition, but his vast hand encompassed mine and tightened like a vise. "Pleased to meet you, Bob. Actually, Philip mentioned you when he was phoning me up about getting a couple of rudder bars from us last week, told me you're a chap we can expect to be looking out for in a year or two."

I could tell I was flushed as I managed to mutter some denial of my right to any praise. Then I felt like a fool.

Bill Parker went on, "Our little company builds aircraft parts. Mind you, it's my ambition that we will be building light planes in a year or two; we're planning for that."

Parker turned to G.W. "Look here," he said. "I've become really curious about this thing you pretend you're making. I'm here to embarrass you, Philip. Let's see it."

"Yes, have a look, Bill," said G.W. "It's real enough, though as to what we'll ever be able to do with it . . ."

I suppose this moment, which seemed so slight, casual, inconsequential at the time, was actually one of great agreeableness for G.W. He was so alone. He had James, superb technician, friend, selfless worker, and he had . . . me. Despite the extraordinary defiance of his lone wolf status in a field populated by large, strongly financed teams, I thought he must have sometimes felt – under the cheerful stoicism of his daily pose – a desolating sense of the world's indifference.

You sensed all this as soon as Bill Parker moved towards the aeroplane with wonder in his eyes. You could see the unguarded eagerness of G.W. to explain all, to get the response of a friend who was an aircraft professional, to be able to talk as fully and as unselfconsciously as he liked – using every form of engineering jargon with the certainty he would be understood – to present his ideas, knowing the other would follow every step with appreciation and understanding. He glowed, he was eloquent. He fielded Parker's shrewd questions with a pleased virtuosity.

Parker shed a sports jacket as big as an ordinary man's overcoat and stepped right up to the assembly. He peered at the cockpit, then ruefully down at his own waistline. He turned to look in my direction. "I see you must have yourself and this stripling in mind as pilots, Philip. No fat old men, eh?"

G.W. chuckled. "Yes, well, we did do our physical anthropology on the cockpit dimensions, Bill."

At the end of half an hour, Bill Parker stood back and looked hard and long. At last he said, "Philip, I'll give it to you straight, as they say in American crime films. I think you've got something here that'll either make you or break you, old boy. And my betting is it'll make you. In fact, I think it may be a sort of a miracle."

G.W. was pleased beyond response. You could see that. They chatted on a for a while, then Bill Parker raised his voice a little, so as to include James and me.

"I just want you all to know that I'll be happy to help in any way I can. If you need standard parts or components we may be able to supply them and could rush them over to you quick. My place is only thirty miles away, actually on the other side of Ashford. And if you want standard parts modified, or some other things made to your specifications, we have the workshop facilities to do that. Actually, we already make quite a lot of stuff for the big companies. And in your case, Philip, we'd do anything for you at cost that fell within our manufacturing capabilities."

"I'm tremendously obliged to you, Bill," said G.W. "There certainly will be a few things."

"Well, you just send over young Robert, here, or James, for anything you need. They might find it interesting to see what we do. And if you can possibly spend a day, all of you should come. And Philip, I'd welcome your advice on what I have in mind for the future of Parker Aircraft."

After a cup of our tea, which he drank as though it was eminently acceptable, Bill Parker took his leave. We waved him goodbye as he drifted silently away in his dark blue Rolls Royce.

"Looks as if there might be money in the aircraft parts business," said James, with a sort of grim smile, as he watched the Rolls.

"Ah, yes. . . true enough," G.W. agreed. "I knew him – in fact we flew together – in the last days of the war; just about the time the Royal Flying Corps was being replaced with the R.A.F. He was slim enough in those days to slip into a standard-sized cockpit. Bit hard to picture, what?

"Anyway, he's going to let me have the rudder bars for nothing. Very nice. His place is easy to find. See, here it is on this map. He's also offered the loan of some tools that'll be very useful. Bob, you can drive over one day soon and pick everything up."

Chapter 17

Our Rolls Royce "motor" had, of course, been subjected to the Company's usual massive factory testing and running-in exercises, and ten days after its delivery to us, Mr Wharton reappeared, this time to stay with us at G.W.'s cottage and assist with final checking and installation. In the workshop he donned immaculate white overalls and demonstrated his personal workshop expertise as he helped us fit the engine to the airframe.

Percy Wharton was a trained engineer with a soundly critical attitude, except about the quality of this Rolls Royce engine for which he was unstintingly enthusiastic. "Based on the R2 that Mitchell used in the Schneider, of course. But better. And much more generally robust. The Germans have no such motor. Nor the Americans. Nor the Italians. This thing is in a class by itself. As an engineer, I'm just a good garage hand compared to you –" here G.W. made a self-deprecatory gesture, but Wharton swept on. "That's not false modesty. But as far as this motor is concerned, I'll stake my word on its quality and performance. It will do the job for you. In fact – and I can give it no greater praise – I think it's probably worthy of your plane!"

"Well," G.W. returned, "I wanted this engine because it is a development from the R2 type, but with a more general application."

"So. When will you manage to begin your flight tests?"

G.W. tapped the stem of his pipe on a table. "Two to three weeks, let's say. We have to do our final cockpit tests. We have taxiing tests. After that we'll have about four weeks of strictly controlled flights, each flight and each set of flights, with specific, restricted purposes."

"And full flight trials?"

"Oh? . . . Well, we'll try to put that together following the tests – say two months from now. But, if the wings are still on, all the final testing will be is to just require that the pilot won't confuse up from down in the heat of the moment, what!"

Wharton laughed with a faint edge of nervousness, G.W. uninhibitedly, with his head back.

For three interminable days we were deafened by engine sounds – despite ear plugs – as a full range of throttle settings was tested. Eventually, after five hours of actual running time, plus discussions that extended to meal times and into evenings over ales, whiskeys and coffees, G.W. and Wharton had thrashed out all aspects of the engine's use and maintenance in relation to its performance requirements.

After dinner on the third day Wharton looked over at G.W., who was replenishing his whiskey glass.

"Who will do the flying?" he asked.

"Me and Bob," said G.W. "The both of us."

Wharton lifted his own glass to us. "I'm not a pilot, but I really envy you both." He turned to G.W. "But, even after talking and working with you for days, I also dearly wish I understood how you've done this thing. It's still a mystery as far as I'm concerned."

G.W. smiled, but was silent.

"What about publicity?"

"Haven't exactly sought it," said G.W. "Let's fly The Beast first."

* * *

The large shed in which we worked was on the edge of a huge open field created by a farmer who had cut down the hedgerows that had formerly divided it into four smaller fields. I forget what the farmer had hoped to achieve, but anyway something had gone wrong and he had abandoned the field, though he did not want to sell it. G.W. had been searching for a long time to find so large an area of unobstructed land in that part of England that he was able to lease for three years. It was flat and fairly smooth, quite treeless now except for four old apple trees alongside the work shed. We had therefore no problems of transporting the plane to some distant airfield. It could just move out of its kennel and exercise itself in its own capacious yard.

Taxiing tests began when Grant and I twitched the chocks from under the wheels and, with G.W. in the cockpit, the plane moved a yard a second for the first time – about seventy yards in all. Later on I took over from him. For the next two days we taxied, covering miles of smooth turf, never at more than 25 mph. On the third day taxiing speeds had risen and risen. G.W. had calculated takeoff speed under still conditions as about seventy miles per hour.

I was in the cockpit to begin several speed runs. G.W. said, " Bob, now we want to try actual takeoff type runs – right up to about five miles per hour below critical."

Soon I was beginning to speed over the field towards the distant hedge. At forty-five the tail came up, smooth as paint. A bit of undercarriage jiggling, but that was just surface bumps. The roar of the engine rose evenly as I opened the throttle. I got towards seventy and then, without further work on my part, she lifted off gently, so gently. I managed not to panic, eased the stick forwards, and got down safely enough about a hundred yards from the hedge.

G.W. and James were waiting for me as I taxied back to the shed. Both were grinning, G.W. with his pipe jutting at a high angle, but neither said much.

That evening, G.W. was thoughtful. "Well, Bob, you've flown her. You did it first! Let's remember the date, and the weather and how we all felt. She's a bit more buoyant than I thought. Hope that doesn't mean we're seriously out somewhere . . ."

It was typical of him to feel critical rather than elated over such an apparent bonus, and he consulted all the notes I had written on how the plane's handling felt. We might be pleased at what had occurred, but it was unexpected, and G.W.'s entire approach was to say: prediction, control, certainty.

Flights continued in rigid sequence. But now they included time in the air: pull up over the hedgerow, long slow turn to left or right one or two hundred feet up, return to a smooth landing. Repeat twenty times. Then take off, climb to five hundred, never exceeding a hundred and twenty miles per hour – really just slipping along, propeller turning slowly, smooth, smooth, almost like skating, turn to right or left (slight bank), land. Twenty repeats. Take off, climb gradually, increasing to forty degrees and more, at a speed of a hundred and eighty, continue to three thousand feet – to brink of stall – then slip away, throttle back, and return to a landing. Ten repeats.

For me, performing these monotonous test flights with care and precision was the way to contain my excitement instead of staring out in triumph – perhaps distractedly – at the countryside. I had, after all, got the plane off the ground first, even if it was unintended. I! That alone would stay with me forever. And now, even if only as part of a long sequence of rigorous and rigidly limited tests, I was taking my turns in flying it.

I had supposed the controls would be inevitably heavier, stiffer than those of the light biplanes and that elegant little monoplane, the Gull, in which I'd learned to fly. I was wrong. G.W. knew what he was about. The plane was so docilely and precisely responsive to the pilot's will that I could sometimes hardly resist pointing its nose at the heavens and opening the throttle to storm the heights, slicing though the clouds at ten thousand feet, and hurtling out into the open sky of morning.

I'm not surprised I felt little physical fear in the test flights. I was like many twenty-two-year-old males in lacking much of a sense of risk – for myself or for others. But tension was there – a tension that weighed hugely upon me . . . at first. We weren't – like big aircraft companies – able to turn out more than one prototype. We had this aeroplane that we had built with our own hands and no immediate prospects that we would ever have another. Many times since those test flights, I've felt amazement that I was not completely paralysed at the prospect of destroying the plane. But somehow, I always managed to get on top of the tension and function effectively in the flights.

Our success with the tests, their essentially smooth progression, reinforced my trust in G.W.'s skill, and soon it dawned on me that since he apparently trusted me I should be able to trust myself. From that point on the worst of my tension began to dissipate, and I was able to become cooler, more critical, objective, detached – better able to concentrate and report on the myriad details and events of every test.

The testing manoeuvres got more complex and technically demanding; it nevertheless became easier to manage cockpit routines and controls, as flying itself was now a familiar daily activity. Now I had more freedom to appreciate and marvel at the simple experience of flying. Now I could watch with joy as the plane raced its shadow until it gathered real speed, and then my heart would surge as I speared it up towards the lower clouds, or as it would reach the point of stall, when it would pause, nose up for a moment, as if trying to squeeze its way over a knife edge before the nose finally dropped and the plane plunged down a long slide of air on the other side.

When I banked into turns, I marvelled at its solid stability, the smooth precision of its handling. The plane's weight, power, aerodynamic perfection, gave a feeling of moving through some medium more substantial – more solid in its support, yet paradoxically smoother, more frictionless – than plain air.

It was addictive to fly it. And I was hooked.

We carefully considered and discussed and logged the results of each flight, and each series of flights. G.W. had drawn up expected performance norms, and the variations he considered acceptable. Departures from the norms – whether better or poorer performances than expected – always required explanation or adjustment.

We went on. Step after step. Apparently without end.

After two weeks G.W. flew to five thousand feet, dived, slowly at first, to two thousand. But before he levelled out, speed had reached two hundred and fifty. Twenty repeats – of which I did nine. Then banks, rolls, sideslipping from seven thousand; climbs at three-quarter throttle; then full throttle. Rehearsed stalls, spins, recoveries. An eighty-five degree climb at ninety per cent throttle to eight thousand feet, from a beginning altitude of three thousand.

How high could we get? We leased portable oxygen sets from the R.A.F. Twenty-five thousand feet was no obstacle in our first altitude test, but to reach it, carry out standard manoeuvres there, and return, took an hour and two hundred miles of flying.

G.W. and I shared these antics, splitting the entire series of tests squarely down the middle. Grant almost went crazy checking, checking. But he was constant, unremitting. No one was going to let the others down now. We were a single mind.

We spent three final days reviewing, talking over the results of all tests. G.W. became didactic in manner, intent on formalizing and generalizing all we knew. He had always conceived this creature of his as a totality, a system, as he put it. Now, however, he wanted to be quite sure he could understand it in its smallest details, as intimately as one could ever know and understand a complex machine – even a machine of one's own creating. He wanted to be sure it would not become his Pygmalion, whose spirit might somehow elude him – even overthrow him.

"So," said G.W., judicially, measuredly, "we have a shorter takeoff distance, and a lower takeoff speed than predicted. The climb rates at a full range of throttle settings and various angles are about right. Good! But at forty-five degrees and ninety per cent power we're four per cent slower than expected. There's a trace of sluggishness in turns –"

"Hardly sluggishness," I said. "More of a stiff feeling . . ."

"Sluggishness," he resumed. "And there's something a bit odd when you sideslip to port. And the cockpit noise level is too high."

His list continued. It was long. But it contained nothing we couldn't either attend to or eventually choose to disregard as insignificant.

Our evening meal on the day before that chosen for the final test flight was a good one. We usually ate pretty well at the cottage thanks to the housekeeper. But G.W. had asked Percy Wharton down; Mary West, his sister, had come from Salisbury; and Grant was present. Bill Parker had also come, and I had picked up Janice from the Ashford railway station in the Vauxhall. The dinner was a casual celebration.

G.W. was in a reflective mood, and talked of the ramshackle biplanes of World War I, of the strange contests during the 1920's between the older builders, who still believed fixedly in biplanes not only as passenger aircraft but for speed as well, and the new builders, who wanted clean streamlined monoplanes whose wings used the self-support system of the cantilever.

Over nightcaps of scotch we considered tomorrow.

"Are you keyed up?" Mary asked me.

"A bit. Though, of course, we have done a lot of it already. But . . . yes . . . I suppose it really does mean something if we're going to put it all together at last." Suddenly I felt my youth, and dispensed with my blasé pose. "Yes. I really am looking forward to it, of course. Terrific, really."

"Yes," said Grant, the calmest of men, "let's by all means not be too cool. This is certainly something for an old boat builder to be thinking about."

* * *

I drove Janice back to the housekeeper's sister's house where, as before, she would stay for two nights. We pulled up and then sat looking at each other under a sky that was still not very dark, a half-moon just beginning to shine.

"You really must be feeling everything pretty strongly," she said. "You look pleased, but not overwhelmed. Why don't you?"

"Feel overwhelmed?"

"Of course."

"I think because we've lived it all for so long now. If you had been able to get down for the earlier tests you'd have just seen us sweating away at it all in a sort of routine way for day after day. See, we *know* it'll fly and fly well. We know that already."

"So what, really, will this flying tomorrow tell you?"

"Mainly, it will let us see what the plane looks like when we put it through all its paces in one session."

"I wish I could have come down," she said. "But, you know, I was pretty busy."

"I know; that's all right."

"Well, it isn't. But you know, listening to all of you tonight, I thought how terribly far away from all this my world is. Most of the people I see most of the time could never begin to picture what your life is like. I find myself a bit tormented over it. I'm fascinated at what you've been doing and also quite fearful of it. The risks seem enormous."

"That might be true if we didn't take the care we do, but –"

"The risks are still great compared to anything people in my field expose themselves to. Let me put it this way, Robert, I like you too much to say 'I like you' and leave it at that. But there are a couple of problems. In my own way I think I may be nearly as interested in what I eventually want to do as you are in what you're doing and – "

"That's no problem," I protested. "I understand all that, and actually I find what you want to do very interesting."

"Perhaps," she said. "But you're only twenty-two and I'm twenty. We've both got years and years of study and work ahead of us and I'll tell you now, I don't want to – "

I reached out and grasped her slim shoulders and kissed her hard and long – a kiss that was returned. I drew back and watched her face, lighted by the rising moon.

"I love you," I said. "And I may be young, but nothing will change that – even if I never set eyes on you again."

She smiled her great smile. "I know you do, and if I didn't know I wouldn't be talking to you in this way.

"But we have to wait. And I wonder just how long that will be for, and how it will affect us."

"Don't know; and I'm not going to try to figure it out tonight. Just be ready when I come to pick you up tomorrow morning."

We kissed again.

*   *   *

When I got back to G.W.'s and was sitting in his parlour, thinking about going to bed, he and James went to his office to check something over for tomorrow. Mary West, who had been sitting on the other side of the parlour, sat down beside me. Mary was G.W.'s senior by five years, a slender grey-haired woman with fine features; her only resemblance to him was in her sudden, intense gaze.

"You must tell me, Robert, just what G.W. is really up to. I mean in ordinary language that I can understand. He's such an enthusiast about the things he does – perhaps 'enthusiast' is too weak a word. But anyway, he tells me nothing of what he wants and why he's doing it. We've been very close in some ways since Mother died when he was only twelve. But on the mental side of things he sometimes treats me as if I can understand nothing except knitting." Then she laughed. "The fact is, I'm mentally pretty lazy, he thinks – and probably he's right."

As I tried my best to explain things to Mary West I quickly realized that she was very bright and, for a person innocent of engineering knowledge, caught on quickly and well. But soon she began to ask the same questions repeatedly – a sign that her attention was wavering. Yes, G.W.'s opinion of her – which she apparently shared with him – seemed correct.

But I also saw that her interest in G.W. – and in me – ran to more personal matters.

"Philip was bereft when Mother died. He was a sensitive child, but in some ways he was very arrogant, sure of himself in things that interested him – as a lot of things did. He was somewhat reckless and took too many risks, but he was lucky. He was only nineteen when he finally got to the front, but his luck held until the war ended, and he did see air action – he was a wonderful pilot, they said. Anyway, he survived – so I was lucky too."

"I know he started at Cambridge before he went to the war. When did he go back there?"

"It was 1919." She smiled apologetically. "They were just starting to teach aeronautical engineering, but despite the love for planes he had by then he didn't do overwhelmingly well."

"No?" I was surprised.

"Too headstrong. But some of his teachers saw something in him, notwithstanding."

She looked at me. "You're very young and you don't look or talk as he did at the same age. But something about you reminds me of him. The eyes, perhaps . . . I certainly admire your pluck in just getting up and coming here alone from Australia."

Then she changed the subject. "That young woman, Janice, who's a friend of yours, seems to be very nice indeed – and she is a great beauty."

I was feeling very self conscious about all this personal stuff; it seemed improper to be talking about G.W. without his knowledge, but Mary went on. "Philip must complete what he has to do; I am praying for a favourable outcome tomorrow. Most of his money has run out. Even though he gives the impression of indomitability, I think he may be closer to . . . well, a sort of 'edge' than most people would believe. In a way, things have been pressing on him for ten years, ever since . . ."

She broke off as G.W. and James Grant came back into the parlour. In a very low voice she muttered, "James knows about this better than anyone else. He'll probably tell you about it some time."

I was left feeling far from satisfied and wishing Mary had never started.

*   *   *

Last thing before bed, G.W. muttered, "By the way, question of name. I thought . . . Vector I. 'Vector: A quantity possessing both magnitude and direction represented by an arrow the direction of which indicates the direction of the quantity and the length of which is proportional to the magnitude.' That's a definition out of an old physics textbook." He smiled. "And a vector's also the direction or course followed by a plane – or a missile."

Chapter 18

We opened the doors of the shed and pushed Vector I out into summer sunshine. The air was warming up and the dawn dew would soon be gone from the grass except where there was cool shade from the four old apple trees. There were the small white cumulus clouds of a fine day in the blue sky.

I examined Vector I almost as if I had never seen it before. I knew it was the most completely streamlined aeroplane that had ever been built, and I'm pretty sure its design has remained the most aerodynamically rigorous of any aircraft capable of only subsonic speeds. In flight, with its undercarriage fully retracted, the plane's "perfect" lines were interrupted only by air-intake, radiators, exhaust ports, and the shining bubble of the cockpit cover. Its flush-rivetted, stressed skin, duralumin covering had a supremely burnished finish and reflected light in dazzling fashion. In truth, the aircraft had an almost "simplified" appearance. It looked dense, as if it were carved and smoothed from a single block of metal. It had the solidity and strength of a winged projectile and none of the usual surface "detailing" common to even the fastest aeroplanes in those days. Its appearance resulted, of course, from G.W.'s having concentrated solely on achieving an optimal aircraft – one in which design and form had inevitably followed from his attempt to combine – in a single compact package – speed, strength, safety, performance, handling, comfort and efficient controls. Therein lay the focus and originality of his genius.

G.W. had put on his fleece-lined leather jacket and quilted overalls from the war. An ancient leather helmet dangled from his hand and he pulled it on as he climbed into the cockpit. He settled himself as he checked instruments and adjusted his parachute harness, then switched on the ignition. As the engine fired and the airscrew spun, Grant and I pulled the chocks away.

He was off then, Vector I bouncing away along brown ruts worn in the emerald grass during all our earlier takeoffs and landings. He accelerated and Vector I sprang into the air and climbed away fast at forty degrees with the engine's characteristic sweet formidable roar, a strong note that faded while we watched. After a few minutes Vector I's course took it above some small bits of altocumulus and we lost sight of it for a little. Then Bill Parker spotted it again with his powerful binoculars, and lost it again, and for quite a while we assumed it had climbed beyond our range of vision.

Mary, Percy Wharton, Bill Parker and Janice had stood silent and well away as we had made our final adjustments, but now James and I had joined them and Janice reached for my hand. She was trembling. James brought out the great teapot and we all stood drinking from white-enamelled mugs. For the first time in many months I began to notice again how harsh the tea tasted.

James sat down impassively on a camp stool in the sunshine, talking quietly with Mary and Percy Wharton. I felt uncontrollably restless and paced off to the nearby apple trees to stand in their shade, rubbing my fingers over their cool, rough bark.

We saw nothing more for half an hour, but I knew G.W. would be trying for maximum altitude, where the propellor would hardly grip the air, where all lift was starting to fail. Above forty thousand feet he would be driving the plane towards its aerodynamic limit, doing all he could think of to force it into aerobatics that, in most aircraft, would not be manageable at more than half that altitude.

At last, out of the clouds, about five thousand feet up, Vector I came diving. My God! I thought, it's going to go straight down! And it did go straight down – until at last the nose came up, incredibly sharply Then without hesitation the plane began to weave a seamless pattern composed of the kinds of aerobatics we had been using for so long in the daily tests.

A half-roll left and Vector I was upside down, flying very close to the ground. Then the nose came up and the plane went into a vertical climb until momentum was lost and G.W. pulled it over into the top of a loop and it began to dive again – a dive that led into a banked turn. The plane drove into a second climb, this time to a greater height, which he allowed to peter out until the aircraft started to slip backwards on its tail, when it was snapped over and fell towards the ground again. The fall turned into a kind of sideslip that levelled out to lead into another half-roll from which followed a reverse loop with G.W. on the outside and centrifugal force pushing blood towards his head rather than his feet.

Only a few minutes, but dazzling, mesmerizing in the remorseless, flowing continuity of the different manoeuvres. Like nothing we had ever seen or dreamed of. In no sense was this exhibition flying – like that of some festival stunt pilot doing a few tricks in a slow, agile biplane. G.W. was seriously, deliberately, ruthlessly intent on driving Vector I to the absolute limit of its flight possibilities, performing a seamless, ceaseless progression of moves that would not normally ever be attempted. This was a private practice, a performance of the only-just-possible. Dangerous, of course, something to be attempted by very few. But also a demonstration of what was now G.W.'s faith in his own creation.

To watch it was to feel fear – but fear overcome by awe and wonder.

At last, with a swelling note that rose to a shattering but musical roar, Vector I came towards us almost hedgehopping out of the east at a speed whose magnitude we instantly grasped. As it peeled away in a shallow bank to the north, not a hundred feet up, leaving a wisp of exhaust, we all began to cheer, and our cheer turned to a bellow as G.W. made it climb in a huge rocketing sweep. The engine's giant power notes boomed back to us as the climb steepened to forty-five, sixty, seventy-five degrees. At three thousand feet, Vector I was drilling up almost vertically, still hanging on, still climbing fast. G.W. flipped the plane upside down off the top of the climb, did a roll, and slipped off into an awesome dive, then throttled back to pull into comfortable level flight. He descended lower, accelerated powerfully, then barrel-rolled at fifty feet – just as he had said, a year earlier, that the aeroplane must be able to do.

I laughed then, a laugh made of terror and relief and admiration, as I pictured G.W. sitting there, momentarily upside down, as he flicked across the landscape, grinning to himself as he kept his promise.

Then Vector I climbed again, away to the west, sudden hard

left. At fifteen hundred feet a long dash began, calculated to lead to a final run over the field. The note from the engine was high, like stressed fabric ripping, yet somehow sweet. Then it turned to a roar to fill our world. And then it was over and going away, away far beyond all of us – into yesterday.

Two minutes later G.W. was climbing stiffly from the cockpit to raucous shouts and slaps on the back and a hug and kiss from Mary. At first he was silent, reflective, just a tiny quiet smile showing.

"Well, yes," he said at last, as he fumbled his pipe from his pocket. "I think so. I really think so." He stretched towards Grant and their hands met. "Good show, old man. And thanks!" He reached out then to me, and I looked into his reddish, weathered face as we shook hands. Now he was grinning broadly at last, blue eyes shining, but with a softening sheen over them. "Thanks, Bob. All thanks, son." I felt the power of his hand.

G.W. was not an intimate man. Much of himself was always obscured, though he was not reserved in ordinary conversation, having neither false modesty nor any tendency to hold back when he felt he ought to be a leading participant, and he was nearly always informal and unstinted in his language. But he neither gave nor sought easy confidences. Yet at this moment, as I gazed at the young, perceptive eyes that belied the ageing face, and felt the strength of his hand and saw his slow tears, I was closer to this being than I would ever be again, perhaps closer than I would ever be to anyone. And we knew and understood each other on what was, for both of us, a young green morning.

* * *

A few minutes later Janice touched my hand and I turned to her. "I never knew anyone or any machine could do such things," she said. "I just never, ever imagined it. Thank you and thank G.W. for letting me see it. It was just incredible."

* * *

It was impossible to fight off publicity. In 1934 you could not fly a loud aircraft at an extraordinary speed low over the countryside without attracting notice. In those days, few people had ever set eyes on small, all-metal, low wing monoplanes with total streamlining. Enormous attention had been created. Suddenly our peaceful retreat became an easily accessible target for reporters, feature writers, radio interviewers, and every kind of enthusiastic crank.

The world came tumbling in upon us.

Chapter 19

"When," she asked, "did you first feel inspired to become an aeroplane designer?"

A Lady Reporter from London had decided I might be intriguing story material ever since someone had sent several newspapers a rumour that a nineteen-year-old wild man from the Australian bush, living at a secret workshop in Kent, had built a marvellous new aeroplane assisted by only two aged rustics.

I was trying to correct false impressions, but she didn't seem to be listening. "Look!" I said, and realized I was almost shouting, "I'm twenty-two. The plane isn't mine. I came to Britain two years ago. I'm twenty-two. I didn't build the plane. I just helped. I've told you and three other reporters all this already. The designer and builder is Mr. Philip Gibbs White. He's an engineer. He studied at Cambridge and worked with an aircraft company. Mr. James Grant is his chief helper. You met them just a few minutes ago. Surely you can take this in?"

And so it went. Our world, so small, felicitous, and self-contained had been invaded by the Goths of the media universe.

G.W., fluent enough in most circumstances, was soon reduced to mutterings that probably concealed curses rather than information. In private he would fulminate over the "press morons". But he seemed more than a bit dazed when being interviewed.

But we got headlines. As soon as famous aeroplane designers turned up to pay their respects and marvel, we got headlines.

And G.W., squeezed into the cockpit in his antique pilot's outfit (immediately noted by the "human interest" journalists), obliged reporters and the public alike with virtuoso performances that gained steadily, from one flight to the next, in diversity of riotous improvisations as he became increasingly confident about Vector I.

As he hurled Vector I around the sky, I began to ask myself

again about the nature and purposes of this man – of his possession. The plane as a creative exercise, that I could accept, could understand.

There had been, till now, this solid pipe-smoking figure who, with his stained worker's hands, had patiently and ingeniously shaped refractory metal to his will. In that role I accepted him as readily as I accepted his brilliant conceptual skills – two facets of his creative power. But seeing him in his soiled and ancient flying suit, and in the splendour of his piloting, I realized I had failed to grasp half of what he was. Now I began to comprehend the magnitude of his determination to breathe life into his creation. When he flew Vector I they came as close to being a unity as was possible for a person and a machine. Who saw them saw feats of flight they would not, could not, see repeated.

As his fame grew, the more sensationalist papers began to spin fatuous tales of the crazy wizard of Kent and Cambridge who was not only a genius with a slide rule but of derring-do as well. Some obscure servant from G.W.'s college at Cambridge was reported to remember him as insane-brilliant. There was something about sinister religious practices that had endowed him with inhumanly great abilities! He had – this unnamed servant insisted – terrified his professors, humiliated them with his wild pranks and intellectual conjuring. Eventually, so one story went, he'd been sent down (this accounted for his not having completed his degree!) on some triviality trumped up by the dons who hated his very shadow. He'd then gone on a wild, depraved spree in London till an ancient widowed heiress with a million pounds to waste had offered him a post as her pet inventor and "companion." It was supposed he had honed his flying skills when he'd gone roaring off to barnstorm drunkenly across the U.S.A. (which he'd actually never visited) with a pair of biplanes bought out of the fortune the old girl had left him.

Poor G.W. He could have been devastated by these mad tales. But he was a man of mettle. Or maybe he was just unworldly and most of it simply went by him. Anyway, all he'd do was forget to light his pipe, stare fixedly at the wilder stories, then give a short nervous laugh and turn to some technical problem.

People came to his flying exhibitions by the horde. Perhaps

they came to see the airborne satanist. But, for sure, they came to see Vector I, the great gleaming aeroplane, and its pilot who could make it play in the air like some giant Man O' War bird. They came, too, to touch Vector I and G.W., like talismans of wondrous times, of great days coming. The Air Age was here – never in higher glory! People felt that no one who was a crack inventor could fail to be rich and have a marvellous life. Hadn't that happened to other great engineer-inventors – Henry Ford, Edison, Brunel and Rolls and Royce? Of course it had. To many people it just seemed like good sense to see and hear, and even maybe touch, someone who was of that genre of technical magicians.

Some of the sleaziest journalists continued, however, to make G.W. out to be a Rasputin of technology – they really gave it their all, hammering the dual appeal of the master inventor who had tapped the dark forces to get where he was.

If anything stranger could have overtaken a person of G.W.'s stripe, I could not think what it might be. Later on I saw it differently. It is the fate of many innocent and clairvoyant people to be misunderstood in their lifetimes, as they may later be venerated. Either way, little of their humanity is allowed to peep out. It was, as I came to see, G.W.'s simplicity and artlessness that, after all, allowed him to be so misinterpreted to an avid public. The state of possession can be sensed in certain persons. Whether it should be attributed to God, Devil, genetic chance, or just the particular circumstances of one's early youth, calls for nicety of judgement. G.W. was – for a time – cast as a diabolist by some. He could as easily have come out as a flying John the Baptist. To me, either possibility was just as comical.

On the solid, detached, workaday side, G.W. did his level best to ignore the nonsense, the craziness, the trivia, and interacted quite straightforwardly with the professional aeronauts who turned up to watch and to meet him. It was this consistent directness and open manner that, after a time, overwhelmed all the journalistic rubbish and placed him more and more in the public eye as what he was really cut out to be – a folk hero if ever there was one.

Of course, the actual aeronauts were, one and all, amazed and tantalized by what they saw of Vector I and heard from G.W. Many of them were dumbfounded, others were excited to an almost incoherent babble of praise. A few strong souls simply planted their feet, placed a hand on G.W.'s sturdy shoulder and looked him in the eye as if to say, "At last!" One of the most famous of the aircraft designers among our visitors said, "Let's face it, Gibbs White, in a profession like aeronautics, it's not every day some fellow just leaps on the stage like a bloody Mephistopheles (bad imagery again!) to unveil a marvel."

G.W. smiled a little thinly.

"I mean," continued our visitor, "you really are the limit, old man. Just consider. Here are all of us professional grinds tramping along on our weary way, slaves of our fat companies, with big budgets, skilled technicians, great workshops. And between us we number – so we tend to imagine – nearly all the worthwhile brains in British aeronautics. Then you, without even a 'by your leave', astonish our weak nerves by suddenly pulling the covers off the aeroplane no one could ever make. The all time stunner. And then by way of really putting the boots to us when we're already down – if not out – you have the gall to show us you're the best pilot we'll ever see this side of kingdom come.

"My God, Gibbs White, have you no sense of proportion? Show a bit of mercy. It's all just too much."

G.W. was by now totally embarrassed. But it got worse as a host of other visitors had similar things to say.

Truly G.W. had spoken late, waiting an endless drift of years to announce himself. But now that he had spoken, it was with a voice of brass, and as if the skies had split.

* * *

But it wasn't the way to "get things done". G.W. may have been appreciated now in the field of plane design, but as a chronic, long-term loner, his talent wasn't going to get him suddenly elected as chairman or chief designer of any big aircraft company. Few of the chairmen were, in any case, engineers; most of them were likely to have been former lawyers, accountants, managers of toy factories . . . and most of the designers had outstanding academic qualifications from some leading university.

So would they even hire him? Not really. How could he have worked with their teams of experts? Would they retain him as a trouble-shooter/adviser and permit him to free-lance? They already had plenty of competent people for that sort of thing. And in more general management roles, what, anyway, would he know of such modern marvels as cost-benefit considerations and building to a budget? Hadn't the blighter spent his own savings to build Vector I? Reckless bastard!

And then, too, the man who can, literally, make anything, perfectly, is unlikely to be patient with, or particularly useful to, those who after receiving long and specialized training can eventually make just a few things fairly well. And this, I believe, was tacitly understood by those one might have perceived as his likely colleagues.

Why didn't someone offer to buy his design outright? Perhaps, just perhaps, there might have been an offer if he had shown the slightest interest. But who, after all, would want to own Vector I? What could they learn from it that wouldn't eventually be revealed anyway? G.W. was quite open about its design features. Nothing was patented. Certainly as it wasn't built to Air Ministry specs, they wouldn't want to touch it . . .

A few months on, after everyone had seen the plane, exulted in its performance and appearance, lavished congratulations on us all; after the last of the scandal-sheet reporters had gone on their way and the public that cared for such rubbish had become sated with tales of the sinister presence underneath G.W.'s old tweed, a certain silence descended. We three knew, of course, that the recent splash in the pool, with all its gaudy excitement now seemingly fading, was just the epicentre of influences and concepts that would radiate silently and rapidly, not only throughout Britain but across The Channel, the Atlantic, and beyond. What G.W. had done would make massive permanent contributions to aeronautical theory and practice when written up by himself and others and when the design of Vector I eventually became common property. But years would pass before these lessons could be fully learned, their principles be generally employable.

Before they departed, our professional brethren did leave us one Great Piece of Advice: "For God's sake, you chaps, get the world's speed record. At least that'll make the Americans, French and Italians sit up and take notice. And you'll begin to get a little of the real credit due to you."

It seemed astonishingly difficult to organize that attempt. It called not only for G.W.'s best efforts, including formal applications to national and international bodies responsible for record attempts, but for prodigious pressure from our new colleagues who wanted a Britisher – even a maverick Britisher – to get the record. G.W. was bored, too. To make a Vector I, to fly it for his own satisfaction – that was one thing. To bother to have to prove to others, through some tedious formal procedure, that the plane could do what he was perfectly willing and able to demonstrate it could do on any fine day – that was an anathema. G.W. felt, looked, and acted dull. He loudly *stated* that he was dull. He was by turns surly, morose, felt he was merely marking time. And for what?

"I'd sooner be off to Athens" (he loved Greece) "or even gardening" (which he hated), he would snarl. "Lots of stupid tommyrot. You know, all of us know, the blasted plane will fly at over five hundred in level flight. What's the so-called world speed record? . . . Well!"

Despite his negativeness, his relative ineffectiveness in this sort of venture, the thing gathered momentum of its own and began to carry us remorselessly – if painfully slowly – towards an outcome.

Chapter 20

With great reluctance at first, G.W. turned his attention to preparing Vector I for speed record trials. "I don't really want this," he grumbled. "I want this aeroplane to fly very fast, but it's not built to be just a speed record breaker. That's not really flying."

He was further irritated by the "bloody ridiculous and appalling paperwork and number of people to talk to just to get the thing set up." But when we finally settled to the task his humour was restored.

Rolls Royce would have provided a new engine for Vector I, with its performance directed solely towards the speed trial. That was how they had built their engines for British attempts on the Schneider Trophy, and success had brought them great publicity and fame. But G.W. wouldn't hear of it.

"This plane will easily break the record with the engine we've got – or it won't. But look, its performance now and in the future will mainly depend on its aerodynamics. If we change the engine, we may have to change the plane's profile and its balance will be upset. That may mean altering the fuselage and fooling with the control surfaces. I'm not prepared to face that."

So our preparations were confined to fine-tuning the engine in the hope of getting a few more miles per hour out of it, installing a new, more specialized propeller, and removing everything of significant weight that would not be of specific use during a speed flight. Otherwise the prepared plane was exactly as it had been.

*　*　*

As the date for the trials began to loom I wrote to Janice, asking her to join us as an official guest. She replied that she was leaving for Edinburgh to look at portraits and landscape paintings in art gallery collections and in several ancestral homes and castles, and she would be away for a month. She wrote that she expected to arrive back about three days before the record attempt. Her letter ended –

I'd love to come unless something unforseen stops me.

I miss you Robert. It seems already to have been ages and ages since that first display of G.W.'s. I suppose you must all have had some fun since then and you will all be thankful that newsrag rubbish has died down. Anyway, I hope like anything to see you in a few weeks.

Love . . .

*   *   *

The commencement and end point of the speed trial was about twenty miles north of Nottingham. A seven-stage, two hundred and ten mile course had been planned according to standard specifications for international record-breaking.

Once we knew the course, G.W. flew over it several times at speeds never in excess of 200 mph. He had no wish to attract prior attention. On his return we discussed what the trials would entail. "What we now have to do," he said, "is to fly The Beast over approximately the same distance down here to get the feel of things at high sustained speed. But, even though this engine is very rugged, we want to keep the speed down to not more than eighty per cent of our estimated maximum for the trial. We can't risk harm to the engine from too much maximum speed running beforehand, what?"

He looked at me then, and smiled. "Bob, you'll be flying half of these practice runs." He put up his hand to hold back my protest. "For two reasons," he said. "First, to fly at high speeds is just a part of your piloting experience that you must get if you can. I know this, because I've only just had some of it myself, remember. And then, say I catch a dose of flu, or measles, or something.

"I want to fly this trial myself, but we mustn't cancel if it should happen that I can't. I've already put down your name as my alternate."

*   *   *

I cannot say what coursed through G.W.'s mind as he flew his practice trials over Kent and adjacent counties, but my own flights were like a waking dream. The slipping effortlessness of this wonderful aircraft beggars description. I thought not of "I" or of "the aeroplane." I thought of "we."

The green and pleasant land of southern England flowed beneath us, the blue glow of the sea mostly in sight, often just beside us as we shot along the coast. These were practice speed flights, but often deviated from a strict course pattern. Sometimes we would swoop down over the landscape and see people walking, driving in cars, riding bikes, sheep in fields, small woods, individual trees, flashing streams, ponds, little lakes, reservoirs. The airman sees as others do not. Cannot. If he identifies with his aircraft, he can also identify with the whole earth, because that is how he sees it. He knows in a direct way, as others do not, as he sees the vast curve of the horizon, that below him spins a single globe, a minute fraction of which is slipping by. He can have dreams of a paradise – a world that is vast and round, made of tiny, lovely fragments of landscapes and living things that he can grasp in their immensity – a paradise that is his. Others are denied the airman's prospect.

Sometimes we would turn and bank and even roll and sideslip as I tried, perhaps with something like success, to see and know what every soaring hawk could know on any ordinary day. . . and wonder again at the price we pay for what we think of as our biological supremacy.

And then the dream would change as I pulled back on the stick and we blasted our way to high skies and places where the sun was always burning – and a mood of transcendence would take over.

* * *

G.W. flew Vector I to Nottingham on the morning of the speed attempt. Grant and I had driven up in the Vauxhall the day before to attend to details of the flight arrangements.

When G.W. landed amidst a publicity blaze and the applause of a large and enthusiastic crowd, James and I were waiting to assist him.

I saw, to my amused delight as he climbed from the cockpit, that he had dressed for the occasion, not in his old flying suit, but in a fairly decent, heather-coloured tweed suit, an Irish woven wool hat, and brown brogues. It was an arresting sight to see this gentleman, clad as for a visit to a country town, stride across the tarmac to shake hands with officials, meet the Duke of Kent, then, still in his best suit, take a kit of oily tools to make a couple of final adjustments to the engine of Vector I. The crowd, now restless and irreverent (many of them were not habitual aviation enthusiasts but had been drawn by the advance media coverage), delivered raucous and amused appreciation of his dress, demeanour and activities.

Soon James and I were no longer needed and we shook hands with G.W. and went to an enclosure marked out for special guests. Bill Parker was there, and Percy Wharton, Mary West, at least a dozen members of the elite of British aviation, plus representatives of the world of flying from France, Germany, Italy and the United States, and soon, moving a bit slowly and self-consciously, Janice got through the mob as I went quickly to embrace her.

"Should I really be here, Robert?" she said, smiling nervously. "I mean, taking up space among all these bigwigs?"

"Darling," I said, as I embraced her hungrily, "try to remember that *we* are the bigwigs in this gathering, and you are our cherished guest."

"OK, " she said, and kissed me. "I must tell you this is a lot more exciting than the art galleries I've been looking at."

"Bloody better be, if you're thinking of marrying me . . . one day."

She blushed. "When this is over, we've got to talk, Robert. I mean really talk."

"Right, " I said. "As soon as this is over." I took her hand and held it.

Bill Parker came over to me then and shook hands. I introduced him to Janice.

"Great day for Philip," he said, "and indeed for all you chaps. What a machine you've turned out. I bet you're fit to bust over it all, eh? "

"Well, yes," I agreed, "but of course everything now depends on today."

"Do you think he'll break the record?"

"I'll eat the bloody plane if he doesn't."

Bill Parker gave a deep guffaw and slapped my shoulder with his big hand. "Well said, son. Good to hear some bold confidence."

And Janice laughed and squeezed my hand.

G.W. had now announced himself satisfied and ready, and went to place his signature on some official documents, wiping his hands on a bit of cotton waste on the way while nodding amiably to all and sundry and waving occasionally with his pipe. At last he gazed wonderingly at the crowd, which was getting increasingly noisy and restless. I saw him shake his head slightly in bewilderment. Then he smiled and waved to those who had been personally involved with Vector I, walked quickly to the plane and vaulted into the cockpit. I put my arm around Janice and glanced at her for a moment.

Then Vector I took off in the few seconds it needed, and G.W. wasted no time in pointing its nose at the sky. The plane went up in a breathless sweep like a launched rocket and there was a great soft "Aaaaah" from the crowd that said something quite different from the earlier irreverent calling.

After that tearing climb, though, there was nothing more to put us in mind of the marvellous aerobatics we had seen before. Vector I was now just an arrow speeding dead straight at constant height. So was it thrilling, or just an engineering exercise?

It was thrilling, because of the circumstances. Vector I was not a machine operating automatically in some workshop remote from human hands. Even the most technically uninformed could grasp that its huge power was under the direct and immediate control of its human pilot. It was G.W. who regulated its speed, kept it on course, made it ride out the effects of atmospheric turbulence, kept it at constant altitude, steered. That was the challenge, the nature of which anyone present who had ever driven a car fast could appreciate.

Unofficial lap times and speeds were called over the public address system as Vector I shot over us, together with the margins by which the existing world's record pace was being bettered. The crowd's great beehive hum soon swelled to a low roar that rose and rose and was punctuated by vast-throated cheering as the plane passed overhead.

But it was not over. I knew that many record attempts had failed, not because aircraft had been too slow, but through engine breakdown . . . or crashes. And if Rolls Royce engines had proved their quality years before, well . . . that was then. And even when Schneider planes had failed without actually crashing, their owners often possessed, or could muster, the resources to try again. We would never have another chance.

So the closer Vector I came to completing the course the tenser we became. Nearly half-way through and only two things mattered: to maintain speed and to finish.

I tried to see G.W. in my mind's eye; to imagine how he looked, what he thought, as he ripped off the miles. He was moving much faster now, in level flight, than any human being in the history of the world. That would be enough for most plane builders . . . and for most airmen. I doubted it would be quite enough for G.W. He would be pleased that it was so easy to demonstrate how fast Vector I could travel. But I knew in this kind of flying, that called for precision but no imagination, he would be close to boredom by now – longing for it to end.

I wondered if he was still wearing his Irish hat or had shoved it carelessly into some crevice in the cockpit. He didn't have his old wartime helmet with him, so I knew he would have stuffed cotton wool in his ears against the engine noise. I wondered if his pipe would still be clenched between his teeth. I didn't expect he would be smoking it, though he sometimes did while flying.

I knew that, whatever his impatience with the repetitiveness and monotony of the simple manoeuvres required for this speed attempt, he would perform them meticulously. That was the thing about G.W. He was careless about his clothes; his workshop was often a jumble; he let books and papers lie in heaps, but in any task he deemed worth doing he was ruthlessly thorough.

Anyway, four laps to go. Vector I was showing no sign of faltering, and we all began to shout out a countdown. I'm not sure that I bellowed louder than anyone else, but I certainly gave it a try.

And it amused James Grant, Bill Parker, Percy Wharton, Mary . . . and Janice, whose now sweaty grip on my hand continued to tighten. In fact Janice began to laugh and cry out in excitement that my own had perhaps ignited in her. I was pleased and surprised by such a strong response in her.

Another lap time was announced. It was still far inside the requirements for a record, and as Vector I wheeled for its third last run, our small group all roared. The crowd near us caught our enthusiasm, and along with laughter and cries of playful scorn, the excitement spread outwards. The second last and final laps began, not just with cheers, but with a thunderous bellow of "Two!", "One!", "Zero!" and ended as Vector I flashed across the line for the last time and G.W. prepared to land.

The crowd began to move then, and Janice grabbed me round the neck and kissed me hard. She broke away then, flushed, laughing – a bit confused, I thought . . .

Then the crowd surged forward and we were swept along towards Vector I and G.W.

Wild scenes accompanied the finale. It was, of course, filmed for the newsreels. And there was the incomparable press photo, that appeared in so many papers and magazines around the world, of G.W climbing tweed-suited from the cockpit, Irish hat still on, cold pipe again in his teeth.

"How a gentleman dresses for air speed records," chuckled the caption. Years later I heard an aviation expert, who had been in the crowd that day, who said with a laugh, "That was the thing about Gibbs White that told you no matter how smart a fellow he was, he was always essentially an amateur – the beggar never dressed right for the job!" Well, it was said with good humour . . . but I think there was envy in it.

*   *   *

G.W., James and I remained in Nottingham for two days, guests of the mayor and local aviation executives. We were entertained lavishly and put up at a luxurious hotel. Someone noted that Janice and I appeared to be more than "just good friends" and saw to it that she was included in our party.

It was a tremendous celebration. The mayor gave a speech that announced how pleased and flattered the city was to be the focus of so great an event. G.W. managed a brief, gracious, appropriate response. Congratulations rained on us.

Recipients of the city's largesse, we ate and drank too much and wallowed in our celebrity.

After a day of this, Janice and I – our inhibitions swept aside, our feelings inflamed by our proximity to each other, and confident, for the moment, that we were objects of everyone's approval – made love for the first time. That it was pleasant, "overdue", the first moment of fully expressed intimacy we had experienced, is easy to say, because true – though trite. But what really happened between us left us not satiated but more fully alive, shaken as we discovered the fatal depth of our passion. We were young. We had a life of unknowns ahead. It seemed we would not marry soon. But this girl was the one whose essence I would carry with me forever.

It appeared she returned my feelings.

* * *

With the speed trials over, the garbage talk about G.W.'s demonic links was now buried under a huge barrage of professional acclaim as newspaper and magazine articles aimed at making a new British Air Hero. In fact there were leading figures in the aviation world who declared G.W. was the greatest thing in aviation since the Wright brothers themselves.

I was no longer hailed as "The Boy Wonder from Down Under," as that persistent Lady Reporter had labelled me following the first flights of Vector I. But I was still regarded with *some* interest and speculation. And eventually it was felt to be all right for a Colonial to do unusual things without full formal training, assuming he was bright enough. "After all," it was said, "look at their cricketers: no coaching, not much form. They teach themselves to hit a cricket ball out on sheep paddocks. Natural talents, fed on lots of half-raw lamb and beef. Rough diamonds – big louts, half of them, if truth be told. Probably the same sort of thing for this young feller!"

Grant, too, got credit. He was ready-made story material for feature writers, this unknown Thames boat builder, picked from nowhere by G.W. – now hailed as spotter of untutored talents. Gibbs White himself was all right now, of course, with the diabolist rubbish all but forgotten. Air Force, then Cambridge (even though he never finished !). Solid enough there. Even his eccentricity of dress and manner (*they* were being talked about in papers now, in substitution for the demon) – perfectly all right and with good precedent, if a chap was really up to the mark in the thing he was doing.

Somewhat to our surprise we found it was all great fun and we began to enjoy ourselves.

G.W. was now in demand as a lecturer, not only by aeronautical societies and professional engineers, but by schools and churches and every sort of inspirational organization that wanted him to tell how he had managed to write yet one more glory page in the Annals of Empire. The French gave him awards. So did the Germans. Americans made him a lavish offer to include a great public reception in New York. There would be a welcome by the mayor, followed by twenty lectures across the United States at a thousand dollars a throw, and meetings would follow, not only with the notables of American aeronautics but with politicians and film stars.

"Well," said G.W. wryly, "one has to admit the Yanks do like anything to do with the air."

I asked, "Then will you . . . ?"

"Accept? No. Couldn't handle all those lectures. And from what I hear, a lot would be to Ladies' Intellectual Improvement Groups and so forth. I'm not a snob, exactly, but . . . that sort of thing . . . not my cup of tea, what?"

Chapter 21

The news came ten weeks afterwards. In the mail. We were drinking our inevitable morning tea in the workshop. The main doors were open on a fine day and Vector I stood outside, its gleaming side mottled by shade from the apple trees. The envelope was of stiff white paper and carried an originating address in embossed black lettering. G.W. looked at it for a moment and said, as he slit it open, "This'll be from the timekeepers, about the record. Official notification."

He extracted a handsomely headed sheet of paper with interesting watermarks – paper that crackled as he unfolded it. On reading it, he silently pushed it across the tea table to us. He replenished his tea as we read.

The letter's gist was simple. Protests had been entered by the Americans and French challenging the legality of the timekeeping. It was alleged that one of the timekeepers at the moment of the trial lacked full international standing.

It turned out in subsequent enquiries that this man's papers had been mailed and were all in order, but due to a postage handlers' stoppage in London, the letter had been delayed in getting to the international body that approved all timekeepers. Some deadline had been officially exceeded by a day or two. The matter was a technical triviality, but in the cut and thrust of international jealousies it proved to be a legally defensible objection to the record.

The rash of indignant headlines and editorials, all sympathetic to G.W., scarified not only those whose petty envies had brought the protest on such piffling grounds, but also the British aeronautical authorities for their carelessness in not attending to every detail. The situation was the more poignant when it emerged that the times of the official in question had been the slowest recorded. Without them, G.W.'s "record" would have averaged a clear one-tenth of a mile more per hour faster.

No matter. The record was declared null and void. As if it had never existed. British aviation authorities received a formal censure for slipshod practice that caused – both in aviation circles and in the popular press – a furious hubbub against the Americans and French.

G.W., to our consternation, steadfastly refused to become indignant, instead treating the thing as a sort of joke, or some kind of ironic judgement on our over-inflated national pride.

"Really," he said, grinning, "is there anything more ridiculous than all the solemn nonsense we subjected ourselves to? We knew, the crowd knew, the papers knew, everyone with even a pocket watch knew, that Vector I didn't just go faster than any other plane by more than a hundred miles per hour, but that it could outclimb, outturn, outdive, and generally fly rings round any other aeroplane that's ever been. Everyone knows all that now. And that's all I ever wanted. Who cares a hang about this other nonsense?"

We tried to persuade him to set up another record attempt, as did all his other backers. The timekeeping body was desperately anxious to restore its shattered reputation. G.W. would have nothing to do with the idea.

"Never go through such a circus again," he laughed. "Cost me a thousand pounds out of my own pocket even with the money put in by the companies."

Pressure and pleading from all the other heavies among the designers – Mitchell, Camm, everyone – did no good. G.W. refused to budge. Eventually even the press, formerly profoundly sympathetic, became judicial even dictatorial.

"Mr. Gibbs White is understandably devastated by what is rightly condemned as an incredible and expensive bungle," declared a Times editorial. "The fact, however, remains, that in his extraordinary plane, Vector I, he has the most advanced aircraft ever built. Mr. Gibbs White and Vector I have, in a sense, both become public property. We honour them both. And we claim them both for the Empire. Mr. Gibbs White must now –"

"Must!" snarled G.W. " 'Must' be damned! Bloody aeroplane's mine. Do what I damn well please with it. Bunch of idiots!"

There it died. Over the whole of the following year public interest in G.W., his aeroplane, the record attempt was sustained – which was, I suppose, what really mattered.

Chapter 22

I wondered what should come next. The things I had joined
G.W. to do were behind me, experiences and insights that would be
with me forever. I had flown the fastest and most agile aircraft ever
made well enough to do advanced aerobatics in it. But though I might
have an outside chance of joining an aircraft company as a test pilot,
my prospects of becoming a professional in aviation design seemed
remote until I had completed my degree in aeronautics. I had to apply
soon to the university if I hoped to resume studies in the autumn.

Meanwhile Janice wrote to tell me she had joined some students
going to Florence on a late summer excursion to study art collections
in and around the city. It was a windfall opportunity she could not
turn down and they would leave very soon. She urged me to finish
my degree as soon as possible. She wrote: –

*I know you think you've done the right thing, and I concede
that you probably got experience you might otherwise never have
got. And I know something else you might not have fully admitted
even to yourself, Robert: the whole thing – regardless of its
"educational" value – was a tremendous adventure for you. It was
very perceptive of you to see from the beginning that you would be
doing things other students would probably never do. But now that
it's over (I'm referring to all that terrifying flying you did) I can only
say I'm glad. I found your elation and sense of achievement and
adventure exhilarating, but I wouldn't want anyone I love putting
himself so deliberately in harm's way for very long if he could avoid
it. I think the strain of it might just about do me in!*

* * *

I continued to hang about with G.W., who was assuming that I
would soon return to Cambridge. James Grant had already been

negotiating for a job with several of the big aircraft companies, but so far nothing had been decided, though it seemed only a matter of time. Meanwhile, the three of us tinkered and fussed over a few improvements that had occurred to G.W. during the recent flying.

"Sneaking towards those performance asymptotes," he chuckled. It was more than that; by summer's end we had increased the plane's altitude limit till it was approaching an amazing fifty thousand feet; the maximum speed – tested in short bursts – was up by fifteen miles per hour, and the takeoff run was shorter.

But I did get my request to resume studies ready to post next time we went to Timley for provisions. I did not enjoy thinking about what Drs Milland and McIntosh might say – though if they were in a generous mood they might concede that my gamble had come off!

There was also the problem of trying to resume my scholarship. It might prove very difficult – even impossible. If that was how it turned out I was not sure what I could do.

And then, one late afternoon, when G.W. and I were getting ready to close the hangar doors for the day, Bill Parker's dark blue Rolls Royce arrived. Bill got his bulk out of the driver's seat with a bit of a struggle and came towards us with his rolling walk, waving a cheerful greeting.

He didn't waste much time on preliminaries. "I've come to tell you chaps something I'm excited about which you may find interesting." He looked more in my direction than in G.W.'s. or Jim's.

"You'll recall my mentioning it was my aim that Parker Aircraft should get into actual building of light planes, yes? Well, it's about to happen. I've finally persuaded a couple of business friends to come into a venture with me to do this. But though we believe the concept is sound and workable, we agree that we must have a good test pilot, who has flown and tested high-performance modern planes. Well," he said, " you, Bob, fit the bill to a T."

Before I could protest, he said, "You've had experience of a kind only a few people in this country could match. And your experience is absolutely current. Now, of course you haven't flown a lot of planes of different kinds and sizes, but I know you and what you can do, and anyway" – here he gave a wry smile – "I am a businessman and I know that we could never pay a high enough rate to pull in any of the top senior test pilots." He glanced sideways at G.W. "But," he continued, "we could pay you wages, Bob, that I think you'd find quite satisfactory. If we got bigger in time, your salary would increase in proportion. What do you think? Worth considering?

"What's your opinion, Philip?" he asked, before I could respond.

"Well," said G.W., "I had been thinking Bob would – probably must – go back to university."

"I thought you might say that. But there is another aspect to this. I and my associates want to do more than just build light planes. We want to design, build and race them in some of these handicap events that are becoming extremely popular. This would bring our planes to the attention of airmen and a wider public like nothing else could. Don't you think?"

"Probably," G.W. said, after a pause.

Bill Parker was watching me now and I realized what it meant. I liked Parker, but he was a businessman trying to hook me into his scheme, and he had shrewdly sensed how much I liked to fly and was counting on this invitation to prove irresistible. And then he played his winning card.

"Bob, don't think it would just be flying. We would use you in our design team too. I'm sure you'd have a hell of a lot to contribute."

He had me now. These were new opportunities that forced me to see that I really did not want to go back to the university – just yet.

Almost as soon as he finished speaking, I said, "It sounds pretty enticing. And thank you. But let me talk it over with G.W."

"Well, of course, but anyway, this just brings me to the second part of what I want to offer – actually what I'm leading up to."

Parker turned now to G.W. " Philip, I'll be blunt. We want to get you to come to us as our chief of design. If you come we'll offer you a partnership in the company."

G.W. looked at him for a very long moment. He did not smile. "Well, Bill, that sounds very fine, but I – "

"I think I know what you want to say. You've made the ultimate small aircraft and you don't want to devote time to something so much less."

"I think . . ."

But again Bill Parker cut him off. "Consider it this way, Philip. If the principles and concepts – to say nothing of the construction methods you've acquired – are to have lasting influence, it'll have to be because designers everywhere are going to adapt and use them. That's how your work and its principles will survive and flourish. With us you could use them in the most direct and immediate fashion possible and we would give them maximum play in any light planes we produced."

"It's interesting, Bill . . . and tempting, certainly."

"And to cap it, we'd encourage you yourself to fly Vector I – or some plane of very similar type – in these handicap races. You know, it's what de Havilland and Percival are doing – flying their own planes, I mean. It's really just a logical progression. Think of the draw to the public that would be. What d'you reckon?"

G.W. was enough of a realist to see the logic of Bill Parker's proposition. But I sensed that though he might accept, it would be hard for him – at least at first – to take the plunge.

"Bill," he said, lighting his pipe and smiling at last, "it's a fine offer, and very unexpected. Give me a week to think things over.

"As for Bob, unless he really does go back to Cambridge now, he ought to grab with both hands the offer you've made him."

Now Parker turned to James Grant.

"James," he said, "for all I know you may already be about to go to work at a handsome salary for some big company. I'm sure some of them would love to get you after the quality of work you've shown here. But we'd love to have you join us too. I can't promise our salary would match what you might get elsewhere, but we'd do the best we could. And we'd like to keep all three of you together with us. Do you think you'd be interested?"

James' surprised pleasure was obvious. He said, grinning, "As long as I can get enough to let me live comfortably nothing would suit me better."

As we shook hands with Bill Parker he said, "Oh, one thing I forgot, we won't need any of you for another month or six weeks, till we get everything finalized on the financial end. Now Philip, you are already getting plenty of requests to give exhibitions with Vector I, flying in air shows and all that. True?"

G.W. nodded. "True."

"So why don't you both get on with that. It will be fun for you, and eventually it'll be good advance publicity for Parker Aircraft. And in fact, we'd be more than pleased if you'd continue these flights after you join us for as long as interest in them lasts."

*   *   *

So we all accepted Parker's offers and began the next week as he had suggested to continue to fly Vector I for fun and for public demonstration of progress in aircraft design.

About this time there was clamouring in Germany for a visit by G.W. and Vector I, and also in France, where there was powerful popular indignation at the trivial legalistic grounds on which his record had been wrested from him. The latter was particularly interesting in view of French nationalistic ambitions for their own planes and airmen. G.W., however, was not attracted by these invitations, though they would have paid handsomely.

*   *   *

The day before we left for our new jobs with Parker Aircraft James and I went out for a drink to mark the occasion. G.W. was busy with some loose ends of business arrangements, so we were alone. I thought, at the end, as we sat over our beers, that I'd come to know James pretty well while we'd worked together, but that was just because – like many of the very young – I was confident I could "understand" people, even when I knew little of their personal histories. The facts were that I'd found him a congenial workmate and an amiable, if reticent, companion. Now that the Vector I project was ending, it was as if the shared experience at last overcame some of his reserve. He looked at me reflectively.

"How many young fellows of your age, Robert, will be able to look back when they're fifty on experiences like you've had recently?"

"I know. I . . ."

"I mean, you're a smart chap. I don't know that you're as smart as G.W., but perhaps you'll . . ."

"No. My God, no! Of course I'll never . . ."

"Oh, spare us the modesty. You're smart, all right. And it's obvious G.W. thinks so too.

I muttered some inanity.

"But whatever you do later, I'm sure you'll think of recent times as representing some high points."

"Naturally. No argument."

"Of course both you fellows are different in the upper storey than most of us."

"Oh, not really. It's just that . . ."

"Don't interrupt, Robert. G.W. and you *understand* what you're doing and why. And you can see round corners most of us don't even know exist. As for me, I'm happy enough doing my work as best I can, and I don't think I'm too bad at it."

"Your work is great, James. Wonderful. And that's something G.W. has often said to *me*."

"Yes, but I'm just carrying out – for the most part – jobs you fellows pass on to me. I can follow them pretty well, but I could never think them up."

He finished his beer, picked up my already empty mug and went to the bar for two more ales.

He seemed to want to go on talking, slowly, quietly. As we moved along to our third and fourth pints I saw that he was becoming slightly drunk. He told me now how he had met G.W., years earlier, one Sunday on the Thames. G.W. had been sailing, and another boat had struck his small craft, staving in the hull just above the waterline. He'd run ashore just near James' modest boathouse and gone to him for help. He was impressed by James' clean and elegant work, his way with wood and metal. "I'm with an aircraft company," he told Grant. "If you ever thought of a change you could do well there. Not many chaps we have can handle materials as you can. Ever think about planes?"

"Not really," James had replied. "I work mostly by myself,

except when I want a hand with some heavy stuff. Then I hire a couple of local lads to help me. My young brother used to work with me. But he went into racing cars. Working with an aircraft company might be more stimulating than this, but I have no formal training in working with metal, though I've taught myself a bit of it. But for a decent job in the aircraft industry I'd be competing with an army of younger chaps who have had the right sort of training."

"I understand," said G.W. "For my own sort of work, though, I find there are too many cooks spoiling the bally broth. I'd like to go it alone, myself. Only it takes more cash than I can lay hands on at the moment to make planes by oneself – especially the sort I'd like to try to make." He laughed, " Maybe I can save up."

Each summer from then on, when he sailed, G.W. saw James Grant. Sometimes, at the end of an afternoon, they went for an ale together.

"He had a lovely lass with him, a few times," said Grant. "Name of Eve. Delightful girl. Very pretty. Charming. Full of smiles and laughs. In her early twenties. G.W. doted on her. It certainly looked like a serious affair." He looked into his empty beer mug and waited, perhaps feeling he was saying more than he should. "G.W. was not as you see him now. Much younger, slimmer, laughed a lot and looked happy and carefree. I soon realized from his conversation how clever he was, but he was a more easy-going man then."

I was listening carefully. In the time I had known G.W. there had been no hints of any romantic attachments, present or past.

"Then it was over," Grant continued. "After two years. And as far as I know there was never . . ."

"Over? What?"

"Well, it was awful, you know. Her brother used to drive racing cars – as a matter of fact, my own brother knew him quite well. Anyway, Eve's brother was an experienced competitor, but one day she was accompanying him for a spin in his sports car near Southampton and a cow strayed across the road. Well, the car hit it. Her brother held on to the wheel, but she was thrown out. Killed instantly."

"My God."

"I saw G.W. late in the 1925 summer. He told me about it then. He was still very upset, but handling it."

"And since then?"

"Since then, there's been nobody else, as far as I know."

"You didn't talk about it again?"

"Hardly ever. G.W.'s someone who declines to look back. He grieved all right. But then he just went on. I don't mean he stopped grieving. I think the fact that for him there was never another is sign enough . . . But he aged a lot, and very quickly."

So this had been what Mary West had hinted at. And there was the picture of a woman in G.W.'s bedroom that I never saw close up.

Chapter 23

We had given several flying exhibitions with Vector I in southern England – for which we had been paid rather handsomely – when Janice returned from Italy. I rushed up to London to see her even before she had time to go down to the Whitcombe family home in Sussex.

She was full of enthusiasm, bubbling over for what she had seen and heard. "It's a marvellous region for an art historian. Just incredible, really. The richness and variety of what's there could keep you busy for a hundred lifetimes. It makes the British art scene look pathetically meagre."

She was far more excited over her work than I had seen before and I did not interrupt her. But as her narrative slowed down a bit, and there were pauses, I said, "I think I'm getting the impression that you'll want to go abroad some more."

"Yes, more and more – and still more. And soon. Because for anyone with serious interest in the history of the arts, the sooner one starts to travel and see what's out there the better."

I thought this over rapidly but carefully and said, "I have to tell you now about a few things that have happened here. And though they are important to me, I'm not sure how you'll take some of them in the light of your last letter."

I told her of the invitations we had received to join the Parker design team. She was pleased and said, "Yes, great, especially for G.W." Then she said, "But I have to wish you were going back to Cambridge. So long a delay seems to me . . ."

"Yes," I said, "but then I wonder what you'll say when I tell you I'm going to be their first test pilot."

She looked – there's only one word for it – stricken.

"What can I tell you?" I said. "I'm in aviation. I plan and hope to get along in this field, and being both a designer and a test pilot are part of it. Most people don't get a chance to do either of these things. I'm offered both at once, I have to grab the opportunity.

"And that's not the end of it. I'm going to be in some air races when we build some suitable planes at Parker Aircraft."

She didn't say "Yes but – ", or make any sort of protest. But her great eyes dimmed a bit.

I think she felt very bad. I know I did.

I managed to extract from her a promise that she would come down to Parker Aircraft for a look at what we were doing, but of course there wouldn't be much to look at for several months.

I didn't stay long in London because I knew she wanted to see her parents – especially her father, as it was with him that she most shared her artistic interests. We left vowing to meet again as soon as her studies had resumed and when I had more to report about my new job. I felt pretty dissatisfied at how things looked, and returned to G.W.'s place still feeling quite low.

* * *

We finally started work at Parker Aircraft two weeks later. The small factory was near the village of Hinxhill not far from Ashford. There we met Bill Parker and his two financial colleagues. I signed documents that would make me an assistant designer and test pilot. G.W.'s arrangements were more complicated, as he was going to become a partner. For this he had to accompany Parker and his associates to a solicitor's office in Ashford. That afternoon, G.W., James Grant and I rented rooms in a flat complex in Ashford where we would stay until something more spacious and comfortable could be located. G.W. had rented his cottage and expected tenants to take occupancy in about a week.

Bill Parker, with his comfortable bulk, rolling walk and easy manner was in fact a dynamo workaholic. In the first two days of our arrival we had met and talked with all of his fifteen employees and were locked in discussion with Bill Parker himself.

"I've got a good crew of people here," he said. "At the level of the workshop they can make aircraft parts to specifications and do a good job. But you, James, I want you to take care of them and show them all the tricks you and G.W. have learned. No formalities here, we try to keep everything nice and friendly. But I also keep people on track, because we do have orders to fill. This will continue, but I'm not looking to enlarge that side of operations. We'll want you to bring them – most of the better ones – round to working in more advanced ways, so that we'll eventually have a dozen chaps who can build just about anything we'll need."

Now he turned to G.W.

"Philip, as you already know, we want to have you design – and here Bob can join you – three light aircraft. They'll be much lower-powered than Vector I, and have simplified cockpit equipment. The idea is to have one of them small – a two seater, one a bit larger to seat three, and the largest to seat four. All of them should have aerodynamic design characteristics based on the principles that you've already deployed wonderfully in designing Vector I."

"OK," said G.W. "But of course they'll be much wider-bodied and lighter, because with the smaller engines and lower speed and more modest handling capabilities they won't have to be quite as strongly built. On the other hand, because we'll be making several at once – and perhaps many if this venture really works, in the long run we can wander more or less into the realm of assemblyline production. So, unlike with Vector I, we'll be able to preform parts and make up sort of kits for all of them – so putting them together will be much easier."

"Of course," Bill replied, "but what we really want is your adherence to the kind of streamlining and cleanness of profile you've built into Vector I. And though the product might not be hugely different in appearance from, say, Percival's Gull, you'll be using monocoque, all-metal construction and they'll have completely retractable undercarriages.

"And let's always keep in mind that we want to fly these planes in the trophy air races – and win with them if possible."

G.W. cleaned out his pipe, refilled it, lit it and blew smoke. "It's a good project, Bill," he said. "Let's all go to your drafting office and nut out a few essentials."

Over the next couple of days we watched as G.W., talking, but in some ways almost oblivious of our presences, drew plans and illustrated ideas and did rough computations almost without ceasing.

It was like a dream. He had subsumed, adapted and – where necessary, modified – all the concepts he had worked so tirelessly to arrive at, all the knowledge he had stored up, and was able to draw on it with an awesome speed and skill.

It was, I suppose, like seeing some great painter who has created a huge and absolutely unique masterpiece, and has grown because of it, acquired powers beyond anything he had before, so that all subsequent works inspired by it can be done with a brilliant ease and economy of effort.

If I ever wished Janice could see G.W. at work it was now. From her I had gained enough appreciation of art – and of the way artists worked – to know that she would have been transfixed by the sweep and elegance of G.W.'s sketches and scribbles. I felt that, without doubt, she would have seen him now, not so much as an aeroplane builder, but as a powerful artist.

Bill Parker stood or sat by G.W.'s side. He said little, but occasionally his great hand would pat G.W. lightly on the back or lie on his shoulder, and he would utter a grunt or slight whistle of appreciation.

As the question arose of the precise angle at which the wings should be set in relation to the long axis of the planes' fuselages – the dihedral angle – G.W. worked for ten minutes, discussed it for ten more with Parker – and then it was decided. Parker stared. "You've done in a few minutes, Philip, what I thought might be the work of weeks."

G.W. grinned. "Yes, well let's just hope we're right, what?"

But somehow we knew we were – that he was.

* * *

Of course, we had to transform sketches and notional drawings and scribbles to final plans, measurements and specifications, and finally to blueprints, sometimes full-scale. We had to do and redo calculations to arrive at final, hard numbers. Loose approximations evolved into exact plans or numbers. James and the other workshop crew had to fashion wooden or metal full-scale templates against which to shape components like fuselage frames. And all these procedures required months of effort – sometimes much drudgery – to complete.

But we were getting there.

* * *

I worked with G.W., but not all the time. Nor did he work all the time. He continued to fly Vector I in exhibitions and I accompanied him, contributing about one third of the flights. Bill Parker had no problem with this; he wanted it. The publicity was very good for him, as our association with Parker Aircraft was becoming known, plus the fact that G.W. was designing planes for him.

G.W.'s own reputation was also boosted in other ways. He was invited to write several papers on the design, construction, and handling characteristics of Vector I for the Royal Aeronautical Society. These papers, when published, were immediately recognized as vital contributions to aeronautical theory and practice. He also gave lectures to the Society and eventually received their highest awards and Life Membership.

There were also some serious-sounding mutterings about a knighthood, but nothing came of them. It would not have meant much to him anyway. For me, the other main activity was to attend trophy air races. Such races had been growing in popularity in Britain since about 1930. They were popular on several counts. They permitted the entry of aircraft of a great variety of forms and range of performance. This was feasible because of the handicapping procedure. Although – as with horse racing – this could never be completely fair, it made for spectacular aerial theatre. It was an incomparable sight to see some tiny, ridiculously slow aeroplane stuttering its way towards the finish, while some high-powered, streamlined, state-of-the-art arrow came sweeping up to try to catch it at the line. Whichever way the win went, you could be pretty sure of some marvellous finishes.

Now my excitement was rising. I was getting almost desperate to try my hand at it, feeling again – and, I had to admit to myself with great relief – that the career I was following was, for me, the right one.

Chapter 24

G.W. and Bill Parker had seen plenty of races in their time but for me an air race would be a new experience. Soon we took a day off and went in Bill's Rolls Royce to Hatfield, north of London, where I would see one.

We arrived at the airfield to find a scattering of aeroplanes being readied for the start of a race of four laps that totalled eight hundred and thirty-one miles. The sight of it gripped me from the first. None of the planes were military types. The smallest, lowest-powered and slowest planes like De Havilland Moths and Avro Avians, nearly all biplanes with tiny engines and top speeds around 100 mph, naturally received the most generous handicaps. Planes of somewhat higher power and performance, like Comper Swifts and Percival Gulls, their top speeds around 140 mph, were heavily handicapped, and the fastest – planes like the Messerschmitt Taifun and the Lockheed Vega, a big and beautiful American high-wing monoplane, both capable of about 180 mph, were the most heavily handicapped. Most of the faster planes were bigger and heavier than those of lesser speeds, though a Chilton, a tiny plane with only a 44 hp engine, had been cunningly designed as a racer and could reach 180 mph.

I was overwhelmed by the shining polish and vivid colours of so many planes, their engines revving and roaring, everywhere the smell of aviation fuel, engine oil and exhaust; pilots of various ages clad in a range of flying suits; throngs of ground crew and owners. And nearby, a milling excited crowd.

"My God!" I thought, as my pulse surged, "is this what I'm getting myself into?"

The course to be flown was of four laps. The first lap, the longest, had four parts of approximately equal lengths and ended at the return to the starting place – so the lap formed a square. The three remaining laps were triangles of diminishing size; again, each lap began and ended at Hatfield. The idea was to fly the straight lines of the course as faithfully as conditions allowed, cutting around the corner markers along the way as sharply as possible, while trying to conserve speed – and avoid crashing.

The first planes made ready to start, pilots in their cockpits or cabins, crews, if any, in their seats. Everything shone in the light of a golden morning with a clear blue sky, and around the airstrip the flash of green grass and the stirring of windsocks half-filling in a moderate breeze.

With many sputterings and some false notes, the smaller planes taxied to the start to be waved on their way by race officials. With a high buzz of their little engines they got going, bouncing into the air within a few yards – that is, most of them. One or two fired on less than all cylinders, stopped, and resisted all efforts to get them restarted. These efforts were moments of fury and frustration for pilots and ground crew – and sometimes of high comedy as people started to fling tools around in desperation to find the right ones, while pointing fingers at one another and shouting blame.

About two hours after the slowest planes had gone, the first of the faster ones took to the air. After nearly another hour the Taifun, the little Chilton and the big Lockheed got away. Now the crowd would wait, tense and faithful to the end, to see if a struggling survivor or two of the underpowered Moths and Avians would somehow hold off the Percival Gulls or the Taifun, or that great marauding Vega, in the last desperate run to the line.

The first planes to complete the first lap were all small stuff, buzzing along like bees to the hive. But just as the slowest of this group grumbled its way out of our sight, engine labouring, a Percival Gull, with its beautiful, simple lines flashing silver in the sunshine, came sliding into view. It slipped effortlessly round the lap marker and bolted off in hot pursuit of the small straggler ahead.

As the laps increased, more and more of the faster aircraft began to be seen among the slow ones. At various stages, aircraft judged to have no chance of finishing among the top, were eliminated by race officials.

Late in the day, towards the end of the finishing lap, we used a

pair of powerful field glasses to spot the first of the leading planes
several miles away.

"By God," said Bill, "it's a Moth."

Yet, ten or fifteen seconds later, a second, far faster-moving
shape appeared in the field of his binoculars – "It's that bloody Taifun!"

Then the little Chilton flashed into sight.

Now our glasses showed the three planes tearing towards the
finish – two predatory hawks rushing in deadly pursuit of a desperate
sparrow.

At last we could see them without the aid of binoculars and we
could hear them, too. As they came on, the Moth pilot drove his plane
into a sharp ascent that seemed a strange move as it meant forward
speed lost, but then he put the plane into a sudden, engine-screaming
dive that flattened out close to the ground. He was gambling this gain
in speed would more than compensate for what he'd lost in pursuit of
altitude.

As they drove towards the line, the Chilton on top, the Taifun
nearest the ground, the Moth the meat in the sandwich, they bounced
in the turbulent air of each other's wake.

Then it was over. The Taifun – by a nose.

* * *

In the aftermath, after all the people Bill and G. W. knew had
shaken our hands, or slapped us on the back, we went off again in
Bill's Rolls Royce.

"How long was it, Philip, that you saw your last race before this
one?" asked Bill.

"Not sure," said G.W., "but some years, certainly."

"Well, I'm glad we saw this, because we needed it to wake us
up to what we'll be facing soon," said Bill. "And you, Bob, if not the
rest of us, should attend several more, because you have to pick up all
the tricks there are in this sort of flying. You may not appreciate them
just yet because they probably look like a piece of cake after the
aerobatics you now know, but it's all in the timing – knowing exactly
where and when and how to turn. If you lose any time on the turns,

that can ruin everything. In races like this, where you can have anything from ten to more than fifty turns, you can lose a lot of time if you don't get round them cleanly. Time you'll never make up no matter how fast you fly the straight bits."

"True," said G.W., "and Bob, did you notice how that big Vega wallowed on the turns? That's why it finished well back. Yet the Vega is a great plane and a very advanced design, considering it's already seven years old. Yes, tactics are crucial. Another thing you have to do is make sure you don't get in another plane's wash. That can be very difficult – it's even been known to be fatal."

"Well, enough of all these solemn warnings, I suppose," said Bill. "What, in short, did you think of it – I mean as something we want you to do in a little while?"

"Marvellous," I said, caught up in the excitement of the moment.

Chapter 25

A week later I had already mapped out a twenty mile triangular course with three sharp turns in it. I could either fly the straight sides at top speed, and pull round the turns as fast as possible or, if I wanted more turning practice, I could take several runs at each turn.

But this was just a map exercise. I had no plane. We had moved Vector I to the site of Parker Aircraft where a hangar for it was under rapid construction, but none of us wanted it to be used in such routine exercises. In any case, the planes I expected to be racing eventually would all be enormously slower than Vector I.

Then Bill came in one morning when G.W. and I were just beginning some plan draftings and said, "Bob, I want you to come to the airfield near Ashford. That's where we'll have to begin all our flying from. You need to see their facilities. Why don't you come, too, Philip?"

It took us only a short time to get to Ashford and not much longer to see around the "facilities" – which were indeed very simple. Then we went into the aerodrome manager's office to meet him over a cup of tea.

After ten minutes Bill raised his hand and said, "Listen."

He said nothing more, but there was the distant hum of an aeroengine that rapidly intensified to a roar, which then ceased abruptly. A plane had certainly landed nearby. We all went out to look.

A new Percival Gull sat there, from which a pilot was emerging. He waved to Bill and approached us rapidly. " Here we are then, Mr Parker, and here's the paperwork. A twelve-month lease I think?"

Bill thanked the friendly pilot, gave him a cup of tea, signed the papers and got one of the Ashford manager's workshop crew to drive the pilot to the railway station. Then we went out to look at the Gull.

"Not a *really* fast plane," Bill said, "but you know that already. But it's a great little aircraft that will be one of the faster types you'll fly against, so OK for practice." He gestured at it, and then glanced at me. "Like to take it up now?"

* * *

A couple of days later, when I was making small adjustments to the engine of the Gull, a letter arrived from Janice. There was a long week-end coming and she was intending to visit her parents. She wanted me to come and meet her father. She seemed to feel this was important and I felt I must accept. There was no difficulty about this from Bill or G.W., so I caught a train to Eastbourne at the end of next week.

* * *

Janice introduced me to her father in a somewhat ceremonious manner that told me it was, for her, a meeting freighted with more significance than the one with her mother had been.

I was thinking about the meaning of this for me as we shook hands.

Henry Whitcombe was a tall, austerely handsome man, with what I'll call Norman features. He had a reserved demeanour, though he shook hands warmly enough with a strong grip.

"Pleased to meet you at last, Robert," he said. He had a deep voice and a precise way of speaking.

For a while we spoke those bland pleasantries that many English of the time employed as a semi-formal ritual at a first meeting, before allowing themselves to be more relaxed and direct.

So he was very polite, but careful. He meticulously avoided staring, but I knew he was taking me in carefully. I was taking him in too.

After the inevitable cups of tea – very good tea for a change – and a biscuit or two, he began to unwind, and asked me about my work. He was very intelligent and knew a lot more about aeronautics than Janice did, or than I could have expected.

Eventually, I got a bit tired of the oblique way we were addressing each other and, reverting to my natural manner, I said, "I thought of you as interested in church architecture, but you're asking things about aviation that laymen hardly ever do."

He smiled, became more relaxed.

"You see, my first training was as an engineer, and it was partly during that time that I became interested in the history of churches and how they were constructed. My engineering gave me a basis for understanding the principles church builders had employed over the centuries. Most churches are made of stone – which is very heavy. And though, in a sense, such buildings are strong and may last a long time, their heaviness can make such things as walls very difficult to stabilize."

I knew I was under examination. Henry Whitcombe did more than show polite interest in what I had been doing: he promised to look in on us at Parker Aircraft one day. And then, to my astonishment, he brought up the cricket match I had played in during my first visit.

"You certainly left an impression in this corner of Sussex," he said with a slight grin.

"All I did was go out and have a bit of a slog. Anyone who . . ."

"Yes, but you see quite a lot of people that live hereabouts know their cricket. It's been widely talked about that – out of form or not – you managed to slog your way very quickly to a winning score, and while doing so hit a very fine England spin bowler out of the ground on several occasions."

"Just luck," I said, though feeling pleased and knowing I was looking flushed.

"Well," he said with a little laugh, "let's hope you never tackle our bowlers when you're in real form."

I felt puzzled. This man was a considerable scholar, able enough to make a very good living in an unusual, specialised field of expert knowledge. Surely it was of little significance to him whether or not I could hit a ball. But then the thought came that he was viewing me with reference to the daughter on whom he doted. To put it crudely, I might be reasonably smart, but was I "a good chap", someone he might one day have to entrust his beloved child's future to, who could fit into her social milieu and not be utterly alien to the kind of life she was accustomed to?

He was too reticent a gentleman in speech and manner – and, for that matter, had too much good taste – to refer directly to any significant future actions, or promises of them, between Janice and me. But there were various hints – things he did say, opinions expressed – that led me to see that being OK at cricket, a very social English game that members of his family and their friends and acquaintances played, might be of some assurance to him

Janice was affectionately amused. "Dad didn't frighten you, I hope. He's really a dear."

"He didn't frighten me. But I had the impression he's sort of eyeing me, measuring me up, as it were. Otherwise he seems a nice man. And he told me some interesting things."

She grabbed my arm and kissed me. "They're going to play tennis in half an hour. I suppose like 'all' Australians, you play tennis like some sort of champion."

"Christ!" I said.

*   *   *

The next morning Janice borrowed one of the family cars and, with a sandwich lunch on the back seat, we went off to visit the town of Hastings. We had half-planned to press on as far as Folkestone in Kent, but just beyond the eastern limits of Hastings, Winchelsea Beach opened up and we stopped there. It was a dazzling afternoon and we pulled off our shoes and socks and just wandered along the wide shore. I kissed her slowly. Held her. And we kissed again. It seemed like years since we had been alone together. And now, under the wide sky, with the blue water and the long beach and the gulls calling, it suddenly seemed just a bit like Australia. And I felt many strange things. I would stand on an Australian beach with my arms around her some day and we would kiss. And peace and love and a life together would be in reach.

I snapped out of this, pretty quickly.

We walked on till we were a long way from our parked car, and houses, and – as far as anyone could see – were alone. We dropped down on the warm sand, at a place where a sandy ridge stabilized by beach grasses loomed a few feet above us.

* * *

That evening after dinner, out on a terrace, I said, "You've got to come soon and see what we're doing. In about a month we'll have some of the plane parts being assembled. It won't be till next spring that we start to fly them in races. And before that they'll have to be test-flown."

"By you . . . ?"

"Yes, by me, of course."

She became silent as we looked up to the stars and half-moon as they slowly appeared in the darkening blue of the late evening.

This didn't feel the right time to pursue what could become a matter of difficulty for us. So I turned into more neutral channels.

"I plan to see Salisbury Cathedral and its ancient clock your Dad was telling me about, one day," I said. "And maybe the clock sounds even more interesting than the Cathedral. Know why?"

"Of course. Because it's so obviously a real machine that still works – and that's where your true interests lie."

"That's correct, as far as it goes. But thinking about it also made me see that everything can always be traced back. I can almost picture some sort of primitive – what do they call them? protohuman? – with its hands chipping away to make the first-ever tools from a lump of some hard rock. The first ever? Maybe . . . And then everything else since – everything! – can be traced back to those basic gestures of invention. That – ancestor of us all – wouldn't have known, really, what it was doing, that it was what we call "making" something. But in a way it was the one to be envied above all, because it was the first. Stood on absolutely nobody else's shoulders."

Chapter 26

So now I had met Janice's father, and because of it I somehow felt older when I returned to Parker Aircraft.

As for Janice, I loved her, and I thought she loved me. But for her, unlike me, the closeness to her family had neither slipped nor weakened. She might not automatically seek her parents' advice on every matter, nor accept it when offered. Nor did they seem the sort of parents to stand strongly in the way of her real wishes. But though it had never been expressed, I sensed that neither of them would view any marriage or other permanent relationship for their daughter with favour – at this point.

And assuming I was reading them correctly, I thought I would agree with them . . .

For if Janice was the woman for me – if she would have me – she was still just a girl. To put it in the simplest, most bluntly honest way, I knew we were not ready for each other.

I think I was beginning to know who I was and I could guess what sort of young woman she would be at twenty-three, but by then she would be in a real life of her own. That would be better for both of us. So I thought, not without wry amusement at my own increasing "wisdom" that the best thing would be for us just to get on with our working lives for a year or so and then come together permanently with everything gained by way of experience and self-knowledge – and nothing lost.

But another question loomed for me. Janice had already expressed her fear of my flying – anyway, the sort of flying I was doing, which I was not planning to stop any time soon. Could she get used to that? And was it fair to expect that she would?

Maybe what I needed was a woman who was much more devil-may-care about the possible dangers in the lifestyle of her spouse. Maybe. The trouble here was that I loved Janice.

I had to push these thoughts to the back of my mind as I got back to work.

* * *

We were getting well into the autumn now and I went to some of the few races that remained before the end of the season. I learned more about tactics but the rest would have to wait until I had a Parker plane of Gibbs White design to fly.

Two aircraft were now taking shape in the capacious workshop/ hangar that had been built to Bill Parker's specifications. These planes were far from being mere copies of Vector I, being considerably wider-bodied to accommodate a pilot and passengers – as many as three in one version. Or seats could be removed for baggage space. The fuselage could have been much slimmed by reducing the crew to a single pilot intent on mere speed. But Parker Aircraft were aiming at planes for an expanding market – planes that, while robust and manoeuvreable, would be attractive prospects for private or corporate owners who wanted speed – and comfort as well.

And what would drive these planes were De Havilland Gypsy Six in-line engines, just then beginning to come into use in high performance, medium-light aircraft.

The features by which the Parker "Falcons" most revealed their Vector I lineages lay in their maximized streamlining, the shape and structure of their wings and tails, their monocoque fuselages, fully retractable undercarriages and all-metal construction, including stressed-skin wing and tail surfaces.

As they took shape, we could see they were going to be extremely beautiful aircraft. And as winter approached we were cheering on our workshop crews under the general direction of James Grant, checking and re-checking G.W.'s design calculations – though eventually it became too late in production for further re-checkings to be useable – and endlessly discussing my responsibilities as a test pilot, and the basic tactics for racing.

* * *

There was no way I could spring the time to get to London, but not long before Christmas – in fact just after her examinations were over – I persuaded Janice to come and see our progress. And then, as we talked by telephone, an inspiration. "Perhaps your Dad would like to come, too?"

She thought this was a great idea, had in fact thought of it herself, but hadn't wanted to seem pushy.

"Look," I said, "he's an engineer. I bet he'll find it pretty interesting."

Janice's father accepted – with alacrity, she reported.

A week later, just minutes after they arrived by car, and with introductions and small talk about weather and the density of pre-Christmas vehicle traffic over, Henry Whitcombe was looking at our Falcons. The somewhat austere, detached manner was gone. Here was an engineer, able to understand very well the principles of construction we were adopting and the reasons for them, and readily fired by our collective enthusiasm for what we were doing.

"Good Lord!" he kept saying, "I had absolutely no idea. This is marvellous work. I've never seen such engineering skill. Absolutely admirable." Then he laughed. "I take it that they are not merely very beautiful, but that you really are confident these planes will fly."

"My God, they'd better," said Bill Parker. "Otherwise, we'll be on the streets of London with our begging bowls. But listen, come down in the early spring when Bob and Philip will be testing them. And then keep us in mind for the air races. I can let you have the schedule before you go. Now come and see our plans if you'd like to understand just what G.W.'s been getting at."

I was glad Janice's father had come. I knew she was. She obviously loved him and I had pleased her by including him. Besides, it was nice to have someone with engineering knowledge, but who was not in planes, to appreciate and admire what we were doing.

Chapter 27

G.W., James Grant and I had managed to rent a three-bedroom flat – sparsely furnished, not especially comfortable – for the three months till our central task would be near completion and we would have more time to pick and choose. We agreed to work through the Christmas and New Year season. Our only breaks were a leisurely Christmas lunch at a nearby hotel and a convivial dinner on New Year's Eve at Bill Parker's spacious home, which ended with a noisy midnight toast to the upcoming air races. Janice had invited me to her home for Christmas and New Year, saying everyone was keen to see me again, but I declined because G.W., Bill and James were anxious not to waste significant time. I hoped she would understand.

And we really did work. All the sorts of trials and examinations we had put Vector I through were repeated now, but with four of our regular workforce to help – all of them young, single men who didn't mind working through the holidays at fifty percent more than their regular wages – the task was much easier.

By February, we were installing seats, making final adjustments to cabin instruments, checking undercarriages. I stuck my head outside the workshop one fine morning for a breath of fresh air and saw that crocuses were blooming.

By the end of February one of the Falcons was ready. The impression it made when we had it transported to Ashford airfield was close to sensational. All the newspapers knew G.W. and me, and now we were arriving with another new aircraft of stunning appearance. Not three hours after we began final adjustments for the first of the trial flights, there were scores of reporters and photographers, and a growing crowd. From appearances, many of the ordinary folk of Ashford were showing up; we could recognize local storekeepers, bank tellers, a publican, shopkeepers, police, and – it being a regular Monday – a couple of hundred women, ranging in age from young to old, most of them carrying shopping baskets.

We probably should have cordoned off an area to operate in that would be a little away from the growing crowd. But we were interested in getting a hint of how the plane looked to a general public.

Most of the comments were praise and admiration and awe. We were pleased, but not exactly surprised. The Falcon – like Vector I – shone with the mirror-like brilliance that only a polished metal-skinned aircraft can show. Its lines, like those of Vector I, were clean, streamlined – but in a way more "friendly." Vector I's form derived from a striving after aerodynamic perfection – overwhelming performance and handling its sole aim. These considerations led to an impression of purity and some sense of remoteness – even transcendence – in its form. People could sense that Vector I was a sort of final statement in aircraft design for its time. Its appearance could lead to wonder and amazement, but not as easily to something that a broad public could understand and appreciate.

The Falcon was accessible. Its large cabin and wide fuselage meant it could carry people and their luggage, like a car. It was entered not through a sliding plastic bubble, but through two perfectly recognizable doors – one on each side. The 200 hp engine, only a fraction of the size of the huge Rolls Royce that drove Vector I, meant a much shorter and perhaps less menacing nose. Yes, this was a falcon, not some glorious, possibly terrifying, eagle.

And when I finally got aboard and started the engine, the noise it made seemed like a warm, domestic hum compared to Vector I's roar of triumph. The crowd – about a thousand strong by now – gave us a great cheer of a send-off, which we could sense (but not hear) by seeing a multitude of open mouths.

*   *   *

I taxied slowly down the airfield, inspecting the limp windsocks for any signs of breezes. There appeared to be none.

I made some preliminary taxiing runs to check out the sound of the engine at different speeds, to see that information from the instrument panel seemed correct, to get a general feel of controls, note any undue vibration, and to be sure the pilot's seat was adjusted for maximum comfort.

"After that, standard stuff, of course," G.W. had said. "For a first flight just get up a couple of hundred feet and circle the airfield. Nothing fast. Probably don't retract the wheels, and for God's sake set the plane down gently. Mustn't do anything to frighten the crowd, what?"

Those were the things I did. Necessary. Minimal. What I reported was that all was quiet and comfortable. It seemed hardly enough to put the crowd into ecstasies, but on the whole they seemed satisfied, and applauded as I rolled to a stop at the exact spot I had started from.

Next day, after we had further checked everything we could think of, I went up again, flew a good bit higher, did two fairly slow banked turns to describe a figure-of-eight over the airfield, flew a bit faster in a short burst, then settled down for a landing as before. This time I had to remember to lower the undercarriage.

To my surprise the crowd was no smaller than the day before. And the crowds did not diminish.

And as I pushed on day after day with our series of test flights, gradually increasing speeds and altitudes, and eventually including loops, vertical banking turns, deliberate sideslips – all the standard aerobatics, it was not just more admiration for G.W.'s ability I felt; it was love for the Falcon itself.

The Falcon was not Vector I. It was a quiet, comfortable little plane that handled like a dream. It was responsive, stable, viceless, forgiving, ridiculously easy to fly. Its engine was only a fraction of the horsepower of Vector I's, but its clean design, smooth streamlining and fully retracted undercarriage gave it a top speed of nearly 250 mph under good conditions.

I hardly dared to tell G.W., but I began to feel – more in this Falcon that I had in the all-conquering Vector I – the glory of flight; that I could have turned the nose of this superb aeroplane in any direction and soared away, over and above the crowded and often despoiled earth, and see it with new eyes, its grossness and imperfection fused into images of colour and beauty.

At the end of my last flight of the test series I remember that I pointed the nose down and opened the throttle to something close to its limit, and really began to rack up some miles. I held on, for about ten miles or more, then dropped to two thousand feet, flattened out, and finally slid lower until the Falcon was circling the field.

I came in for a soft, perfect, three point landing. Neat, if I do say so.

The crowd was only a thousand or two – not quite like when Lindbergh landed in Paris! But all in all, for a British crowd of those times, it's safe to say they were more than a little enthused.

* * *

Again the publicity machine began to roll. Again G.W. and his Aussie protégé had produced a wonderful new plane. And this time the plane itself was more accessible to a reading, radio-listening, newsreel-watching public. This Falcon was a plane that people with the money to buy one – businessmen, air sports enthusiasts – could actually be imagined in, and be seen flying.

Bill Parker shared little of our public glory, but he got what he most wanted: a sudden reputation for Parker Aircraft as a producer of excellent aeroplanes. He was launched; his company would be taken seriously in the aviation world.

* * *

Janice had, of course, known about the flights from letters I had sent her, and now she knew they were over – and of their success. She telephoned me and said all the right things.

But I could tell things were *not* right with her, and I had forebodings of what was to come.

Chapter 28

But then there was a disaster, the seriousness of which, for a time at least, would quite cloud anticipations of whatever might be the future for Janice and me. I received a letter from Janice to inform me of her father's death in a car crash while on his way to advise on some repairs to a small, ancient church in Lincolnshire. The letter was short but full of an enormous sense of loss. I telephoned her at the family home where everyone was in mourning to say I would visit her in London as soon as she was able to return to her studies there.

When we met a week later her slim body looked frail, bent forwards, even shrunken. Her face was strained, drawn, mouth dragged down at the corners, the shine of the large eyes dimmed from hours of tears. G.W. and Bill Parker had urged me to stay near her for a week if need be, so I hung around, not saying much, but listening to her as she recounted her life as a child – of twelve, even five years ago – with the quiet fun and love she had always experienced with her father.

After a few days, she began to think a bit about her work and took me with her to see three current exhibitions.

The first was a collection of Etruscan artifacts. I knew nothing of the Etruscans, but Janice explained they had lived in the Italian peninsula between the Arno and Tiber Rivers and were well known to Greeks and Romans who fought them and wrote about them. The history of the Etruscans was far less known than that of their more powerful enemies, so their artifacts – many examples of which were assembled in this collection – were of special interest to historians. We saw bronze helmets, statuettes, an image in gold of the horned river god Achelous, whose beard was fashioned of thousands of tiny granules of gold fused together to form a patterned surface texture, a terra-cotta head of the god Turms, and several pottery bowls and urns.

From this, we went to Tate Gallery where there were many Impressionist landscapes on loan from Paris, and an exhibition of works by Picasso and Braque from the days when they were friends and working together in Paris early in the 20th Century.

It's fair to say that these arrays of sharply differentiated art objects – many of them beautiful or remarkable in their greatly varied ways – awakened in me a growing interest in a world of crafts and splendours I had been hardly aware of. I might have found them interesting even without Janice to inform me – though the likelihood is that I would never even have seen them. But, anyway, it was through Janice's insight and knowledge and sense of wonder that my eyes were opened to these things for the first time – things that were other than those I had so far been inclined to worship.

*   *   *

Janice said nothing at first about the Falcon test flights. Eventually, I mentioned them myself. She then admitted she had seen newspaper reports and congratulated us for getting so far so fast. But her remarks were muted, with nothing of the enthusiasm she had shown when Vector I first flew. I did, however, extract from her a promise to watch the first air race in which I would compete during the summer. Before that she would be going to Paris to study some of the enormous art collections in the Louvre and other museums and galleries.

*   *   *

In the last couple of days we had together we went in the evenings to my small hotel room and made love. At first she seemed hesitant, doubtful, but at last we were comfortable together and the passion of our earlier lovemaking returned, intensified.

I remember the morning before I returned to Ashford when she stood in a thin white shift against the early light of the window, her body still with a sense of frailty about it. And I came and stood beside her and tried to comfort her.

Chapter 29

"The day of judgement" – as I came to think of it – approached. G.W. and I flew the carefully readied Falcon up to the starting point – Hatfield again – on the preceding afternoon. Bill Parker and James Grant came in the dark blue Rolls.

I was pleased beyond measure to find a note from Janice at the airfield manager's office to tell me she was staying overnight at a nearby inn. I telephone briefly to thank her for coming. I had thought her father's death might still be affecting her enough to put her off.

G.W., Bill, James and I stayed at a small and not very good inn that was right alongside the aerodrome and were up and about well before breakfast at six a.m. We went at once to the airfield though our plane was one of the most heavily handicapped and we would not be starting up for a long time. When we arrived we were immediately swept into a scene of frantic activity that continued all the time we were not actually in the air.

The course had been laid out differently for this race – the Prince of Wales Cup Race, one of the most important of the season. This time we would fly an inverted triangle with its apex – and starting point – at Hatfield and pylons to mark the course at Buntingford and at Barton in the Clay and finishing at Hatfield. The triangle was equilateral, with a total straight path distance of fifty-one miles. Twenty laps of this gave a total race distance of a little over a thousand miles. It was a course laid out for speed, with breaks for refuelling every five laps. Clearly, one of the most exacting aspects would be the high speed turns. A loose turner would be savagely penalized.

Janice soon came to where we were assembled. She seemed better than she had when I'd last seen her, but still had a sort of haunted look. It worried me.

Soon, however, we had to give our full final attention to the Falcon.

"Fine day forecast," said G.W., "but a bit breezy. Want to watch out for that on the turns, what?"

Our time came round at last –it was the final start in the race – and after a feverish hug and kiss from Janice, I climbed into the cabin of the Falcon alongside G.W., who occupied the passenger's position, strapped myself in place, and gave a last wave to everybody. Then we were taxiing to the start.

The Falcon took off in what seemed like the length of a cricket pitch and climbed with a soft, sweeping ease to what would be our operating altitude – which was very low indeed.

I took the greatest care not to crowd or be crowded by any other aircraft – this was, after all, my first race experience, my first experience of flying among many other aircraft. I deliberately allowed the Falcon to fall back a bit so I could see how experienced racers ahead of me handled the turns and other hazards. I knew we had speed in hand to catch most of them later.

I noticed at once that planes were sometimes considerably bunched up as they approached the turns and that this was bad medicine, to be watched for at all costs. G.W. quickly pointed out that by watching the planes ahead of you very carefully you could often tell, by the way they had ridden upwards a little, that the pilots had detected a helpful tailwind – a sign you could then take advantage of.

"And," he said, "sometimes we'll see them bump about a little bit, which means they've hit a patch of turbulence or a slight rising thermal current. So then we can make allowances to avoid hitting the worst of these.

"Basically," he added, "let others make the mistakes, and don't repeat them if you don't have to. Keep the plane flying as straight and even as possible, and remember where landmarks are that'll help you to do that."

We raced on, gathering speed now, and as we approached the third pylon – the one at Hatfield – G.W. said, "I think it's useful not to bother trying to make one's turns as abrupt as possible by the use of steep banks. Those look good, but you lose a lot of speed and tend to drift groundwards, and that can be dangerous. I think the better way is to come in a bit flatter with a normal turn, but beforehand, while you're approaching with a high air speed, use that speed to climb a little. Then as you come out of the turn you'll have good height and you can sort of swoop down to a bit less altitude at absolutely top speed, what?"

As the race progressed we passed many of the slowest of the slower planes and eventually a somewhat higher concentration of them. Among these we saw a De Havilland Dragon, a large two-engine biplane with a number of passengers. For a little while I was disconcerted as some of the passengers, perhaps over-excited at being part of the race – or perhaps with the slightly base motive of trying to distract us – shouted soundlessly, waved or made other disconcerting gestures. I was glad when they were out of sight. G.W. just laughed. And then, at last, the ranks of these thinned right out and most of the planes we were seeing were those that were only a little slower than the Falcon.

Our plane handled like a dream. Its Gypsy Six engine never missed a beat, just hummed along. Our seats were comfortable, placed exactly right. Our spacious cabin affording us plenty of room and a great view ahead and to the sides. G.W. had installed a rearview mirror that gave us a good sight behind.

And then, in well under four hours we were down to the final sixty miles and could see only a few aircraft ahead of us. I concentrated on the final turn on the Hatfield airfield, climbing my ramp of air on the approach and skimming down as we came out of our turn.

"Well, you've got that right," said G.W. "In fact, old boy, bloody good flying all round. Now just pull out all the stops."

I did, and something came back to us on our starbord side. I soon saw it was the Taifun that had won the race I witnessed in my earlier visit to Hatfield – and we were by it in a rush. I decided that if this was not my absolutely favourite way to fly, it was still pretty good fun.

I realized we had received a tremendously punishing handicap, being last off the mark because of our estimated top speed, and I saw we could probably not bridge the gap between us and two front runners. On the other hand, as we passed the next to last pylon to sweep by a blue-painted Comper Swift, I thought to myself that we would certainly have the shortest time in the air and the highest average speed.

The rest would have to be blamed on too heavy a handicap or to my inexperience. I thought perhaps people would be indulgent in their judgement.

I gave one last glance in the rearview mirror to gloat over the Comper Swift. And it had vanished. Well, not quite. It was there, all right, a rapidly shrinking pile of wreckage, smeared along the ground, with the part of the smear nearest us ablaze and pouring sooty smoke.

*   *   *

We finished the race in fine style, third over all. Another Comper Swift won it by a hundred yards from the onrushing finish of the big, formerly unsuccessful Lockheed. We had almost made up what was generally agreed was too big a handicap, and were enthusiastically greeted by everyone not yet informed of the crash seventeen miles back.

All the official presentations were muted, the usual after-race festivities cancelled, and people went home again not saying much to each other. The pilot who had died had been a very successful and well-known race competitor. An air of misery prevailed that was to colour several of the following races of the season.

It was a sad irony that the dead pilot's final error had resulted from exactly the type of steep, banking turn G.W. had warned me about.

As for Janice, as soon as the crash was announced she seemed to melt away in the crowd, and when I tried to reach her at her inn, they told me she had left.

Chapter 30

The next morning, back at Ashford, I hesitated to phone Janice. The events of the day before had proved intolerable – so much was clear. But then I grew concerned she might be feeling diffident in case she had upset me badly by just disappearing. Of course I *was* upset, but mainly because I could see how she would take it.

I phoned about mid-morning and her mother – who sounded anxious – found her.

"I hardly know what to say, Robert," she said. "It was just that I . . ." and she began to cry softly.

I said, "I get it. I really understand. I only wish we could have talked about it afterwards, because I felt very bad, too, as did everyone. His wife and kids and many of his friends were there. You actually might have felt better to have met them. When will you be going back to London?"

"Tomorrow," she said.

"How'd it be if I took the morning train and we could meet in the afternoon and have dinner?"

"Yes . . . yes, I'd like that."

*   *   *

When I saw her, it was clear she was stricken by this latest death, though she had not witnessed it, and it was only because I had been in that race that it could affect her more than the violent end of any stranger.

But she soon expressed herself and I was floored by it at the time. For she could not have been more direct.

"Robert, I love you. I truly do love you very much, and I suppose – I mean I've been supposing – that when the course of our lives got a bit clearer, we would – well – get married. Unless there was a real change in our attitudes to each other. But now . . . well, now, I don't know what . . ."

I can't tell how I looked at that moment. Well, I must have looked like hell, because she at once hugged me and gave a quiet sob.

"See, the thing is, Rob, that I really, really loved Dad. And though I never dreamed for one second last year that I would ever in my life fall in love with someone as deeply as I have with you, well, it has happened."

I held her.

"Darling, I can't . . . I don't think I can let it go on. After what happened I'll never stop thinking about it whenever you fly."

"I think I understand, but aircraft and flying are my life. There's absolutely nothing else I want to do, anyway, not now." This was where I had said too much, made a fatal mistake.

Then I managed one of the oldest and stupidest ploys that I regretted as soon as I got it out. "I mean, any job has its risks. I could be a cab driver, or a geologist who falls off a mountain. I . . ."

She had the grace and presence of mind to hush me. "Robert, I love you. You know, and I know, that your profession is very much more dangerous than what most other people do. I feel, at the moment, I just can't handle it."

"What the hell do we do? Do we . . . ?

She kissed me gently, then. "Give me a few months, darling. Let's see how things seem by the end of the summer."

I felt wretched enough to avoid putting up much of an argument.

*   *   *

Well, if I had failed to read the depths of distress even in one I professed to love, age, or something, had equipped both G.W. and Bill Parker with superior insight. One look at me the next morning told them something had gone badly wrong. Bill Parker didn't actually say much, but G.W. didn't mince matters.

"The lass was upset, I assume," he said.

"Extremely."

He nodded. "She's probably been on tenterhooks since she saw the test flights. And she has a right to be, you know, old boy. Flying high performance planes may be very pleasurable, but as games go we have to admit it's damned dangerous and a bit stupid."

"But now I don't know what to do."

"Ah, well, that's a royal conundrum. If this was just a pleasant 'girlfriend' sort of thing, I'd say let it go. But it is clear you care deeply about this young woman, and from what I can make of her it's right you should. Why not let things stagnate a bit, like she's suggesting? It looks too important to both of you to get impatient."

* * *

I wrote her a note. In it I argued again, and in greater detail, that planes and flying were my chosen life, that I was not a risk taker by nature, did not fly for "cheap thrills" but for the love of flying, that the mere act of flying fast for its own sake had only moderate attraction for me, but that it was a further test of the superiority of G.W.'s designer skills, and also a major form of advertising for the company that was employing me. I added that, for me, the chief joy of flying was being able to cruise effortlessly at one's will in controlled movements like those of birds. I did admit the dangers but insisted I would do everything in my power to avoid them.

I was not, of course, being completely frank, because not only did I intend to fly again in races, I did enjoy it more than I had anticipated. And while I did not discount its dangers – how could I? – it was clear to me that I was going to ignore them.

I saw her from time to time after that, but now our greetings were more and more like those of friends.

I went back to racing. The Falcon won two of the smaller contests, but despite my greatest efforts and increasing experience, we were too heavily handicapped to win major races. This was beginning to annoy us a lot. We knew there wasn't a handicappers' conspiracy but that the Falcon was being judged as something setting new standards for light aircraft. The handicappers didn't want it to win by margins big enough to make the races look ridiculous. As it was, we invariably recorded the fastest lap times and overall race times. So we got plenty of publicity. And for Parker Aircraft that meant profitable orders.

The most satisfying race of the season was the last one. G.W. had finally yielded to Bill Parker's urgings to enter Vector I. If the Falcon had posed problems for the handicappers that were nothing compared to this. How, some of them asked us, could they possibly come up with a reasonable handicap mark for the fastest aeroplane of all time (and one of the most manoeuvreable)?

"You know," one of the senior officials told us, "you beggars are setting us an impossible problem. Everyone in the world will be waiting to see Vector I and G.W. pulverize all the good planes and pilots there are. And we can't, can't for the good of the sport of air racing, let that happen. If Vector I wins it'll have to be by a margin of about one yard. Seriously! We've got to get away from the idea that other planes are worth just about nothing. Because that's the way the broad public will see it, and that's very bad for the aircraft industry as a whole, and for all race pilots. So please understand in advance why Vector I probably won't win. Nor, in all probability, will its young stablemate the Falcon – for similar reasons. Don't say you haven't been warned, and understand that this is absolutely not personal. In fact, at the personal level, every last one of us has the greatest possible admiration for you chaps!"

* * *

That last race, when it came, was certainly the most remarkable I was ever in. I mean, it was something to be storming off in the Falcon in pursuit of twenty five aircraft, the slowest of which had started on the eight hundred mile trek literally hours before. Yet even more hours would elapse before G.W. and Vector I would be released like some Grand National winner in pursuit of a mixed gang of spavined pit ponies. A fragment of poetry from my schooldays kept popping up in my mind? "The Assyrian came down like a wolf on the fold, and his cohorts were gleaming in purple and gold."

It was only in the very last tearing miles of the race's closing stages that I caught sight of a growing speck in the far distance and realized that G.W. was on course and coming up at five hundred miles an hour like a bat out of Hell. I knew by then that I was not going to be able to run down all of the two or three that lay ahead of me, though I might just make it to third place, but really I was more intent on what G.W. was doing in Vector I than in anything else.

I tried to picture him, relaxed in a way but utterly intent, as was his fashion at moments like this. I could almost see him lighting his pipe as he peered steadily ahead.

I don't think the crowd were disappointed. In fact, from what I heard later, they cherished, for ever after, the memory of this incredible aeroplane screaming towards the finish, closing, closing on the Falcon and also on the eventual winner, at a totally unheard of rate.

They – G.W. and Vector I – lost; I mean they came in third by three seconds – say half a mile behind, having already got by the Falcon and me at a speed two hundred and fifty miles per hour faster than I was travelling.

We all felt sorry for the winner. He had flown a great race and he and his plane had, after all, won. But no one – no airmen, no competitors, nobody in the crowd – could erase the heroic memory of that vast, storming finish. Talk about glamour in the air. G.W. and his creation – their appeal, their glory . . . Everything was kindled anew.

Chapter 31

Things were not kindled anew for long, because G.W., while not declining to fly Vector I in the occasional airshow, did not want to fly in races – for which he simply lacked the sustained competitive zeal. Besides, the idea of having planes of different speeds and handling qualities handicapped seemed to him ridiculous – even if the public loved it and it brought great publicity.

I was not as purist in outlook. I continued to fly one or other of the two Falcons in air races until the end of 1936. I flew to win races and I did win several. I placed in the top few in four or five more races and always posted the fastest lap times and the shortest total times for courses completed.

But though I flew to win, it was – as I had mentioned to Janice – one of the ways in which we gathered increasing information about the performance of the Falcons when flown at prolonged high speed, information that could be passed along to G.W., Bill Parker and James Grant. They all worked continually on improving the Falcon prototypes, or on including what we were learning in the new versions of the Falcon design that were on the drawing boards. I assisted in this.

The changes to the prototype Falcons began to improve their handling – which had been excellent from the start. These changes were slated to appear in the "Mark 2" models, together with improved pilot and passenger space and comfort. We also planned for more power and speed from engines of new design and from different types of propellers, and were aiming at minor changes in wing shapes and dimensions and in fuselage construction. Undercarriage retraction would be more rapid and the cabin would have improved ventilation.

We all worked hard, and orders grew, and though we could at first produce only a few planes a year, we began to make real money.

But as I saw G.W. each day, I knew he was changing. He would never give less than his best to any job he had accepted, but the quality of the challenges he was now confronting were – for him – trivial.

Bill Parker saw the changes, too. But what could he do? He, at last, had a great product. In five years he could be recognized as a manufacturer of superior aircraft, his products sought all over the world by fliers with enough money who were looking for great planes. Later on, he would be interested in seeing other new designs for different kinds of aircraft, but for now Parker Aircraft had to stick to Falcons.

* * *

G.W. flew little now. He declined to fly Vector I in races. "What's the point? Handicappers will never really let us win. We've been told why. Not that I care a damn about racing – though having a genuine chance of *winning* the bally race is supposed to be the point, what?"

* * *

I saw little of Janice. She was very busy in her career. She had gone for almost an entire summer to see and study art collections – Italy, Germany, Russia, finally France again. She wrote enthusiastically of marvellous French Impressionist paintings in Russia that had been bought before the revolution and somehow survived it – paintings of great beauty and the widest historical and cultural significance.

She said she would see me in the early autumn before she wrote a report, part of which had been commissioned by a magazine of fine arts.

I did, however, get a phone call from Janice's home just before she returned from France. It was her mother; she asked after my health and hoped I still found my work rewarding. I thought she seemed pleased at my replies.

"It was such a pleasure to see you down here, Robert. I don't know whether you know it, but everyone in the family liked you. Including Janice's father . . ."

"I liked him very much, Mrs Whitcombe," I said. "I was absolutely appalled at his death."

There was a long pause on the line, then she said, "Janice was devastated. Worse than any of us. We all were terrified of what might happen to her. And then . . . there was that awful accident at the air race. Well, she seems all right now. In some ways."

She paused again, so long that I wondered if the line was broken. The she spoke again, her voice unusually husky.

"You know, Robert, all of us who saw you and Janice together got the feeling that you were . . . well . . . just right for each other. I hope I'm not being too presumptuous, speaking like this . . ."

"Of course not. I thought it was going to work out myself."

"Robert, my dear, is there any hope it may yet?"

"I'm not sure," I said. "But the prospects seem unfavourable." I felt very hollow at hearing myself say that, and wondered when my voice would falter.

I said, "I really can't tell what will happen."

"I know what she thinks – or thinks that she thinks – but to leave it like that seems so . . ."

I couldn't handle more. I cut in, "Unfortunately, any decisions are out of my hands."

Chapter 32

At summer's end, in 1937, I decided to return to Cambridge, to Engineering – if they would accept me.

I had had enough flying races to last me a lifetime. I had nothing further to prove there, did not believe I could become significantly better at it.

As for working with Bill Parker, I had found him an admirable employer, a good friend, an astute adviser. But it was clear that Parker Aircraft, with Bill and G.W. in partnership, was going to be almost wholly involved for years with making more and better Falcons. It was time for me to further my basic engineering education.

When I told G.W. he nodded his head.

"It'll be strange not to be working with you, old man, but in all honesty, seeing you go will be a ton weight off me. I've never for a day failed to think about my responsibility in allowing you to join us. You've done a great job, but the time when chaps like me could somehow manage a career in aviation without completing our major credentials was really just a hiccup of history. You younger fellows – no matter how smart you are – just have to get a comprehensive training in engineering.

"So, though I'm sure we'll often see each other, and though I'll be looking for my right hand for a year or two, go! And Godspeed."

Bill Parker equally understood, and for him it was actually more difficult, because he would have to find a new test pilot. But his approval of my decision also contained a warming spice I had never expected.

"It's a great idea, Robert. And don't ever forget there'll always be a place for you with us here. And as for your fees for tuition and college accommodation, they'll be taken care of by Parker Aircraft. You'll just be one young, highly valued colleague we're sending off to complete his engineering education."

So I left with all sorts of good feelings and gratitude at its fullest.

*   *   *

I entered the Engineering Department at the beginning of the 1937 academic year with trepidation. I could almost picture Drs Milland and McIntosh waiting just inside the main doors ready to cast me out physically – with or without imprecations.

I certainly wasn't expecting to be greeted with the degree of cordiality that awaited me. Yet, I suppose they had to be cordial. If I wasn't exactly a national hero, G.W. certainly was, and I was his chief acolyte. And I enjoyed a minor share of his glory. What was more important was that I now had state-of-the-art knowledge of design principles and "hands on" technical skills that few lecturers in engineering, let alone undergraduates, could lay claim to. In short, I was welcomed more like a junior colleague than a prodigal . . . and something like a celebrity.

So I resumed my studies and my life at Cambridge.

*   *   *

But there was no resumption of what I had shared with Janice. We exchanged a few letters, but if I had thought she might re-examine our relationship now that I was back at university I was mistaken. It seemed cruelly clear that a page in the book had been turned forever.

*   *   *

My studies began to absorb me, and as my understanding of more general engineering principles deepened I was able to appreciate better many things G.W. had done, and could marvel afresh at the sureness of his engineering intuition. But I was also now beginning to get a flow of ideas about future aircraft design that I had lacked before. Proximity to genius had inspired me, but a more complete formal understanding of engineering physics would now perhaps help me to find, and go on in, my own way.

Well, all this was dreaming, really.

By 1938 the war clouds in Europe were beginning to pile up. I resumed my flying practice – by now I was a volunteer instructor in the Cambridge Air Squadron – and at the end of the year I decided again to suspend my studies by joining the R.A.F.

In terms of personal war readiness, I had long decided on this course of action as preferable to alternatives.

I might have got a job in warplane construction but was advised that, regardless of what I had done with G.W., without a full degree in engineering, my work would inevitably be of a lowly sort.

I could have become a test pilot, but there were many available, partly because most of them would be considered too old to serve as fighter pilots. As for risks, I knew they would be substantial. But while I did not feel exactly reckless from my concealed depression over losing Janice, seeing active service if war broke out was almost guaranteed to prove distracting.

*　　*　　*

With my known history as a pilot I was welcomed in the service. My formal instruction in flying was rather ludicrous. My instructor, a grey-haired Sergeant Pilot from WW I, knew who I was and simply said, "For Christ's sake, Sir (I was a Pilot Officer), I've seen you fly exhibitions in Vector I, and those Falcons in air races. We have to go through this, but please just take the bloody controls and let's fly around for a few hours while you show *me* how to do some of those fantastic aerobatics you do and we'll call it quits. If that's OK with you."

I was soon promoted to Flying Officer and after a couple of months to Flight Lieutenant. But at the same time, like any other new member of the R.A.F., I was learning how we would fight in combat, how to use aircraft radiocommunication effectively, how to recognize and understand the flight characteristics of enemy aircraft and to fly several kinds of fighter aircraft we might use in combat. The R.A.F. had some wonderful pilots in its ranks, and though I was more than conversant with most aerobatics, there were many combat tricks they knew that I had never heard of. Also, I began to learn to shoot and soon realized that, while not a bad shot with a rifle or pistol, I was far from being a good marksman with wing-mounted machine guns.

My learning continued and I made new friends and came across a few old ones, among whom, to my surprise and pleasure, was Pete Randall who, it turned out, had joined the R.A.F. in 1937.

"My God, young Robert," he shouted as we recognized each other in the mess two days after I appeared in the Kent base aerodrome where I'd been posted, "I've been following your amazing antics in the papers and everywhere, but now here you are, just a humble bloody R.A.F. type, like the rest of us." His big oarsman's hand slapped me on the back. "But Jesus, old boy, it's great to see you."

Over beers we regaled each other with stories of the recent past. Pete, never a fearfully serious student, had graduated in Arts with a modest academic performance. But then, without warning, his father had died of a heart attack and Pete – always a happy-go-lucky bon vivant — had become, at twenty-three, what he told me he had always dreaded becoming: Lord Randall.

"That," he said, "is a technicality. I'm just Pete to everyone. Always was and will be. But I was sorry as hell when the Dad pushed off, because he was a great bloke. However, I have to say, Robert, it turned me round with a vengeance. Suddenly there was this estate to manage and about a hundred tenant farmers and their families – altogether about a million responsibilities to see to, not counting looking after Mother who was devastated at being left alone while still a fairly young woman. Then there were my brother and sister, both of them living an even freer and easier life than I was. I had to somehow get them to grow up a bit, while not being grown up myself. Not easy."

He looked thoughtful, serious, with significant lines in his forehead, his formerly unmarked, boyish face now that of a man capable of concentration, though still able to display, as before, unconfined mirth.

He was avid for details of what I had been doing and shook his head as I told him of the flight tests and races. And of what had become of Janice and me.

"Who the hell would have thought it?" he said. "I mean, you could always speak up in your own defence. One might have guessed that if you really wanted something . . . I'm sure you shocked the wits out of a pile of guys who were trying to ingratiate themselves with Janice when you just walked in there that night I introduced you and waltzed her off her feet. You . . ."

He stopped himself suddenly. His face looked grim. "Sorry, old boy. None of my business. Actually I was truly delighted to see you two together. Loved that girl myself in the way a brother would. You know we grew up . . ."

"Yes, she told me."

His face cleared. He laughed. "And when you came down to her place and beat the living hell out of the bowling. D'you still play?"

"Never."

"Pity, because you've got it. I loved cricket myself. Only took up rowing because I could never have made it as a real cricketer but was big enough to row fairly well."

Again, his expression was serious. "Can I ask what happened? I haven't seen Janice for a long while, but her Mum was nearly stupefied when things seemed to go wrong. Of course it was a bad time for their family."

I was hesitant. I had not seen Pete for years, had never known him very well. I liked him, but was not sure I could or should try to explain things that were still not very clear even to myself. I ended up telling him as little as I felt I could get away with – which, in his empathic and remarkably insightful presence – was not a lot. Still it was nice to see him. And I knew he was sorry for both Janice and me.

* * *

Then three things happened: the R.A.F and other services started to prepare for war; I was asked to do quite a lot of instruction of new potential pilots who were joining up; and G.W. wrote me a letter.

At the beginning, G.W.'s letter rambled on in a manner uncharacteristic of him about activities at Parker Aircraft. He said that they had been doing well, but had recently been approached by the government concerning their possible role in future air defence of the country and so on. The letter went on –

You know, Bob, I've become very tired of doing this. Bill is a friend and a great chap to work with – never a hard word and all that. But there's no prospect now for me to do the sort of thing I really want, because with this bally war beginning to loom, the firm will not have the opportunity to try some really creative new things of the kind Bill and I wanted to see eventually.

So until the international situation firms up a bit into whatever insanity those who decide our fates will decree, I've decided to pull up sticks here and go to Greece. I went there once, long ago, and really never got over it. Always meant to go back, but never managed to. Over the years I've read a lot. It's the antiquities that interest me, of course. If I had my opportunities over again I think I'd have done archeology and art history, like Janice.

That was a splendid girl you had there, old man; damned sorry it didn't work out for you both.

Well, he planned to go to Greece in April 1939 and stay for six months, but as conditions in Europe began to crumble, he put his plans on hold.

Chapter 33

After the appalling fiasco of Dunkirk, I found myself part of a Spitfire squadron. We were stationed uncannily close to where G.W.'s workshop in Kent used to be, which made fighting in the skies overhead seem a peculiarly personal matter – the defence of hallowed ground.

But those were strange days, made stranger by the unusually sunny and warm summer of 1940 – "classic holiday weather" as has been endlessly remarked on by historians of the air war.

If it was a time to die it seemed like a good time.

I was a good pilot but, nearing twenty eight, past my first youth, I felt almost of another generation to that of my companions. And by "good pilot" I mean of great experience and technical skill, but therefore wary, careful, full of the designer's and the test pilot's insights into the constructional limitations and flight characteristics of the planes we flew, insights – I can say with all modesty – far beyond the range of most of my companions.

On the other hand, many of the much younger pilots were my superior in speed of reaction, acute eyesight, marksmanship, a juvenile reverence for teamwork, youthful self-confidence, even a special kind of luck.

When we attacked the bombers – Heinkels, Junkers – and their Bf 110 fighter escorts, I know I was more conscious of the stresses on wings, tail surfaces and airframe of a Spitfire than my friends were. My flying movements were neat, reliable, executed by an expert, but I would sometimes hold my machine below its maximum level of stress when many of my squadron companions would push theirs beyond their supposed design limits. Often they got away with it – sometimes not.

For if these reckless friends were sometimes more effective in attack than I, the soundness and perfection of my evasive movements gave me a better survival chance in the crazy maelstroms of air battles. And because I survived, I continued to get chances to shoot down enemy planes. So although I was not a "natural" as a fighter pilot, I was "safer" than some and my score kept gradually mounting.

But war changes everything. For what seemed an infinity of weeks we scrambled daily. As I mixed constantly with younger, wilder and – in essence – braver (or more foolhardy) men, I began to behave in ways that were younger, wilder and, yes, braver. This trend was reinforced by our brief, disturbed sleep that would find us not fresh and poised in the summer dawns, but dry-mouthed, weary-eyed, eventually desperate with fatigue, endlessly and depthlessly apprehensive.

Ever more abandonedly we would fling off the ground, sometimes neglecting cockpit drill, takeoff form, our heavy little planes lurching, twisting, sometimes bucking in the low crosscurrents of far-from-ideal wind conditions. The climb would be a stomach-grinding hurtle, as we raced skywards as steeply and as fast as our howling Merlin engines would drag us without stalling or slipping to doom. No grace. No ease. Just get up there, to ten, fifteen, twenty thousand . . . higher.

I felt my twenty-eighth birthday marked – in some vaguely formal way – a point in the aging process that distanced me even more from my boy companions, whose average age decreased as they were continually killed off and succeeded by ever younger and less well-trained replacements. I seem to have watched this distancing with a growing detachment and not much concern. I only knew that, through constant fear, I was becoming brutally exultant as I became an ever-more-efficient destroyer – and survivor.

But I knew in moments of clarity that my heart was becoming cold – and felt as old as the world.

*   *   *

Our one principal tactic in air fighting was to get above the enemy bombers. To have to climb up and attack them from below usually foredoomed our success, because we were then open to attack from above by their fighter escorts. If our fuel had lasted we would have stayed indefinitely at 20,000 feet or higher, forever waiting to pounce out of the sun.

Our strikes, when they came, were remarkable. In a mental state almost approximating serenity as we patrolled on high we might see approaching marauders. Or else their whereabouts would have been spotted by radar and radioed to us. Then, our battle tactics long discussed, agreed on, endlessly practiced, we would slip away to fall on the foe, often bellowing personal accompaniments to the roar of our overtaxed engines. There would only be a few seconds to make good our strike as we plunged on down, closing on the enemy formation at hundreds of yards per second. Only when we had gone by or through their formations did we pull out of dives, bank or roll to climbing positions, try to regain height in fast spirals, and start looking for targets of opportunity.

But the second and subsequent tries were never as good as the first. Now they waited for us, those Luftwaffe gunners, as coldly and matter-of-factly efficient as the electricians, plumbers, junior bureaucrats, pork butchers they once had been.

The Bf 110s seldom broke away from the bombers to pursue us. To strike back with a simple vindictiveness must have been an almost ungovernable urge. But only rarely could we goad them into fighting us one-on-one when the advantage would be all our way, since the Bf 110s could never match the Spitfires in agility. Theirs was an escort duty. And, as good Germans, they stuck, with rigour and bravery, to their bloody, inflexible job. The discipline required of the Luftwaffe exceeded that required of us at the time. If we were no longer free men in a free world, in our attempts to be efficient killers, at least we enjoyed a semblance of democratic choice in some of the tactics we could employ at close quarters as we smashed at these welded formations of bombers and their escorts – these creatures-of-many-creatures.

And then it would all heat up and go crazily to pieces as the air got thick with tracers and cannon shells and bits of tattered metal and the occasional whole human being turning over and over in a slipstream as he bent himself double in a last dying try to get free. And here and there would show the blossoms and fruits of this turmoil of deadly youth – the red flowers of explosions against the thick soot of smoke, and sometimes the white puffballs of filling parachutes.

* * *

My first leave came with me physically whole, but close to madness.

I went to London, the place for secular celebrants of all the remaining rites of the sensual life. There I met and mindlessly caroused with unknown armies that even included a few Australians, a couple of whom I had actually known in Sydney – lifetimes ago.

The initial charm of being well met in these bizarre renewals of uncompleted adolescent relationships was gradually dissipated as it bore in on me how truly remote "Sydney and all that" had become. Somewhere inside me was an old-young hunch that in some far future I might return to Sydney to look at it again – and perhaps love it once more, but I felt – and talking to the Australians I met told me so – that, if the war ended tomorrow, it would be much too soon to try to integrate the diversity of my experiences, and that I would be rash to try.

So I drifted, not away from the Australians, but more and more into the orgiastic company of all and sundry, where the eyes of one are the eyes of many, and the heart beats and swelling blood are not one's own but part of some giant music that goes nowhere but may never quite cease . . .

But in the end everything palled.

* * *

To clear my head I made my way to Parker Aircraft. Bill Parker was still there with about four of his original workshop people. No more Falcons had been made. There was an R.A.F. need for that type of aircraft, but Parker Aircraft had lacked the critical size and workforce strength to fill large orders and other, larger companies were supplying the required – though inferior – planes. Parker Aircraft was doing again what Bill Parker had thought to say goodbye to forever – making needed aircraft parts.

As he said to me, cheerfully, but also ruefully, "Here we are then, Bob, just as we were when I first met you. And I really don't believe we'll ever regain the momentum we had – even if we do somehow manage to win this bloody war."

He frowned for a moment. "I couldn't myself be happier to see you, but in the spring they sort of dragged G.W. away to be a technical adviser/ troubleshooter with several teams in three or four of the big production factories. I haven't heard just where he is at present; things are getting mighty hush-hush. But there is an address I can give you that'll get letters to him eventually.

"In the meantime, Bob, come home with me for lunch. We haven't anything fancy to eat, except some decent local bread and a bit of cheese I've been storing in a cool cellar since 1937, and also a bottle or two of pre-war sherry."

We drove off to his house for some cheese and sherry. He still had the dark blue Rolls, though he said he only had enough petrol to travel the couple of miles between work and home.

Chapter 34

The cockpit cover was jammed. I tore off my gloves to get a better grip and took hold of the cover again, and still tugged in vain. There was blood. I wondered where from. My aeroplane seemed about shot to pieces but I didn't think I had been hit. Then I started smashing at the cover with bare hands. And then the plane was turning almost horizontally, the same clouds seeming to pass by every few seconds. Soon it would . . .

With terror-driven strength I tore and battered again and again at the cockpit cover, but it remained immovable. Then, for no obvious reason it slid freely in my hands and I flung it back. I took hold of the windshield frame and heaved myself up to try to struggle out against the rush of the air. But no go. My legs felt very weak, perhaps numbed from the shock of the cannon shell that had smashed through the cockpit an inch of two from my feet.

In fear and fury I dragged myself part way out by arms alone, but then I could get no further. I would have stayed there, helpless as a pinned insect, but then the angle of the aircraft's turning plane changed a little and I tumbled out. I flailed furiously, striving to shove myself away from the still-turning aircraft.

These days people fall from the sky for fun, many alone, sometimes in pairs, or even in parties, their hands linking them together to form down-drifting rosettes of bodies. Some do it with multicoloured parachutes of bizarre shapes. A few practice delayed drops, getting preposterously close to the ground before opening their parachutes. Still others try to land on targets.

I have fallen away from a disintegrating plane once only. Quite enough. And it *was* a delayed drop. My parachute didn't open till I was only seven hundred feet up. Once only. An aircraft going to pieces around me was the one thing that could ever have got me willingly into the air without an aircraft.

Anyway, I was out, with nothing around me but air – I was well below the aircraft now, and there, underneath me, and before the parachute opened, I watched the green earth coming up. I was somehow transfixed as I realized how close it seemed, and for a while just lay in the sky, relieved to be alive, overcome with the strangeness of it all. At last, as the ground grew very close, I thought to pull the ripcord.

I landed hard, knew no pain, but nevertheless sprained both ankles. Later on, the ankles hurt like hell.

*   *   *

A portly, elderly gent in tin hat and threadbare battledress – he told me a bit later he used to run a haberdashery in Southampton – saw me coming down. He was a home guardsman and his only weapon was an old rifle with a single bullet in it. He rushed up to me and, once assured I was British and could manage, led me through a meadow to a shed where two of his companions gave me tea. Then I screamed, because someone daubed iodine on a gash in my thigh a shell splinter had caused, that I hadn't noticed until then. It was the source of the blood I had seen. I opened my mouth to scream again at the iodine, but just managed not to. Now soaked with sweat, they let me telephone my squadron commander, Billy Bates.

Billy, always buoyant, was accustomed to address the world in a cheerful bellow, as if trying to be heard by a deaf octogenarian aunt of whom he was inordinately fond. He did so now, causing me to snatch the receiver from my ear. His roaring, perfectly audible throughout the shed, startled my Home Guard companions, who then listened avidly as if to some amusing and obscene story. I supposed life could get pretty boring for them.

"Robert," Billy exploded, "you're OK? Good show! We thought you might have bought it. Get back here toot sweet. The sawbones can see to you. But look, as long as you still have your head on your shoulders we'll have to get you back in an aeroplane by tomorrow. Jerry thinks he's on the brink of sending us the way of the pterodactyl! Got to discourage him. Kite totally pranged, I expect . . . ? Yes. Well, you're about due for another gong, my lad.

Come home to Mother at once!"

Yes. Well . . . There were no cars or trucks for shot-down pilots. This was England at war. Poor. Battered. Looking all but finished. Fighting a last round above the island's backyards. Limping badly now, feeling the pain and the shock, I trudged half a mile to the local station and stumbled aboard the noon train.

As the green peace of the countryside slid by, stared at wonderingly by the few passengers, I fell asleep. Waking in time to get off at the village nearest our airfield, I located an off-duty comrade in "The Miller's Delight" and scrounged a ride back in his old Austin.

I felt like the inside of something that was badly in need of cleaning.

* * *

Next day I had a new aeroplane – I mean an aeroplane that had been constructed from the cannibalized parts of many unairworthy aeroplanes and, as promised, found myself flying again.

The gash in my thigh, with eight stitches in it, throbbed a bit, and ankles and feet ached badly even though firmly strapped. But I took a pile of aspirin, balanced by many cups of coffee, and was able to manage the controls. My nerves seemed OK. But fortunately we failed to engage the enemy. It wasn't till the day following, when I was finally able to get a bit of rest, that I came unstuck at last. It was good that there was no one near to see – or hear – at the time. After that I slept like death for nine hours till somebody woke me around ten in the morning. It was a lovely day and I felt all right again.

* * *

My crashed aeroplane turned up. What was left of it was in a field, nastily close to a farmhouse on the outskirts of Eastbourne. I didn't get to see it, but though totalled, it had not ignited and most of the bits were there. But bits. They stripped off the guns – only the guns were salvageable.

I wouldn't have minded seeing the plane's sad remains one more time – it can be good for your morale under some circumstances to be reminded of how you managed to survive something – but no one could get away. The Luftwaffe bombers just kept coming. And coming.

* * *

About a month after I bailed out, Mick Main, our squadron adjutant, brought me a little parcel wrapped in brown paper. "Thought you might like to have this, Robert."

I weighed the parcel, light, but fairly stiff. "What the hell is it?"

Mick shrugged, "There may be a simple way to find out." Mick was older than I, which, apart from Squadron Leader Billy Bates, made him the oldest man in our group. I was next. Mick had been an architect in Leicester before 1939, hadn't flown, still didn't, but he was a very intelligent and helpful adjutant

Taking his suggestion, I ripped off the paper.

Inside was a battered piece of duralumin fuselage skin bearing the number of my downed aeroplane. I didn't really want it.

"My God! thanks Mick!   Bloody great! Makes a man think a bit."

"Yes, well, I thought you might want to have it. Your one and only prang, eh?"

We both chuckled uneasily.

Lunch was near. We strolled towards the mess together.

Mick cleared his throat. "By the way," he sounded very casual, "I was talking to Billy Bates yesterday – as you know he's had to go to Headquarters for a few days – and he asked me to tell you your D.F.C.'s coming through."

"Oh, really? Good show . . . very good." I felt ridiculous, hoped I was manifesting a suitable blend of modesty and gratitude. Knew I wasn't.

Fortunately, Mick Main was a mature man, in some contrast to our esteemed leader, Billy Bates, and was not one of the heroic children who now comprised most of my fellow pilots. I believe he appreciated my distaste for much of what I found myself doing in a bloody and appalling war. He took my elbow as we entered the mess. "Congratulations and all that, Robert. Let me buy you an ale." I didn't think he really sounded congratulatory, and was glad.

We drank, and Mick looked at me speculatively. "Well, you're twenty eight – practically an old man to be a fighter pilot. Of course I know you know planes in ways these kids you fly with never will. I've never asked you about your time with Parker Aircraft and, before that, with this famous Gibbs White person I see from your files you used to be associated with. What was the strength of all that?"

* * *

Mick Main and I were on our second ales; we were relaxed by this time. I had explained how I had met G.W. and how that had affected me. I was surprised Mick still appeared interested. "And so," he said, "you went down to Ham Street in glorious Kent, the wonders for to see! And after all this that you've told me, can you say you did see wonders?"

"Yes," I said, after a moment. "Yes, I did, actually. Many wonders, in fact.

"And things were never the same for me again."

* * *

At this comparatively late stage in The Battle of Britain, it was widely understood throughout the R.A.F. that, with Beaverbrook as Minister of Aircraft Production, there had been huge shifts from the way things were being done immediately before the war. In a way, though, there was still surprise, shock and amazement when an air-craft carrying R.A.F roundels – an aircraft of a type none of us had ever seen before – was cleared for landing at our aerodrome one morn-ing. It was more its "different" appearance and structure than anything else that held our attention.

The civilian pilot who delivered it had a brief session with our Squadron Leader. Then both emerged from his office and he called me over. "Bob, this is Mr Culpepper from the F.G. Miles company. He's taking this plane around to various squadrons to let 'em get the feel of it as a possible fighter for production. I want you to fly this, because you were a test pilot yourself and you'll know, as none of the rest of us would, how to give this thing a real try-out. OK?"

I nodded. "OK," and I put my hand out because I knew Culpepper quite well as a very good pilot from my racing days.

Culpepper, very cordial, gave me a short but succinct briefing on the Miles M.20.

"Bob, this plane's been designed, built and flown in 65 days, because my chief, F.G. Miles, approached Beaverbrook with the idea of producing a cheap fighter plane made of wood as a 'utility' fighter in case supplies of metal, or production delays due to bombing, were cutting badly into Hurricane and Spitfire production."

"OK, Tom," I said. "But this thing's got wheel spats, for God's sake."

Culpepper laughed. "This aeroplane may seem to lack lines, and not to have much of a pedigree. But forget about the sort of long skinny appearance. And the spats; they'll disappear and be replaced by retractable wheels in production models. Meanwhile its got a Merlin XX engine – 1460 hp – can carry twelve guns, and, well just you try it!"

It took a bit more takeoff space than the Spitfire, but it had astounding handling and a top speed between that of the Hurricane and the Spitfire. Its fuel tanks gave it twice the range of its rivals, and it could fly very high. I hurled it all over the sky, tried every standard stunt I knew and a few extra dirty tricks I had picked up in dogfights. It was a joy to fly, had no vices, wonderful view for the pilot, and with twelve guns would have been a very deadly weapon as far as I could make out. I wondered what it could have done with no wheel spats and with larger flaps to shorten landing and takeoff.

I flew Spitfires. They were great warplanes, but I had helped build Vector I. I was not closed-minded about plane design. I said to Culpepper, "Remarkable bloody plane, mate. Get rid of those stupid spats and it would be terrific. When's it going into production?"

At this point, Tom Culpepper's pleased, open red face clouded over a bit. "In fact, Bob, no one knows. It may never. The point is that it'll probably only happen if things look bad for the Hurries and Spits. It would otherwise take too long to get a production line started – and there are still doubts about aeroplanes made of wood in many quarters."

I had time to think about all this later. Almost at the same time as the Miles M20, the all-wooden De Havilland Mosquito fighter-bomber flew as a prototype, and eventually became one of the great wartime success stories in aircraft production and use. I suppose, as I thought of this and of Vector I and the Falcons, two things came to me; first the necessity of luck and timing in getting designs – no matter how great – accepted and adopted, and second that it was about time to admit to myself there were other great and original designers out there besides G.W.

Chapter 35

We lay back in deck-chairs in the morning sunlight, or sprawled on the grass. We were fully dressed for action – even wearing our inflatable life jackets ("Mae Wests"). Our parachutes were already set up in the cockpits of our Spitfires, arranged so that the harnesses could be secured at once.

Some played cards, others read, a few talked quietly. I lay supine on the rather damp ground in a state of half-daze, not so much a condition of exhaustion as a wish for escape. I would have been supremely thankful to sleep, dream – if only for a few minutes – of some silent, infinitely lonely paradise: say, an empty, medium-warm beach under a faultless sky. But my mind wouldn't cooperate. Waiting each day for certain danger, it was as though my spirit had gone brittle. I had to hold it delicately in place. I could not talk, or read, or play cards. I would not move if I could possibly avoid it. My feeling was of extreme inner fragility. If anything disturbed me I might – I felt – break into fragments.

Well, that was the feeling.

However, when I had to rouse myself I was able to do it without coming unstuck, and once I was able to act I was soon all right again.

We knew they were coming. Coming in waves. A maximum effort. Already our fighters thirty miles to the north east were engaging them. We knew that as our own call came.

Then we were running towards our planes. Ten yards to my right someone stumbled and fell headlong with an alarming thump. He swore furiously, with maximum obscenity and at length. It could have sounded funny, but in the circumstances it sounded awful. It sounded like the pain and anger of someone who has reopened a wound that has already taken a long time to heal.

I slipped myself then, though I did not go down, but soon after, as I lowered myself into the cockpit, I banged my knee on something hard that hurt like hell, and my language, too, reflected my anguish. In fact the pain, though brief, cancelled my recollection of taking off that morning. I remember only that we were a couple of hundred feet off the ground and I was shouting over the intercom for my flight to close up their formation and climb at full throttle to twenty thousand feet, and make sure they weren't dropped on out of the sun.

It took us about ten minutes to get our aeroplanes to the required altitude and then sort ourselves out again. We'd been told to look for and take care of an advance formation of Bf 109s whose job was to clear the skies for the bombers and 110s that would succeed them.

We craned our necks in every direction, hoping to God they weren't somehow concealing themselves above us. But that seemed unlikely for the sky was clear.

At last, Smithson, who was off my starboard wing, bellowed over the intercom that he could see specks eight miles away at about our altitude.

"Climb!" I bawled. "Two thousand more. Now! Full throttle!"

Our planes struggled upwards like cavalry steeds urged, flogged, driven up a slope of air by their furious riders. And, like cavalry horses, planes could be literally shot from under you – or anyway, from around you. I'd seen that happen once; the machine just shivered into bits and the pilot was left, looking unharmed, seeming to sit alone in the sky for a moment before falling – like some character in a Disney cartoon.

When we had achieved altitude we all fired a short burst to test our guns, and kept watching the specks that were specks no longer but clearly 109s.

Our numbers seemed roughly equal, but they evidently had not seen us, because they had let us get our altitude advantage.

"Tally ho!" I roared – which always seemed a stupid bloody thing to yell, and repugnant to me as I never killed animals for sport, and had only scorn for fox-hunters. But it was an accepted signal and we all pointed our noses at the 109s and started a long dive towards them at full throttle.

The trouble with this sort of thing was that it was so fast. Admittedly, up in the air there were no static objects by which to gauge your speed, but though the enemy planes at first grew larger with deceptive slowness, they would eventually come to you, over the last half mile, in a few seconds. And if they were coming at you head-on the distance might shorten in what seemed like no time at all. Either they or you could, of course, complicate matters by taking evasive action and simply run away at full throttle; then you might never see each other again. Or, as you came close to them, they could skip out of your way like startled houseflies.

The cruel miracle, in an unlimited sky, was that any two pilots could ever actually arrive at a point where one could fire at another with any prospect of a hit.

Of course most of the passes you made in air battles were misses. The best shots, among R.A.F. and Luftwaffe pilots alike, had the ability to take advantage of those half seconds when an enemy aircraft was anywhere near being in their sights.

So we reached them, on this day, with some advantage from having dived at them, and tried, desperately tried, to hit them. Sometimes, as now, you could fluke it and get right on another aeroplane's tail and follow its every move while trying for a shot. This happened to me that day.

I didn't know whether my flying was exceptionally good or my antagonist's skill was below average, but wherever he went, however he turned, climbed, banked, or dived, I was behind him. Only thing was, I couldn't hit him . . . It seemed incredible. Time and again he came, for an instant, into my sights and I would fire a burst. Yet somehow he would move in that same instant and most, if not all, of my bullets would pass him. This went on for so long that my ammunition was three quarters gone. By then I was feeling certain someone else in his group would notice us, conclude that I was totally preoccupied, and rake me from behind, the side, above or below – from anywhere, in fact.

Before that could happen my target suddenly put his nose down almost vertically and dived away at full throttle, introducing a tricky spiral into his escape manoeuvre. He didn't come out of the dive, just kept going down, and because he'd accelerated so fast he pulled far away before I could respond, and I had to let him go.

I was very fed up, shaking with anger – more at my own ineptitude than at his luck. And then, in the lightning way ideas can sometimes flash through your head in battles, I thought perhaps he was not lucky, or a poor pilot at all, but actually a very good pilot who had just managed to weather an attack few would have survived. And that I had in fact been flying exceptionally well to have held on to him for so long.

This idea was – in a way – encouraging, but before I could think more about it, another 109 flew at great speed towards the centre of my line of sight. I didn't aim, just pushed the firing button. The 109 blew itself to bits.

By now, they had got two of ours and we had downed three of theirs. The rest of them took off home, because their fuel must have been getting low and they still had the Channel to cross. We didn't chase them. We had driven them off. For the moment our job was over.

* * *

As we flew back to our home field I was aware of the irony of the events. I had lost my first target because – though I had flown well – he had outflown me. Fair enough. But then I'd taken the life of another, almost by accident; there had been no engagement between us, except for the bullets I fired that flew across a hundred and fifty yards of high cold air. What I had done, and would be officially credited with – one more kill – had been like swinging a golf club at someone in a dark room and accidentally braining the poor bastard.

I felt angry, abstracted . . . and ashamed.

We were, however, as the Americans liked to say a year or so later, "in a shooting war."

The time for philosophy and spiritual self-examination was past. We were the young men of a society in which wars were declared and administered by old men. And half a century later people would still bicker about the legal, ethical and spiritual meaning of it all. And whether it had a meaning. And why it could not have been prevented in the first place.

*   *   *

Next day I had calmed down a bit. Fortunes of war. Better him than me, and all that.

Anyway, our standard job – bread and butter stuff, so to speak – was not to fight other fighters, but to intercept bombers. We often had to attack escort fighters to get at the bombers, of course, but it was the bombers that were supposed to be our meat.

There have been many attempts to analyse the way in which this particular air war of 1940 and 1941 was conducted. A recurring dispute has concerned how the fighters should have been deployed – whether in the flexible formations of smaller units, or in "big wings" with less flexibility but the potential for enormous hitting power. This question was never satisfactorily resolved.

As for us, those who sat in cockpits at twenty thousand feet, outstretched wings full of guns that fired three kinds of bullets – ordinary, armour-piercing and incendiary (which made bright yellow flashes as they hit a target), we at first flew line astern, but later – thank God! – in finger four formations, which were flexible attack arrangements that removed the problem of defending those who had been at the end positions in "line astern" formations.

Whatever; our basic mission was to concentrate on shooting down enemy aircraft.

We were the killers.

Many of our tactics resembled those worked out in World War I. A principal move was to get as close to the enemy as you dared before firing. I suppose that took nerve, but most of us who were effective just viewed it as the best way to survive, less risky than opening fire from too far away. If an enemy plane survived your first shots it was still there to kill you. Yes, somehow you needed the skill to get close.

Some were good at judging where a moving target would be a fraction of a second after sighting it and aiming so as to hit it as it reached that point. It was the ability that allows a good sporting shot to hit a bird on the wing. I was not good at it. All I did was try to use every piloting skill I possessed to get close enough to aim directly at the target. I had my guns rigged so the lines of fire would converge to maximum effect at a closer range than many of my companions favoured.

* * *

By the time I had survived a number of daily flights and numerous battles I began to think little about my aeroplane itself. Controlling it in a fight had become automatic. It was *I* who was flying, *I* who fired the bullets. When the plane failed me, it seemed it was my own body that had let me down. If I triumphed, it was as if my body had proved stronger, more athletic, more physically resilient than that of the enemy. Or that luck had smiled my way for a moment. Anyway, it was the swordsman, not the sword!

Yes, well, metaphysics and aphorisms aside, I sometimes used to pull out a dresser drawer and open the little case to look for a moment – with a feeling of . . . embarrassment – at the D.F.C. with Bar. A badge of glory, some would say. But what it mostly said to me was that there were moments in which – though constantly fearful – I had not utterly succumbed to fear. At other times, when I was feeling more cynical, it seemed to take on the look of a badge of Cain – when I would close the case in a hurry, hide it under half a dozen shirts, and push the dresser drawer shut.

Chapter 36

We sat up there at twenty thousand, almost seeming to hang there, trying to conserve our fuel – waiting. We knew the Heinkels would soon be in range because our radars had told us so. We dived as they hove into sight but for once we were out-positioned, for while we dropped, someone was screaming a warning over the intercom as a pack of Bf 109s fell on us out of the sun. Like everyone else, I was heading towards the Heinkels and their Bf 110 escorts; now I pulled out the "boost" handle and went for them at full bore, simultaneously praying I could outrun the 109s.

I saw not a Heinkel but a Bf 110 escort coming into range, and tried a burst. The bullets hit home, and as I flashed past the 110 it flipped over and died nastily in a gout of oily smoke.

Then a 109 was at me. I managed a nice twisting turn, then sideslipped away into perhaps the neatest, fastest turn I had ever managed. But still he turned with me.

We began an insane circling of each other. According to some, Bf 109s were not supposed to be able to turn as well as Spitfires. Perhaps they were wrong. Or perhaps he was just a very good pilot, because he turned tighter. I felt some sort of blows in the lower legs. There was a numbing pressure and sticky warmth rather than pain. I kicked the rudder left with all I had, then vertical-banked and hung on to the tightest turn I could ever have imagined. More blows. Bits of things were breaking off near me and being torn away in the slipstream. The plane's nose was dropping as the turn robbed it of speed and lift. Somehow, as it began to come to pieces, I turned inside the 109 at last and got a glimpse of its tail end in my sights. For half a heartbeat I fired. I could see no effect, and lost him, and we held our deadly merry-go-round. Then I saw that big parts of him, too, were coming off. His circle widened wildly, and for him it was over as he went chopping away to my left, smoke pouring.

It was over for me, too. I couldn't feel my feet. I coldly instructed them what to do, but could be sure they were doing it only because the ruined plane turned sluggishly homewards while settling inexorably to lower altitudes.

I left behind me the savage chaos of my dying companions and those they were able to take with them. I was alone now. Five thousand feet up. Winging it home.

They said I got down well. I don't remember it at all.

*   *   *

On my first day in hospital they drugged me to the point where the pain was just bearable.On the second day, though I didn't feel like dancing the fandango, my wounds, still agonizing when I moved, didn't require me to be as heavily sedated and, in between sleeping and dozing, my thoughts drifted to other times and places and persons and things.

I remembered the models flying over Centennial Park . . . and the plane I had built for the neighbour's son's birthday.

And then I remembered, in my last battle, that final tight turn that got me inside the Bf 109. And I thought – dreamily and detachedly – how Vector I would have behaved in turns like that. How, with a touch of the controls, it would have scampered skywards from the 109, then banked and sideslipped down and away, then turned up again to strike like a taipan at the enemy aeroplane's exposed belly. And I felt an instant of disgust at the constraints that governed Air Force specs, that resulted in producing planes that turned out to be suboptimal compromises – including even, in some ways, Spitfires.

*   *   *

Three days later Squadron Leader Billy Bates visited me in hospital – for the second time. He was a decent fellow, Billy, despite his happy roaring voice that made you want to put your head under the sheets.

"Well, old boy, damned well done. You've now got nine certain, plus a half share in two more. Official. Oh, and three probables. And I've put you up for another gong that you'll get for bloody sure. How're the legs today?"

Chapter 37

Both my legs were shot up with cannon shell fragments. I would spend six weeks in hospital, two months more on crutches, followed by a month with a heavy cane. I expected at the end to return to action, but while in hospital my orders had been simple: get recovered, get fit, get back to active duty. These things I assumed would happen, but my recovery took longer than my optimistic superiors had supposed it would.

*   *   *

To be wounded during the war, if the wounding did not, finally, endanger your life, could place you in a unique setting, a limbo, which, if physical suffering was not devastating, could lead to reflection, self-examination, while insulated from the deadly mainstream. For many young men who had been injured, such interludes of suspension from past and future, from the need for daily action, were the first they had known as adults. Indeed, it is only recently, having finally reached a reasonably hale old age, that something of the detachment and mental ease I experienced during those months of recovery from my wounds has returned. But only something of it . . . The world has turned too many times.

Soon after being injured, still dulled with pain and truly weak, it was simply reassuring to pass lucid intervals in the company of wounded comrades. Magazines, novels, films, a bit of desultory talk, the occasional chess or card game, were the only activities one fancied. Otherwise, lots of sleep.

Initially, my greater-than-average age and my experiences as an expatriate colonial gave me a certain edge in conversations. This edge partly resulted from an interest of some of my new companions in Australia as a place where they might one day want to settle. I was pumped for factual information, the problem here being that my first hand knowledge had only ever been of the Sydney region of New South Wales, and was anyway a decade out of date. Once it was realized how slim and stale my information was there was less special interest in me. For a time, however, as I regained my strength and began to indulge in some shop talk with others at a similar stage of recovery, I briefly became again a central figure in rambling, anecdote-ridden, conversations. This was when my prewar experience with plane building emerged. As my companions discussed what they perceived as the misadventures that had brought about their own downfalls, they turned to me as a technical expert to check out their assessments of supposed mechanical failures. Why had an engine stopped during some manoeuvre of a dogfight? If a wing dropped off during a dive, at four hundred and fifty miles per hour, did that mean it must already have been weakened by bullets, or was there some inherent structural defect? My ability to answer at least some of their questions fully and technically astonished them because, although they could fly planes, very little in their training had given them insight into aircraft designs and strengths.

Gradually, though, the novelty of having a resident expert palled, and special interest in me again declined. I confess that I regretted this. It had been pleasant, flattering to find oneself more or less at the centre of things – even if it was only in a hospital for wounded airmen. And soon it became clear that the trivial talk of every day would become one of the hardest things to bear about a convalescence.

But then, even though still on crutches, I began to feel better, and native restlessness and curiosity impelled me to greater activity than was the norm among the recovering wounded.

I was passing my convalescence near Oxford, and as soon as I could struggle about, doctors encouraged me to get as much exercise as possible. I began to explore the University, the town, and the surrounding countryside. I still knew little of Britain, apart from aerial views of some southern parts; now I had the leisure to drift around a local countryside, talking to people in pubs, looking at churches, yarning with farmers, meeting village folk. All of them were friendly, pleased to talk with a decorated fighter pilot. Some of them even remembered my name from the Vector I days and from the air races. A warm wave of fellow-feeling and of healing caressed me wherever I went.

I first became mobile in the winter, and though it was painful to get around and sometimes very cold I spent as much time hobbling in the open as I could endure.

As strength returned, and it was safe to assume full recovery, I began to think back to G.W., and to what might happen when the war was over. During the years we had shared I had had the idea that, by some marvel of osmosis, a little of his powers might enter me. I was less confident now.

Yet it seemed unfair! I had intelligence and technical ability. My wish to succeed in a similarly creative way still burned. What right had he, anyway, to whatever it was that had blessed him with his talents? I became rather depressed. Even my ward companions and the doctors began to notice it. Eventually I broke through to the other side of what could have settled in as despair, with the sudden conviction that, after all, luck also must have been a decisive factor in G.W.'s story. And perhaps I still had some of that to draw on.

It now seemed to me that he had come to his maturity at a time especially favourable to his aims – allowing him not only to conceive his particular goal, but to have the technical sophistication and the historical milieu for him to achieve it. This sort of thinking, it later became clear to me, was a psychological face-saver that permitted me to shift my attention from my own deficiencies for a while. Necessary at the time, but artificial.

Later on, when I was cooler and more detached again, no longer disposed to depression, I could examine the facts of our difference more realistically. Then I knew it hardly lay in the area of intelligence. Oh, G.W. was smarter than I – perhaps quite a lot – though in posing questions, in analysing a situation, I don't believe there was all that much difference between us. But, somehow, he could force himself to see solutions. His ability to synthesize allowed him to reach forward to answers, and I began to wonder if it was likely I would ever be able to think like that. G.W.'s powers were simple. Like water. Like the air. Like sun or sky. He saw things and possibilities with the directness of a clairvoyant child.

I resented him for a while as I thought I grew to know these things of him – and myself. Later, as I graduated to a single stout cane and, later still, was able to throw the cane away and trust to my own weak but striving legs again, my full affection for him was restored, and I felt once more able to find some pleasure in my own achievements – modest as they had been.

Much later still came the realization that only in a superficial way could *any* of my analysis, at that time, of G.W.'s work and performance be regarded as true.

Chapter 38

I was still feeling the effects of my injuries, but had basically recovered and been sent back to my squadron. Billy Bates had asked me to help our adjutant, Mick Main, until my re-assignment orders came through. One morning a telephone call came for me.

The voice was familiar, though it seemed quieter and firmer than when I'd heard it last.

"Hullo, young Robert. Pete here, Pete Randall."

"Pete! Good to hear you. What's going on, mate?"

"Not a hell of a lot, old man, but I just saw the notice of your D.F.C. Wanted to congratulate you."

"Thanks, Pete, thanks very much. Listen, we should get together some time soon, have a couple of beers."

"Yes," said Pete. "Actually I was going to suggest something like that, but also to ask you to come to – ah – meet me in London one day soon."

He was silent for a moment. Then he said, "Look, I don't want to interfere with your private life and all that, but I've run across Janice, and I get the strong idea that she'd like to see you again. I'm throwing a small party on my next spot of leave in London. Can I persuade you . . . ?"

I thought about it for a long moment, then I said, "Of course. Very nice of you. When is it?

* * *

When I saw Janice, I neither made a bee-line for her, nor even contented myself with sending, or looking for, subtle signals. But when we had finally worked our ways to each other through Pete's "small party" of about fifty somehow squeezed into his London flat, we joined our hands with a gentleness that reminded me of the way very young children do it, and I knew that – at least for the moment – things between us were much as they had been.

She told me she knew I had not renounced flying. She did not indicate disapproval, but I assumed her feelings would have remained the same. She looked at me carefully, rather shyly, taking in my uniform, the D.F.C. ribbon, and at last, my face.

"I'd still have known you anywhere, of course, but you do look quite a bit older, my dear."

"Dammit, Janice, I suppose you do too, just a little. But you also look marvellous. What have you been doing?"

"Well, after I last saw you, I went on to finish my undergrad studies and then did post-graduate work in the Middle East and Alexandria. And I was out of Britain for quite a long time. Then I caught some wretched bug in Cairo and I was unwell for about six months. After that it was well into 1939 and I was looking for some kind of job. But I got approached by the civil service to help make a catalogue of various kinds of art objects that might be put at hazard if and when war broke out."

"Sounds like a big task."

"Yes, but I'm only a small cog in a very large machine."

"And now?"

"Well, for a year I've been working with a group of civil servants. I can't tell you the details, but one of the broad objectives is to determine how much art the Axis may be stealing from occupied countries and where it is going to end up being cached, or for that matter, sold for huge profits – profits they can use in the war."

"Art detectives, then, that's what you are?"

"That's it," she said. "And the potential values of these things are enormous – and will become that much more enormous, by orders of magnitude, as they become older and scattered because of the war, and increasingly harder to find. And because, when artists die, production lines of their work stop as . . ."

"As if they were bombed out aircraft factories," I said.

"That's it, mate," she said, smiling, and at last threw her arms around me.

*   *   *

We lay on the spring grass that covered the hillside, trying to soak up some warmth from the hazy sun. We gazed down at a peaceful scene. There was a dale in which a beech copse glowed fresh and green. Beyond the copse was a dense, dark plantation of pines – the only dark note in an otherwise softly bright landscape that stretched away towards the west. The sky was blurred with a high film of cloud, but peeping through it in a place where it was very thin was a faint full moon. There were also vapour trails from some high battle just above the cloud. They were spreading like cuts in cool iridescent fabric.

Sometimes we glimpsed moving dark specks. Gradually the specks worked their way downwards as the fight settled to lower altitudes.

Janice lay beside me. In the three weeks since Pete's "small party" we had seen each other several times. It was still not clear what lay ahead for us. Former attitudes had to be reconsidered, serious declarations had yet to be made. We were both guarded for unstated reasons of our own that were perhaps as obscure to ourselves as they were to each other.

We were able to be together on this week-day morning because each of us had managed to wangle two days leave. I had spent my recent time in locating stored aircraft spare parts and cataloguing their whereabouts wherever they might be in the whole of Britain. This, I had been thinking, had some sort of parallel with what Janice was doing in the art world – but was colossally more boring. Basically, of course, I was still waiting for reassignment to an air-active role.

We lay on our backs and watched, transfixed – yet almost relaxed. When Janice spoke, her voice sounded remote.

"Will there ever be such a time as this again?"

"If there is, they can expect my immediate resignation."

"From what?" she asked.

"The bloody human race."

She laughed a bit uncertainly. "You're quite a cynic for a war hero."

"I'm a war coward," I said. "I've been involved in too many

killings and close escapes. I just want it all to cease and desist."

I don't think she took me as seriously as I meant it.

She rolled over on her back and said, "What I really meant was. . . we're here and . . . up there . . . there's a beautiful pattern being traced. And we know its cause and still we can't connect it to earth, or us.

"And you *know* the real thing. But it really is very strange to me. I've hardly ever seen a war plane up close."

As if on cue, as a personal rebuke to Janice for her self-imposed ignorance, there came a distant loud report, and to the west we saw a dense black trail corkscrewing earthwards. A parachute, then another, and another, opened.

"Ours or theirs?" asked Janice.

"Theirs," I said.

"How can you tell?"

"My God, Janice, can you really be that ignorant about war planes? Because there are three – at least, a bomber's crew, or part of it . . . We've only got fighters up there. Don't you know even that?"

She flushed. "I'm sorry, I should have . . ."

She was interrupted by a clattering roar that told of hot metal overworked to breaking point and, as we gaped, a Heinkel and its pursuing Hurricane came – almost as if connected by a length of chain – racing crazily into our field of view from right to left, in the culminating seconds of a desperate long chase. The Luftwaffe machine must have been battered down from great altitude by the Hurricane, stage by deadly stage. All of this last part would have started miles away, and they must have followed the contours of little hills and valleys as they raced across the landscape to burst now wildly upon us.

My imagination encompassed both airmen. The bomber pilot would be smashing at his shot-up, leaden controls, desperate to squeeze some non-existent ounce out of his foundering machine, hoping for a miracle with all the fervour of those-about-to-die as he tried to change his machine's direction by just that tiny interval that would let one of his gunners – if any were alive – get in a single, last, second-long burst at the tormenting Hurricane as it flashed by.

But the Hurricane pilot knew his business. He hung behind, waiting, not firing. He would be down to his final rounds, sitting it out till the bomber pilot made a last mistake that momentarily exposed his flank – or flew his plane into a hillside.

The planes dipped out of sight as they ran into a hollow. Then it ended. As the Heinkel emerged, the pilot was compelled to climb – he had hugged the earth's contours a bit too lovingly. The Hurricane pilot had remembered to keep a few feet higher. Now he had a half-second when more than just the tail end of the target crossed his line of fire. There would have been no time to aim, but, as I say, the Hurricane pilot knew his business. Now, at last, he got off a short burst.

Hurricanes were not that fast as fighters went – appreciably slower than the Messerschmitt Bf 109 or the Spitfire. But they were, as so often said, "a good gun platform". That was what showed now – a rock-like steadiness as the pilot got off his burst. It was enough.

The Heinkel quivered like a poleaxed bullock. Its nose pulled up sharply as its racing propellers strained skywards. Then it stalled and dropped a hundred and fifty feet on its tail.

We were perhaps two hundred yards away – it seemed less. Over the crack and crunch of breaking metal, flames burst, black smoke lunged upwards. There was a scatter and rain of bits, an appalling roar.

Janice and I flung ourselves down on the soft earth among the wild daisies. She was screaming and holding on to me with hands and arms and legs and feet, her teeth clenching in the fabric of my jacket.

The Hurricane bank-climbed steeply to about five hundred feet, waggled his wings, and began what was obviously a long landing approach towards Oxford.

I tried to calm Janice. Briefly, I pulled her close; then held her off.

"I better go down there. There could be someone."

"No. No! Please . . . No."

"Got to."

I pushed her away and walked down towards the burning wreck, past bits of smouldering debris. I knew damned well it was no use.

But I also knew if it happened to me, wherever it happened, I'd hope someone would go over for a look.

I was not yet walking quite nomally. It took me two minutes to get there, another three or four to inspect the rubbish, smell the smell that meant just one thing, and return, feeling nauseated, to Janice.

"Nothing. Just bits."

"Oh God!" she cried. "It's so hateful! God . . ."

I put an arm around her as we walked back towards where we had left our bicycles just over the hilltop. After nearly a half-mile of walking she smiled at me. "I feel okay now, Robert. Sorry."

"That's all right."

I kissed her. She tasted salty with dried tears. Before we reached the bicycles I drew her down into the still, soft grass and we made love in the sweetly natural nest of the hillside, not only with abandon but with a flowing tenderness I had begun to doubt would ever be ours again.

* * *

Late that evening, alone at dinner, we ranged back over the afternoon, and other matters.

"What do you feel, Robert?" she asked. "I mean, you build planes – or would in peace. And you used to race them. Don't you feel they're just a gun now? I mean, before the war, at least some of them carried families, parents to their children, husbands to wives. Now – my God!"

"That really hasn't been their image for some time. But in peacetime I hope we'll forget all this stuff–"

"But you fly them. In war now. Isn't that sort of a betrayal?"

"Well – it's just because I know how to . . . If I've got to be in a war I have to fly if I can. It's what I know how to do – and that puts me in a fighter plane."

"OK, but why do you want to *make* them – and fly them the way you do, whether in peace or war? Things that can be used this way? Why?"

"Ever hear of Icarus?"

"Of course. But he always seemed such a dope. All that wax and feathers – and flying up near the sun. What did he expect? Surely that's pretty stupid stuff!"

"Yes. Okay. Not a perfect myth, though actually it was Daedalus, the father, who made the wings. And did fly successfully. But the impulse. To fly. Not to fly somewhere, or particularly fast, or to carry goods or people. Or do good or harm. Just to fly. I wanted to help make Daedalus wings that wouldn't come off in the sun. Wings to fly with. Just to do it. Something pretty small, really, to fly as no one else had. And to do it with wings we'd made."

"And do you really believe you managed to – I mean to your own satisfaction?"

I considered the question carefully, for I was not sure yet what might hinge on it.

"Yes," I said. "In a way."

Chapter 39

But still things were not resolved

We saw each other a few more times, even though it was assumed I would return to my squadron and fight again. Then I learned that because the question of my promotion had come up my file had been re-examined and, as had not been the case with earlier promotions, this time someone had read it carefully. The report that came to me noted I had served with distinction in the air, had been seriously wounded and was fairly old for aerial combat. It also said –

Attention has been drawn to your active association with Mr Philip Gibbs White in connection with his distinguished contributions to aircraft design and building. While it is understood that you suspended your formal engineering training at Cambridge University when you joined the R.A.F., it is also recognised that you have unique experience and skill in the design, testing and maintenance of small aircraft of advanced performance (confirmed in communications from Mr Gibbs White and Mr William Parker, owner of Parker Aircraft). It has therefore been decided that, from now on, your greatest usefulness to Great Britain's Air Defence will be to remain with the R.A.F. and serve as an aeronautical and technical adviser to several aircraft factories in order of a rotation, the details of which will be forwarded to you in the near future. Your duties may eventually call for your posting to locations beyond Great Britain. Meanwhile, you should hold yourself in readiness for your new appointment.

* * *

So I was promoted to Squadron Leader, but with no more combat duty. My new job was that of trouble-shooting problems at the interface between the R.A.F. and the aircraft industry, advising on how to get them eliminated. It was necessary work, perhaps vital work. On several occasions I had trips – to the Middle East, the Med, France after D-Day – all to pinpoint aircraft performance problems on the spot. I worked like a slave at these jobs, and was good at them. I even got an M.B.E. afterwards, to go with my D.F.C. I also got to know a horde of other men doing similar jobs, some of them civilians, and there were many excellent and talented people among them. But many of us were constantly irritated and frustrated by stubborn and arbitrary opposition to change or improvement from certain bureaucrats with rigidly conceived interpretations of official procedure.

* * *

I thought my being relieved from combat flying (even though it is true that I did do a limited amount of test piloting from time to time) would at last allow Janice and me to come together again. But, despite the day of the air battle we had witnessed – or perhaps just because of it – this did not happen. Janice had me now fixed in her mind as an incorrigible flier, who would always continue to fly and therefore continue to be exposed to the associated risks no matter how clever, competent and careful I might be.

I had not heard from or of her for months, but late in 1942 I received a letter from her mother. It read in part –

I'm writing to tell you that Janice was married last week to Howard Bell, a colleague of hers in the civil service. Theirs was a quiet and private wedding with very few guests. I think I am happy for Janice because she has been lonely for a long time and Howard seems to be a sincere and thoughtful man. Yet, I dare to add something here, because I know you will never betray my confidence: I had continued to hope that it would one day be Janice and you. Sad things happen in life. They happened to Janice. They happened to me. I know they have also happened to you. I feel sure you will join me when I say that I greatly hope Janice will find the life she has needed.

Please pay us a visit if you ever have the time and inclination. I would love to see you.

If ever an event in one's life felt like the slamming shut of a book one had loved, this was it for me. I suddenly faced the fact that as long as I lived things would *never* quite work out as I had for a long time believed they eventually would.

You know about the advice given to those who have experienced a violent and disorienting shock? Just put one foot in front of the other and stumble on. Well, I did – not from any refined sense of self-discipline or anything like that, but just because it was my nature.

* * *

I had thought G.W.'s and my paths would cross fairly often, but I saw him only rarely. His job was one in which he spent much time at the highest levels of consultation among the designers of fighter aircraft; it continued throughout the war, even though it resulted in very few new designs ever reaching volume production. That did not mean that all such work was in vain. It was necessary because no one could be sure when the war would end, and therefore when the aircraft in current use would become completely obsolete. Most of the results of such work, however, did contribute to continual improvements in performance of several types of aircraft already serving. Nearly all of G.W.'s contributions were at the drawing board or in the test laboratory. I never did find out all he had done, but I know it was held in high esteem and that he eventually received an O.B.E. for it.

* * *

One other thing happened not very long after I received the note from Mrs Whitcombe. Parker Aircraft's buildings were small as such factories go, and were – though near Ashford – actually in the countryside. And they were so effectively camouflaged that, even when I flew over them one day, I had great difficulty in locating them.

Yet one day, perhaps by sheer bad luck, an enemy bomb hit the factory. Several of Parker's workers were killed, others injured. Bill Parker was not seriously injured, but Parker Aircraft's production capability was destroyed and the aviation authorities decided not to attempt a reconstruction at that time.

Vector I had been housed in a special small hangar near the main workshop building. The bomb blast destroyed it. Gone from the world forever.

For the one and only time in those years of the war, Bill Parker, James Grant, G.W. and I all met for a day at the devastated site. All of us, Parker included, paid scant attention to the main destroyed building. We just stood among the rubble of Vector I.

It was hard to say anything. We stood around, shuffling our feet a bit, pointing now and then at some barely recognizable feature.

I felt that book had slammed shut again, and I was suddenly anxious and unhappy. I thought perhaps I should throw the book away and start another one. One that was small and modest, that did not already contain an imaginary tale that would demand fatal amendments from time to time.

None of us dared look for long at the others, though we all knew there would never be a time when a "Mark 2" Vector I would take to the air. But as I glanced at my companions one thing became clear; G.W. was taking it differently from the rest of us. Was it from stoicism, resignation, or some sense that a main thread of his experience and existence had now been cut forever? All that comes down to me from that moment with total clarity is that, after a little while, G.W. looked up, tipped his head back to stare into the open sky and said, "Well then, nothing more here for any of us. I see your Rolls is still running, Bill, despite a few surface scrapes. What about taking us into Ashford for a couple of beers?"

* * *

The shocks of the loss of Janice and of Vector I stayed with me for many months. But of the effects of the end of Vector I on G.W. I heard nothing more, except that those who saw him said he wasn't interested in talking about it.

By all accounts he just went back to work and did a job of legendary quality. After the war, for the second time, there was talk of a knighthood. But then it was decided that, to get one, he would need to have been head of something. As before, I'm sure he couldn't have cared less. But one or two of his admirers were outraged.

* * *

As for Janice, her image, everything about her, continued to haunt me. I found it very hard to think of her with another, and agonizing when I did. I felt I had failed by not saying something fairly simple to her, like, "I love you to distraction and cannot bear the thought that we can possibly miss getting married and living together forever." Why hadn't I? Perhaps for two reasons, both of them stupid. I had not – as I now confessed to myself – formerly understood that I loved Janice to the distraction I now often felt, because like many an ambition-driven young male, I had carelessly interposed that ambition between me and my love. I had had too much of that inhuman detachment that can frustrate the emergence of one's adult soul – sometimes forever. It was now, too late in the day, that I knew the true depth of my love for Janice.

But if much of the fault was mine, part of it was hers. The problem had been that each of us had misgivings about the other, and had held back from unreservedly giving and receiving love. And now, as I saw it, the problem, which was one we should have solved with patience and resolution on both sides, had been rudely snatched away.

I met Howard Bell only once, two years later, at a cocktail party before he and I were to receive M.B.E.s. Janice was present and looked very beautiful, if (I thought) a little strained. She smiled her smile, however, and managed to introduce each of us to the other with grace and good humour. I shook his hand and wondered if he knew as little about me as I about him.

He was a decent enough looking man, perhaps six years Janice's senior. I could see little about him to dislike as we chatted briefly about nothing much, but without hating him I detested his existence.

After the word of Janice's marriage got about, our mutual friends tended to criticise Janice and admire my evident stoicism. In my head at the time there was – in point of fact – a crude and bitter mix of my undeclared love and – now inexpressible – passion, and also of simplistic, and defeated, male competitiveness. All of it, stirred by the cruel ladle of defeat, resonated in my mind for many months. Later on, that resonance broke out into a self-revelatory internal chatter of reproach, to ruin serenity and concentration in my waking mind, or drive my sleeping mind awake in sweating fear and fury – and regret.

Janice and I had both been wrong. She had failed to appreciate that I was doing what I must do, and had asked too much of me. I had been too patient, had assumed her attitude would change of itself if only given time.

My youth, for all its adventures, had frozen my movement towards manhood. Now, perhaps permanently sapped of spiritual energy for further growth, I found myself in an emotional trap.

At last I drew a line in my new, more modest, mental book and closed the account with a final sigh: too little . . . too late.

Chapter 40

I returned to engineering at Cambridge, turning thirty-three, in the autumn of 1945. The atmosphere was still abnormal; kids who had come straight from school were in awe of us ex-service types. We felt nothing for them at first – how could we? They had been school children while we fought a war. Yet, five years later, veterans were only slightly more employable than the kids were – even if we could still count on a bit of preference and more rapid advancement.

Some lecturers had, of course, been in the war themselves, and it was easy and natural to be on fairly close terms with them; it made it easier to resume a life of intense and uninterrupted study.

I had known some of my lecturers when they were working in the wartime aircraft industry. Others knew well of my former life in aviation, especially working with G.W.; all who had met him admired him extravagantly. A bit of this transferred itself to me, so I was on very congenial terms with many lecturers.

But if I hoped to run into an academic version of G.W. among them, I was disappointed. Most of my lecturers, no matter how clever in questions of aeronautical physics, had not the essential "feeling" for making an advanced whole aircraft as a functioning creature, and were unable to touch my mind in the way G.W.'s free creative spirit had done.

* * *

My problem was that I had no real place in the world. Australia was remote. I had not seen members of my family for many years. I knew Bill Parker felt too old and tired to return to plane building. Except for that one time when I had met her husband, I had not seen or heard of Janice since her marriage.

I became confused about how I should lead the rest of my life.

If it was to be in aviation I had to acknowledge that, unless I was prepared to return to the world of light – essentially recreational – plane manufacture, the builders of planes of advanced design were racing, torrent-like, to the age of jet propulsion, an age that had already been under mainly secret development since the beginning of the war. No matter that a whole generation of builders had grown up, many now old or gone, who had been imbued with the romance of the propellor-driven aeroplane, the design paradigm had shifted. Anyone striving to stay among the new leaders would have to shift with it.

* * *

Well, Cambridge was still a crystal sphere, a realm of static beauty and serenity, where I could get over the war for my remaining year and a half of studies before finally deciding what kind of a life I could make in post-war aviation.

My university time did not work out, however, in the matter of women. Already in my thirties, I found it hard to take girls seriously. Even though many of them were articulate, clever and pretty, most of them were a dozen or more years my junior. I met some women closer to my age, most of whom had been in the W.A.A.F. and the Navy. Some were very nice. A few were just man-hungry. There were several with whom I could have found pleasant and harmless relationships, but that sort of thing was not for me. My wish for a strongly sexual relationship would need to be part of something else – I didn't know whether it would be marriage – but deep, final.

Chapter 41

Near the end of my time at Cambridge I saw that – regardless of my aviation dreams that were based on memories of Charlie and G.W. – it would only be among the big plane manufacturers that I could look for a career. My wartime experiences had introduced me to some influential figures in the industry and somehow I found myself caught up in the spirit of things. At least, I *let* myself become caught up. That, as I later saw, was an important distinction . . .

British aircraft manufacturers entered the post-war peace in a buoyant mood. The industry had many great designers, was in good technical shape, and was poised for conversion to peacetime needs. If you could just accept the enthusiasm for the coming of jets, the upbeat imagery, then it was easy to accept that huge jet airliners were about to shrink the human world and, by annihilating the limitations of time and space, revolutionize social, economic and international relationships. Britain was seen as having a great role to play in European, Transatlantic and global airlines developments. It was assumed that Commonwealth countries would continue as an inexhaustible, expanding market for British industry.

It was all a long universe from G.W.'s and my earlier ideas of what planes were for. And at thirty four I was basically detached, even cynical, about the blandishments of the marketplace. But I did respond to the flattering idea that such skills as mine would be in prime demand in the industry that was beginning to appear. Also, notions of power and influence and money became, for some time, strong inducements to me, as they always have been to many people at some point in their lives.

Like many others I shared the misunderstanding that in Britain future success hung not just on talent and ambition but on a few throws of chance combined with the changing social, political, and economic fabric of the country.

Take the Bristol Brabazon, a giant turbojet that flopped because of production cost overruns – the sort of thing that was, perhaps, the beginning of the end.

The real end held off for a few years. In the early fifties came the first generation of the lovely British jetliners. They went straight to the top of the class – led the world. But then, horrifying failures and crashes! Statistically, British airlines still owned the world's best safety record. But the De Havilland Comet crashes, occurring when they did, and so greatly publicized, broke public confidence at a time crucial for the future of the British commercial airlines.

So it went.

When Commonwealth countries turned to jet airliners they had scant option but to go with the Americans. The Americans noted and did not repeat the British mistakes; Yankee enterprise paid off. They had planes with longer range. Their after-sales services offered comprehensive facilities, maintenance and parts replacement anywhere in the world. They would fly their technical experts wherever required in their companies' interests.

In the rough game of international trade, the successes of the Americans were eminently deserved. It seemed incomprehensible to many. But it was a fact.

But I'm getting ahead of myself . . .

Chapter 42

It was 1946, getting close to graduation time when I received a letter from Pete Randall that said –

Dear Robert,

Seems like a lifetime since we got together – mate! I am now not as you knew me, having lost (or buried) most of my boyish impetuousness – a characteristic which, I dare say, will continue to bedevil the memories of my friends for the next forty years or so. I am now a "serious person", who is learning to totter in the Dad's firm footsteps in the matter (hallowed for centuries!) of Family Business. No, we are not quite the Mafia, but you get the idea. Anyway, I need, and am insisting on, a short break from my "so necessary" duties. Please find some clean underwear (if you have any), put on a shirt and pants (if you have any) and come to London next week where I am proposing a beer and whiskey bash for a dozen or two fellow wartime layabouts, such as yourself. Come! or I shall be severely hurt – and so shall you next time we do meet. Two thirty in the afternoon on the 27th, at the Eagle's Claws (you remember the place), until they throw us out.

Affectionately,

Pete

The venue, appropriately, was to be an already familiar London pub. It seemed a pleasant idea and I phoned my acceptance. I went alone, though I knew most of the others would have wives or girl friends.

Pete greeted me as usual, with a slap on the back, loud merriment and what also appeared to be a genuine feeling of comradely renewal.

When I looked across the pub lounge I saw Janice was there, also alone. She wore a plain, well cut, short-skirted suit of dark smooth wool and a white sweater. She had on a green scarf and carried a black shoulder bag. She looked cleanly elegant as she always had, and still very beautiful.

We hugged briefly.

"Long time no see, Janice. How do you happen to be here, then?"

"Well, Pete invited me, of course. He said all his old playmates."

I nodded at what she said, trying hard to pierce its meaning.

"You look good, Janice."

"And you, Robert. You look great. Younger, somehow. . . Perhaps it's your hair – longer and more casual. Oh, but something else about you, too . . ."

I didn't say so, but Janice looked older. Decidedly. I didn't mind. The immaculately beautiful girl had become a woman. The great eyes were now defined by tiny lines. The skin at the corners of the smooth mouth was very slightly creased. The whole face was more expressive . . . and sadder than before. I felt a sort of pity, but was also stirred and touched. It occurred to me as my heart pulsed once – heavily – that if we ever made love again Janice's response would not be merely sensually satisfying but might also reveal much more of that depth and tenderness I had caught glimpses of but had been able to reach only once.

I took a deep breath.

"Well . . . Drinking?"

"A scotch and water, please."

I asked for two. We sat sipping for a couple of minutes and I waved briefly to a few people. Then we were as if within a cone of quiet outside of which the others rattled on around us.

"How is marriage?" I managed, finally. It was grotesquely awkward, but the best I could do. Anyway, I needed to break through to something real.

"Done . . . Finished, I'm afraid."

"Oh. How so? And When?"

"Last year, officially. But it was already long over."

Damn you! I said to myself. Damn you, you little . . . Damn the years you spent with that. . . whatever he was. And damn you for not . . . not what?

I harked back to what I had learned about myself. Paused. Cooled, a bit. This needed caution. Here was this blasted girl . . . The same one that threw me over. Were the delicate lines near her eyes, the faintly dimming lustre of the luminous skin, really signs of a sea change? Could compassion and love – and even understanding – flower now behind the crystal of eyes that had grown faintly bitter but were shining with a swelling glaze of something I had not seen before?

I sipped my scotch and glanced at the several tables around which our group had gathered. Nearly every one of our companions knew about us from the years before. Pete Randall was watching us without showing it . . . I knew that. I supposed they were all watching us.

"So . . . I'm sorry." I could have sounded gracious, but I couldn't be bothered!

Janice smiled faintly. "Me, too."

"Well . . . what are you doing now, Janice?"

"Oh, I'm in a publishing firm. I'm an assistant editor, with prospects of becoming an editor in a few years."

"Sounds . . . interesting." What I knew about publishing you could print on a postage stamp. "What sorts of things do you do?"

"All sorts of things, really. Novels, technical books, children's stuff. Just getting general experience. And I'm continuing to write a book on Eastern European art and what may have happened to it during the war. I probably won't be able to approach a publisher with it until I can get a security clearance for some of the documentation. Might take years for that."

"I see. Do you like it a lot – publishing and writing?"

"Quite well. It's a good firm. They try for quality books. You meet interesting people. And yes, the writing is a great challenge."

"I bet!"

She looked at me for a very long moment.

"Robert. I want to tell you something . . ."

Here it comes. "Tell away," I said.

"It died hard."

"What?"

"What I felt for you."

"Really?"

"I'm not trying to be funny, Robert. I mean it. And it's hard to talk about."

I looked into my scotch, trying to hold my tongue.

"I mean it, Robert. Perhaps you could help me if you –"

"Bloody nonsense, Janice!" My voice undoubtedly was loud. People looked directly at us now. I ignored them.

"Look, it's not what I . . ."

"Sheer bloody nonsense – and utter bullshit!"

"I meant . . ."

"You married that chap, Janice. You just up and married him." I was very angry now, luxuriating in the release it gave, getting angrier. Soon I'd be shouting. I felt I wanted to lean across and strike her. Hard. A blow that would leave a stinging red mark on the saddened, fine-boned, beloved face.

"Robert. Please. Can you believe this? Can you try? I didn't understand you, or myself. I was vulnerable, and didn't want to be hurt . . . especially by you. Because I loved you. But I feared you, too, because I didn't properly understand you. And I feared *for* you. And for us."

"And now . . . now you know what you want?"

"More or less. What about you?" She looked at me, her lips quivering, tears seeming to erode her eyes. She looked almost old.

I got up, not looking at the others. Not daring to. But I looked down at Janice, briefly. Just once.

"I'm off, Janice. If you want to come, get up now and come – where we can be quiet. Otherwise . . ."

I pushed my chair back and walked away. I desperately wanted her to follow, and had no stomach for what I was doing. Yet do it I must. For under all failure to resolve things in those earlier years, one thing was clear to me: Janice had discarded me – for whatever reasons she was then, or now, prepared to believe – for another. I had seen his face for months – and then for years. And I believed that, though she might never be able to view it as betrayal, Janice had betrayed us; instead of having the guts to work our problems through, had thrown me over for someone she had not cared about or loved as she had me. And though others might construe it differently, to me that was a betrayal by my most deeply loved.

I had few illusions left about myself, about the limitations of my brains, inspiration, courage – or my future possibilities. Oh! a few perhaps, that might yet lead me somewhere new. Or not. But I had loved this girl. Had continued to love her, without hope, to this moment. But if I had once been prepared, given only a consistent affection and understanding, to love on terms of simple mutual trust, now I had different, more exacting terms. Now I looked for sure evidence of a fealty that would endure, that could not redeem the past but would help to exorcise it by placing it in its correct perspective as part of a process in our lives. And enable both of us to live with it.

I had loved this woman, loved no other and did not expect to. But now I had to put behind me her sudden and arbitrary action that had blighted both our lives – nearly forever. Particularly was this necessary, since now she confessed she had abandoned me while loving me. I even felt angry on behalf of the man she had married. He, too, had been betrayed.

Janice sat mute as I made off towards the pub door. I glanced back just once.

And I saw that she rose quickly and came too, tossing the rich light mass of her hair with a strange gesture that I never saw her repeat, a movement as if she was shaking her head clear of water . . . or dust.

The afternoon was cooling as we strolled near the Thames embankment. Later we sat in a café, and over coffee I inspected her face. It was ravaged by the emotions of the moment. I could hardly believe the change. And yet, a glow was coming, not the surface shine of the immaculate girl of years before, but something from deeper down. It was what I had always hoped for, looked for in that earlier time, and had never quite found.

She looked at me, trembling. I gripped her hand and she returned my grip fiercely, though her hand was shaking.

Soon afterwards we went to her flat.

As I lay over her long sweet body, mouth to mouth, breast to breast, I thought numbly of the missing years, and of the other man, and tried not to picture them as we were now, and failed. And I grew angry in my love and embraced her so fiercely that she cried out and raked my back with her nails as we kissed frenziedly and I muttered in her ear, "Bloody little fool . . ."

Chapter 43

I met G.W. in London not long after Janice and I were married, and though he still looked much the same as he always had, there was something that seemed a bit withdrawn about him. I guessed it might be because so much was now behind him, was history.

His face lit up as we spoke of Janice. "Can't tell you, old man, how good that is. I was very sad to think you two had broken up. Everyone who saw you together in the early days thought you seemed perfect for each other. You're very lucky that it came right somehow."

When our talk got round to planes it was different. Parker Aircraft was gone forever. G.W. was living near London now, working as a design consultant to three aircraft companies. But the disasters in the large commercial operations meant that he was being progressively edged towards nothing but military designs.

"It's understandable, of course," he said. "In the more highly conceived commercial planes, the Americans are going to dominate now. Nothing to stop them. In Britain, all the pioneering jet stuff will be in applications to the air defence system. Production runs won't be huge. The emphasis will be on quality."

"Well, then – ?"

"Well, it never was military planes that interested me much. I was pleased to be involved with them during the war. Doing my bit, what? But for myself it's always been just what you can do with general aeronautical design – the principles of optimality, the unavoidable compromises while maximizing performance and handling.

"What I find myself doing now is working on the maximization of those characteristics, of course, but in the direction of military needs. In fact, building the specifications for weapons systems – something I always wanted to avoid."

"Why couldn't you set yourself up again and build a Vector

II?"

He looked at me in disbelief. Then he laughed.

"Where could I go with that?" he said. "I haven't got the money any more, I'd have to be making a jet – for which you need enormous facilities. The propeller-driven planes they produced near the end of the war, while they didn't surpass the performance of Vector I, could approximate it. That, to me, proves there are certain maximal design criteria that we got close to in Vector I, that really can't be improved on in an aircraft that isn't a jet – or a rocket."

"Perhaps in America – ?"

"America, you think? I don't see why. We're talking about universal, inescapable performance maxima here. I think they've been reached – or at least we got near those asymptotic figures we used to talk about."

"Doesn't what happened to Vector I and the Falcons haunt you?" I said suddenly.

"I don't think so. We built them. Plans of them still exist. The lectures I gave to the Aeronautical Society are all in print. There are hundreds of photographs of them, even newsreel films of them in flight. We know those planes flew. They're like Greek ruins. Only a shadow of what they once were, but enough known about them that we *could* build complete replicas of them if we had the time, money and interest. But of course we don't."

Then he grinned. "Actually there are three Falcons in private hands, still being flown. One of them's in California. My guess is the others will eventually end up there, too. Only the Americans have the money for this sort of thing nowadays.

"My contracts run out soon. Then, I'm going to get a bit organized, get myself a car that combines comfort and ruggedness, and bloody well drift across Europe to Greece, as I was planning just before the war."

"You really are going, then?"

"Really. And not before time."

So he didn't exactly say he would never again be concerned with plane design, but it appeared to be what he was implying. A hard thing for me to swallow: unconcern for the notion that anyone could anticipate, even expect, his going on from triumph to triumph. His position – unstated but pretty obvious – was that having set the toughest possible challenge for himself and met it, he would bestir himself again only if he discerned, and cared to accept, another comparable challenge. And there was another factor that, though he did not state it explicitly, I deduced from other things he said or alluded to: he was still not interested in joining the research or building efforts of large teams, no matter how talented such teams might be.

At that time, and for the first time since I had known him, his attitude disappointed me. To be sure, he had genius; but perhaps his stock of it was spent on Vector I. For that single venture he drove himself with the passion of a Bach, the insight of a Da Vinci. Then it was over.

His analytical judgement was still acute, his ability to comment critically on numberless matters as sharp as ever. But such qualities are, of course, part of the common mental apparatus of a small horde of "clever" people everywhere. G.W. was one of these, but no longer one apart.

Some who had not known him in his earlier life might have found it all too easy to underrate his true ability, or to compare their own quite favourably with what they could now perceive of his. But the fact was that in his heyday his mind had not been of that second order brilliance that produces enough innovation to keep patent office clerks out of the ranks of the permanently unemployed; it had been something much rarer – and much more strange.

* * *

Well, he went to Greece. He stayed there for months. And it was no over-delayed itch he needed to relieve. He went back many times.

He had sold his cottage, but in 1948 he repurchased it, did it up, tidied the wild garden, and lived there as he had when I first knew him, though a bit more comfortably. In all the later years when I was able to visit him, it would be to find him tinkering with his car (he had acquired a Jaguar which he seemed mildly to enjoy), reading anything from poetry to astrophysics. Each spring he would travel to Greece, or North Africa, or the Middle East, to look at archeological sites. He was never involved with professionals, even though his archeological knowledge became quite profound. He would grip his cold pipe in his teeth and stare at some jar, or figurine, or amulet, with something of the old concentration of features. His ideas about the minutiae of the way in which they must have been constructed were powerfully original. The way he spoke about them as his hands traced the patterns on these artifacts said that at least a part of the ruthless mind that could grasp and interpret technical procedures with utter sureness remained intact. But now he was no longer an eager plane maker, just an ageing gentleman of limited but sufficient means who maybe attends cricket matches at Lords, drives a car he tunes expertly himself, travels for fun and enlightenment, and continues to observe the world with an ironic, and increasingly detached intelligence. In his presence I felt myself almost awkward because, affection aside, I could no longer find very much common ground of consuming interest. And, seemingly, he was content.

This almost angered me. I still had an enormous lust for that secret power of his and believed that I, also, somehow deserved to get it – and *must,* at last, because of the force of my dream.

Chapter 44

My first real work after graduation was in a small government-funded aeronautics research laboratory about thirty miles from London. I commuted there by train each day from a station near the London flat Janice and I were living in. She had now been promoted to a full editorial position and was deeply involved in producing a profusely illustrated book on the sort of Etruscan artifacts she had taken me to see before the war. She was also continuing to write about what the Nazis had done with purloined art, awaiting the release of some documents that were still secret. We saw G.W. from time to time and she had got to know him well, and of his interest in Greece. An illustrated account of the history of domestic architecture in the Greek islands was something her firm was looking towards, and she asked G.W. if he was interested in co-researching and writing it with her. He seemed to like the idea.

But this venture never really got started, because one day a designer from American Star Aircraft met me at my workplace and took me to lunch. He somehow knew about my association with G.W.

"What a real shame, Bob, that he was never in the States," he said. "We could have laid things on for him. Too old now, I guess."

I didn't respond to this because, though I knew better, I also knew what G.W.'s response would have been.

"Bob," he went on (Ed McGuire was his name), why don't you come work with us? We're expanding like you wouldn't believe. And we could offer you . . ."

He named a sum that stopped me in my mental tracks.

"We can provide you with facilities and a workplace you just won't find in Britain anywhere I've seen. We're just poised to take off into the wild blue. Know what I mean?"

"It's nice here. And my wife's career is going very well."

"Yeah, but look, Bob, in the kind of work your wife could do here, I'll bet she could do even better in the States. You just ask her and I bet she'll have to agree with me."

"She has family here . . . her mother . . .they're very close."

"Yeah, well, of course I can't comment on that sort of stuff. Obviously the choice is yours. But let me tell you just what we could lay on for your own work."

At the end of the meal, as we sat drinking our final cups of coffee, I promised Ed McGuire I would get back to him soon.

"I'll think on it, Ed. It will largely depend on Janice. Anyway, thanks for asking me. It's very flattering."

We finished our coffees, told each other a couple of current, deeply mordant jokes about building planes, and shook hands.

I was already pretty sure of the answer I would be able to give him.

* * *

When I recall the Seattle years, several strands of experience still shine. First, an unexpected bonus – Washington was a beautiful state. In its soaring physical spaces, the nobility of its coasts, forests and mountains, Washington somehow seemed the sort of place an aircraft engineer and former pilot ought to be living in.

The children began their childhoods there. James was two and Philip three when we arrived. In Seattle they soon ran free. They rapidly became young Americans, of course. Sometimes we used to wince at that. But, all in all, the Seattle years were good years that none of us regretted.

As it turned out, I worked for American Star Aircraft for only a year. Then the university offered me a research and teaching appointment. The salary was much less, but the position was well-endowed for research. I broke my contract to go there, though I retained some working links with American Star in an advisory capacity. Two more years passed while I became accustomed to American university practices and graduate students.

I was an Australian but so far gone in British ways and manner of speech that my roots were at first barely discernible to Americans.

To most of them, however, Janice was an unmistakable Britisher – which largely acted in her favour. And she was also more adaptable than I. Or perhaps I mean she simply pressed on with her essential style intact wherever she found herself, and people either liked and accepted her, or they didn't. Because of her beauty, confidence and apparently democratic-though-upper class manner most people were charmed by her. I used to laugh myself sick at this, because in fact she never gave an inch in things that mattered to her, while persuading nearly everyone of her sweet reasonableness.

I don't believe either of us became particularly Americanized. But I found I had reverted to some of my Australian modes of speech and manner that I thought I had long lost. Some of my Americans colleagues liked this. They thought Australians were like Americans. All that stuff about space Down Under . . . just like Texas. And in certain ways they were right.

American academics tend, for the most part, to be a better-mannered lot than their British or Australian counterparts, many of whom can, on occasion, be splendidly rude. But one of my colleagues was a brash, opinionated New Yorker, loud and superior. Many of my other colleagues recoiled from dealing with someone they found so unpleasant if thwarted or opposed in any way. As an incorrigible scrounger, he would wander into labs and take – one should say steal – other people's apparatus. If caught, he would unhesitatingly invent some ridiculous excuse – anything.

One day this man entered my lab where I was busy with a research associate, a couple of graduate students and an observer from industry. Wing airflow dynamics had now become my principal research interest, and we were – predictably – watching the behaviour of an experimental model of a newly designed thin wing section at critical air speeds in a wind tunnel. He began to grope in drawers, in cupboards. I looked hard at him, but he only glanced abstractedly at me and said, "I'm looking for that pressure gauge you lent me last month. I need it urgently. Where in hell can I find it?"

I said shortly, "I'm pretty busy, Ernie. Could you come back in an hour? I could probably find you one then."

"I need it right now."

"I can't help you now." His groping fingers found what he wanted. He grinned wolfishly. "Got it. See you . . . " He was holding in his arms a very expensive unit that I used constantly. I had cheaper ones that I wouldn't have missed too much.

I said, "Just a minute. That's one I never lend. As I say, come back in an hour and . . ."

"I need it now. You can have it back tomorrow." He made off towards the door.

I shouted, suddenly. "Listen, you miserable bastard! Get your stinking, cotton-picking fingers off that or you'll be eating it. And piss off!" I moved menacingly towards him.

He staggered back, hastily laying the unit on a bench, backed into the door frame and hurt himself, and got outside in a hurry.

My associates, all of them, considered me carefully, with expressions I found hard to fathom.

Later I realized that word had quickly got around. I became an instant celebrity with the many who detested this pest; and for a while I found myself a sort of hero – or at least someone who "wasn't to be messed with". Some people put out exaggerated stories about my war record. They seemed to think they had a John Wayne on the faculty.

I was amused by my new reputation and also horrified by it. But I found that it gave me a certain influence in the department that I had not sought and might not have earned in twenty years of more mundane exchanges.

A few of my colleagues even told me that I was "just the sort of guy" who was fair enough, and tough enough, to run a big department, and that they would be happy to back me strongly when the present department chairman's term ended in a couple of years.

Chapter 45

In Seattle, Janice blossomed. At forty, outdoors living had slightly weathered her English complexion; the lines in her face – especially laughter lines – had deepened. Her rich blonde hair was lighter in response to the sun, and her blue eyes still looked as clear as they had more than twenty years before – the faint signs of the bitterness of 1946 had long gone. She smiled readily and radiantly as she had when she was a girl. She was about to publish the book on which she had worked so long and it was being looked forward to by many art historians and curators. But she had quit her work in publishing years before, when the kids were very young. Now, however, people who admired her intelligence and personality were trying to coax her to return to it. Up to this time we had both decided that young kids needed the full time efforts of at least one parent. But it was reaching the time when wives and husbands could feel fulfilled only when both were working at challenging jobs. So it looked as if she would be in publishing again.

I suppose I was a child of my times – an unconcernedly, politically incorrect male by today's standards. But I think that neither of us, at that time, felt that. We were remarkably happy. I don't suppose we *deserved* to be. But in such a world as we have wrought, we must be thankful for any personal windfalls.

And my work went well in Seattle. Through losing my temper with a colleague I had established a view of myself among others which made it much easier to go my independent way. Though the work was neither outstandingly exciting nor greatly challenging, I had come close to reconciling myself just to having an interesting job that paid decently, and indeed counting myself lucky to have that. Sometimes I wondered what had happened, just where my imagined future had gone to, and why I could no longer manage to conjure it up.

But Janice and I were happy in each other in a way that continued to contain the best of our original reasons for loving, and living with one another, but which had deepened and broadened so that our hours together were a oneness of pleasure and trust. I felt blessed.

And then, in 1958 I did become Chairman of the Aeronautical Design and Engineering Department in the Engineering Faculty. The Department had a good reputation, and my own research work prospered. If there were no more peaks around, my reputation, for what that was worth, was very good. I had executed some highly satisfactory research contracts for the aerospace industry which netted me considerable approval and money. My major skill was as a troubleshooter. Given a problem to solve I was in my element. My experience with G.W. – the incomparable analyst – coupled with my wartime experience, probably accounted for this ability.

Seattle was home. I felt that, as I had never felt about any place since I had left Sydney.

*　*　*

It was 3:30 on a fine, glowing Saturday in late May. Janice and I sat in the shade of our patio which was well-planted around with shrubs that shielded us from view. We lived on high land in a green landscape, with a blue view of Puget Sound below us. I touched Janice's smooth arm and was rewarded with a sleepy but affectionate smile.

"Who'd have thought we'd wind up here?" I said.

"Do you ever hanker after Australia?" she asked.

I was about to answer, when a car entered our driveway. It stopped before the front door and a man got out. As he probably couldn't have seen us through the shrubs, I stood and called to him. "Over here, please." He came, walking smoothly towards the patio, powerfully built, dark-faced, a man of about forty, with a pencil-thin moustache, sportily dressed in a light-coloured leisure suit open at the collar to reveal a muscular brown neck. He held out his hand to me. "Professor Bruce? Professor Robert Bruce?"

"That's right . . ."

"And . . . Mrs. Bruce?"

"Right again," said Janice.

"I'm William Montessori, and I must apologize for barging in on you at your home on this beautiful afternoon."

He smiled evenly, revealing many shining teeth.

"Yes, it is lovely," I said. "What can we do for you?"

"Well, Dr. Bruce, first let me say I *could* have called you at work."

"Yes?"

"Yes. Well, I preferred not to. Or for that matter call you at home. The thing is . . . I've got a confidential proposition to put before you. And because of whom I represent I felt it best to see you in person even though it meant breaking in on your privacy . . ."

"Yes. Well let's hear what's on your mind. Then perhaps we can discuss it. Sit down, won't you.?"

Montessori sat with alacrity. He folded one leg over the other, folded his hands round the upper knee, looked from one to the other of us, and said, "I represent the Defense Department and I . . ."

"Excuse me, do you have some identification, perhaps?"

"Of course. Certainly."

He produced a neat black pocketbook and I perused the documents in it with some care. They seemed to state that he was indeed a Defense Department official, but not in what precise capacity. I said so.

"Well, it's better we don't discuss that point too fully – as long as you can accept my basic credentials."

I felt myself frowning. "As you wish. But if that's the case, what can . . . ?"

"You do for us?"

"Precisely."

Janice half rose. "Would you like coffee, Mr. Montessori? We were about to have a cup."

Montessori nodded. "I'd love some, Mrs. Bruce. But . . ." – she paused – "you needn't feel you should go. In any approach like this, to a person who is married, Defence will always look at both partners."

"Thanks," said Janice, crisply.

"And," Montessori went on, "there's no bar at all in this instance to your hearing what I have to say to Dr Bruce."

"OK," said Janice.

"And so . . .?" I said, feeling very irritated.

Montessori looked at us. "Well, Dr. Bruce, we know very well what you are up to in your studies." He laughed in a strange way, looking down suddenly. "We know your work, that is. The Department has a full record of it, and . . ."

"They're welcome to it. Nothing I ever do is under wraps."

"We know, Doctor, we know."

"And so before you go any further and run the slightest risk of compromising yourself, I must tell you I have no intention whatever of working for Defense; now, or in the future."

"Well now, Professor, you know you really are anticipating quite a bit." He smiled. There was an edge of a new note in his voice; his smile was a trifle strained. I began to tell myself Montessori was a major in counter espionage or something, that this moment was the time for a painless break, before something else, painless or otherwise, became necessary.

"I repeat. I don't . . ."

"Please, Dr. Bruce, hear me out . . . Please."

I looked at him. I didn't look at Janice, who now said, "I'll just get the coffee, I think," and went away.

"Go on, Mr. Montessori."

"Well, we know about your work for a long time back. Right back to that incredible stuff you did with Mr. Gibbs White in Kent, England, before the war."

He became ingratiating. "Those must have been extraordinary times for you. You weren't much more than a boy, I understand."

I looked at Montessori closely. Indeed he knew altogether too much for my liking. I answered carefully, "Yes, it was a rather remarkable time. I mean, to look back on."

"Anyway, Sir, we know too of your great war record and the brilliant work you did for your engineering degree at Cambridge. And we also know what terrific things you've been doing here."

"Well, nice of you to call them that. They're not, of course.

But . . ."

"Well, now, Dr. Bruce," he gave me a lopsided smile that did not quite fit his hard jaw and mouth, "nothing secret about any of it, is there, as you said? All your work has been out there, an open book."

I was growing very impatient. "I'd like you to come to the point."

"Of course. Sorry. Well, we know that you left a lucrative job to enter academia because your work preference lies in areas where public funds are used and you just like to lay out your results for general use."

"I believe we've already covered that point, so what, exactly, are we leading up to?"

"So . . . one thread that runs through your work is your great interest in wing design."

"True."

"You still are . . . interested, in wings, I mean?"

I nodded. "All there in the record, as you say."

"Well, Sir, we want you to go right on doing what you've been doing . . ."

I stared. Was he being funny? He didn't look like a humorous man. More like a man who might suddenly flourish an ominous microfilm and, after that, confront you with, perhaps, a Luger.

"I fully intend to go right on doing it. What of it?"

"With, we hope, just one little difference."

"Which is?"

"We would like it if you could essentially just quit teaching, except for, maybe, your very best graduate student, and do your research for Defense – full time. We would fund all your work, much of which could be done here at the university."

"I see."

"I mean, Defense would pay you a stipend, too. Pay you appreciably more than your present salary – in addition to your salary, I mean." He named a figure that was nearly twice what industry had paid me.

I stared. Not because I was particularly tempted, but because I realized the urgency he believed must underlie his proposal.

I said, "My contract with the university requires that I teach as well as do research."

"Oh, I imagine we could square that with the university authorities."

"I see."

I had a curious feeling of remoteness and realized I was rubbing my chin. Montessori smiled – should I say encouragingly? I pulled myself together.

"The catch?" I looked at this hard man with his leisure tan, his natty sports suit, his grey and pink striped socks, white patent-leather sports shoes. I looked into his shining brown eyes.

He answered me evenly. "No catch, Dr. Bruce. Defense happens to like what you do. We had anticipated from your record that we probably could not tempt you into joining us in more – let us say – directly security-based operations. So we simply want you to continue as before, but without the need to stint your work for want of funds, or because of your teaching duties."

Janice came out with coffee and cookies – impeccable timing – and we fussed with our positions around the table and muttered pleasantries till all of us had coffee and sat at ease.

"Mr. Montessori's just been asking me to go on with precisely what I'm doing – which of course I have every intention of doing – and he'll see I'm paid outrageously more if I just kick out my students and get on with things."

"Oh," said Janice, "goodie."

Montessori smiled a bit thinly. "It's just that Defense is very impressed, Mrs Bruce, with what your husband is doing."

"Lovely," said Janice, smiling brightly.

I looked hard at Montessori. Could he be made to jump?

"Actually," I said, "I must tell you – despite what I just said – that I'm really getting fed up with wings. I was thinking I might drop them and do something different. Even quite outside aviation. Maybe become an author – a writer of fiction; secret agent thrillers." I smiled encouragingly. "I'm looking for characters among people I meet. Would you be interested in being written about?"

I watched closely to see if the mask moved. No eyelash batted.

He simply said, chuckling, "Well, Dr. Bruce, I really hope you're just kidding to see what I'll say."

I laughed myself. "Sure. Just kidding."

"More coffee?" said Janice.

* * *

We sat staring out at Puget Sound, after Montessori had left. Above us, jet trails were stark white in the darkening blue sky.

"A bit sinister, eh?" I said.

"Perhaps. But what will you do?"

"Hold onto my job. Let him come back. I won't ever work for them. Of course, if they want to 'help' me, they can make a hefty donation to the lab, no strings attached. And I'll be happy to use it, on almost exactly the terms they want. I mean, simply continue as before. But I'll remain at my present appointment and salary, too, and not take anything from them for myself. Wonder what they'll do with something like that."

Janice looked at me. I thought because she was proud of my acumen. In fact, I soon realized she was looking doubtful. She said, "Why do they want you to work on wings, anyway, if not directly for them?"

"Because wings are limiting design elements all the time, my dear. Ever since the Wrights warped theirs at Kittyhawk. Ever since G.W. and Reg Mitchell worried about wings in high speed monoplanes and Willi Messerschmitt put thin ones on his Bf 109. Ever since Barnes Wallis proposed swing wings for jets. But, my God, woman, you know all this! I've told you often enough.

"Anyway, it's military stuff, of course. They're getting into the whole question of revising airfoils and wing structures, now that Mach I is commonplace and even Mach 2 or Mach 3 can be had. The lovely streamlined planes we've known are giving place to a new set of creatures. They'll be to the old planes as vultures are to sparrows."

Chapter 46

If I thought I was probably through with Montessori I was wrong. He came knocking on my office door a few days later. This time he was dressed in a snappy blue suit with a crisp white display handkerchief. He wore a patterned red tie and highly polished black shoes. Quite a dresser, I thought, as I sat in casual cotton shirt and pants at my untidy desk and stared at him over my glasses in what I hoped was a fairly unfriendly manner.

"Well, Dr Bruce, I wonder if you've thought again about what we talked about."

"Only a little bit," I said. "I mean, did you really expect my position would change?"

Then I checked myself with a laugh. "Well, there is one thing you might like to consider."

"Yes?" he said hopefully.

"Well, look, if all you truly want is for me to get on with my work a bit more effectively, don't ask me to get rid of graduate students. Instead, pay into my research grant – with no strings attached – enough for me to take on several *more* students and I'll guarantee you we'll make more progress in research on wing design and you won't have to pay me a cent."

But he didn't like my proposal. I said I couldn't see why he didn't like it.

"After all, if what you want is simply that I continue doing what I'd anyway be doing, but with more research money, where's your problem?

"Sorry, I can only tell you what my principals asked me to relay. I have no authority to make alternative offers . . ."

"Maybe I'm just dense, but your people must have guessed I might take this tack. Surely?"

"It's possible they could be persuaded to look at a slightly higher salary . . ."

"I absolutely assure you I'm not making a devious pitch for more money. I just want to remain independent. And how on earth could that matter to you if all you really want is for me to continue as I have been but at a higher level of productivity?"

"We do want that, Professor."

"Then . . .?"

"Look, Professor, I'll just have to check with Defense is all."

"Okay. I'll await their response with interest."

I said to Janice that evening, "The Defense hit man came to see me again."

"What did you say to him?"

"What I said before."

I didn't hear from William Montessori again. I was happy to have seen the last of him, though his just fading away was less satisfactory than if he had told me flatly Defense was not interested in my suggestion. With nothing in writing, no formal approach, there remained a sort of sneaking unease in my mind. The whole matter seemed bizarre, with an astringent aftertaste.

"Suppose they had agreed to my proposal, how do you reckon they'd have proceeded to get me into their clutches a bit more securely?" I asked Janice.

"Dunno," she said. "Perhaps by a very slow escalation of encouragement? If you accept a lot of money from someone, especially if it's not for carefully defined work – even if the money isn't for your own profit but simply for use in your work – well, there's no such thing as no strings attached. There'll be a feeling in you – at some level – of an undefined favour you owe. And someday that undefined favour could just take on a definite shape. I think the pressures would be there."

I nodded. "True."

Chapter 47

The early 1960s were busy years for me. The jet age called for ever-increasing interest in wing design. I remembered G.W.'s frustration at being unable to get the metals he had wanted for wing spars; now there was a wide range of alloys that combined lightness and strength and other virtues. Driven by the general push to obtain the most highly functional supersonic strike aircraft, ultrathin, swept back and variable geometry wings were all being tried out. People came to consult me from all over North America and from overseas. It was flattering, but in a way I felt cold about it. Many people of good intellect were doing as well in wing design as I was. It was really a game of demand and supply.

Seattle was a prime centre for the aircraft industry, and you didn't have to be a seer to realize that world militarism was on a stampede to produce more, ever faster and more deadly planes in this time of The Cold War. That was how I came to realize the true nature of the message inherent in Montessori's propositions as I found myself in a pleasant, fairly interesting, but probably deteriorating situation. My job was secure, I still had enough money for the research I was doing but it was clear that, of the total funds available for wing research, an increasing proportion was going to firms competing for military contracts.

*　*　*

And then at last – surprisingly gradually – I began to think critically about, and take stock of, what I was doing.

I came to see that, for all my "success", I had – really since the war – set aside my central ambition. I had concluded that changes in aircraft design, the developments following jet engines, were inevitable trends in which, if I were to have significant achievements as a professional designer and engineer, I must necessarily participate. After all, wasn't that what G.W. had done?

Well, he hadn't.

G.W. had looked with a scholar's care at what had been achieved in aircraft handling and performance in the three decades preceding his own endeavours, and had then applied the conceptual grasp and soaring imagination of a genius in making not just a breakthrough in some aspect of design, but a complete and wonderful plane. It was the magnitude of his grasp, the greatness of his daring, that had enabled him to do this.

And I marvelled afresh – almost as if I were realising it for the first time – at the size of the contribution to design logic he had made all by himself.

And I confessed to myself that – no matter how much money or help I received – I could never, never do anything that would resemble it.

I don't know if the times were wrong, though that was what I wanted to tell myself – that no one could, all alone, ever again match such an achievement. But what came out of this were questions. If all I could reasonably hope for was to contribute in a limited way to the making of ever bigger, stronger and more refined versions of wings, what was I doing – and why was I doing it at all?

I wrote to tell G.W. about some of my thoughts and how I had arrived at them. I left many things unsaid, knowing it would embarrass him if I mentioned my personal inadequacies or opportunities I had missed. He was an old man now and, though seemingly sound in body and mind, I think he found it hard to answer me. But he did reply and agreed that –

Yes, perhaps the times are wrong now for people like you and me. Jets have certainly changed the whole face of serious advances in aviation and it's true that the military designs and applications are uppermost, and I wanted nothing to do with that side of things. I don't know quite what to tell you, Bob, except that I got out of the plane business when I'd reached a point where I could no longer see just what role I could play that would really engage me. Are you perhaps getting to that point?

You might find it hard to believe this, but in my recent trips to Europe I've become nearly as interested in this Greek stuff as I was in planes. Why? Well, look at it this way: what always interested me about planes was the opportunity to do something that – at the time – others hadn't quite managed. Wanting to be creative, I suppose you could say, though at the time I'd have thought that was a bit too extravagant to claim. But now, when I look at what the Greeks and others like them were doing, or trying to do, and having regard for their lack of modern science, and the mythological notions they had – what you could call the limitations of their "world view" – they came up with stuff that certainly displayed colossal ingenuity. This is the part of Greek history (and the history of other times and peoples, too) that really intrigues me most – how they managed to produce what they did. It seems to me you would find all this of interest, too.

Janice, as we all know, is also very taken with the artifacts of this part of the world, but more from the artistic standpoint. Perhaps you, too, might find something in it to stir your interest. Could you consider something like that? Maybe you and Janice and your boys could join me some time; I know my way fairly well around this part of Europe by now. Think about it.

Give my love to Janice; it will be good to read her book. Tell her I'm off to Sicily for a couple of months in the early autumn. I'll be thinking of you both.

* * *

We continued to enjoy life in Seattle. Philip, at fifteen, was tall and willowy-strong in the West Coast way. He seemed entirely of the place and time with his short blonde hair and tan. His hair was soon to become long in accord with the popular trends of the times. He resembled his mother in looks and personality – handsome, strong-minded, yet sensitive. James, two years younger, was a more tractable person, stocky and dark and not much resembling either Janice or me. The environment was an easy one for kids and I suppose we let them run pretty free. Yes, Seattle was nice – or anyway, the overall ambiance of the place was.

But now, not much over a year since William Montessori had come to call, there was already an expansion occurring in military aircraft production. The U.S. made warplanes. Therefore Seattle made warplanes.

It was easy to recall G.W.'s 1933 predictions of the war that would come to Germany and Europe, and his declining to work on warplane design. Long gone days. Neither G.W. nor I could at that time have been described as approaching pacifism in our attitudes. We were willing enough to fight for our country or community if called on. But now we had a world of imperialisms, hegemonies, false political allegiances, spheres of interest, support of dictators in the name of freedom. Doublethink. Leading to horrors. I wanted none of that.

* * *

When one of Montessori's associates surfaced in 1962 I was ready. Well, half ready. Unlike that bronzed smooth operator, Montessori's successor was a slender, austere, intense man of about forty-five, with carefully swept-back pale blonde hair, a pair of staring grey eyes, and thin hands with fingers that he held inbent, so that they put me in mind of pale hooks. As he entered my office we shook hands. He held onto my hand for a long time, as if hoping to detect some significant pressure or vibration there, and gazed at me while saying, "This is a real privilege, Professor. Your name in the field of aircraft design is becoming one to conjure with."

I decided to treat this piffling flattery with jocularity. I'm a simple soul. But I'm also a suspicious colonial from a small country where acerbic manners sometimes prevail – not about to buy lead nickels from some fulsome American booster.

"Glad to hear you say so," I said. "I'm always trying to tell some of the more stupid bastards in aeronautics that I'm a genius. They don't seem to understand. But I'm sure your Department has excellent intelligence, and if you tell me nice things about myself, I'm only too delighted to believe you."

His smile became a trifle fixed; his laugh a bit tinny. I knew he was put off, if not actually anguished, by the roughness of my approach – and I was not unhappy.

His name was Carstairs – which amused me a bit. I felt anyone called Carstairs should have come from an English Public School. This one, to judge from his accent, was more likely from the Middle West. He had Wilbur as his first name; that, I didn't like, because there was at least one Wilbur – another American – whose memory I had long revered.

Enough. Wilbur Carstairs was not to be thought of as a man: that led to a conceptual grotesquerie. No, he was an *agent* of something. He, of course, claimed it to be Defense. But when he produced his little black pocketbook containing his formal ID, I passed it quickly back. How did you check such stuff, anyway? I should have realized that with Montessori. People like Montessori and Carstairs could, in this world – for all I knew – have been female transvestite members of the CIA. I returned his documents and allowed myself to sigh.

"Well, Mr. Carstairs . . . What is it you think I may be able to do for you?"

He sat up very straight in his linen suit, Panama hat on lap, formal and tight compared to Montessori. His narrow, rodentish face was pale, his gaze concentrated.

"Professor, I'll come right to the point."

I nodded encouragingly.

"Defense is more than just interested in the work you've continued to do – this brilliant work . . ."

"I suppose you saw William Montessori before you came here, Mr. Carstairs." I was pretty sure of his response but, in 'lifemanship' style, I wanted to break the flow of his thinking, introduce a block, however slight, right at the outset.

"I'm afraid I don't know Mr Montessori."

"Oh, you surely must. He came from Defense a year or so ago. To my home one Saturday afternoon. My wife gave him coffee. You'll be certain to know, anyway, that we talked, and of my responses to his proposals. I mean, my answers at that time might still serve for any questions you'd want to put now. Even forestall them. Certainly my basic position remains unchanged."

"Professor Bruce!" There was a hint of asperity in his tone. "I really know next to nothing about Mr. Montessori or his mission. I just want to tell you about what my Department might want to negotiate with you. Whatever Montessori said, could we, please, regard this as a wholly new discussion?"

"Fire away," I said, feeling resigned to the nonsense inherent in this approach.

Carstairs laid out a grander, more detailed plan than Montessori's had been. It at least had the merit of not sounding quite so phonily simple. Defense, in Carstairs' telling, was simply enthralled by the future of wings – swept wings, swing wings, thin wings: wings! There was nothing remarkable about that as far as I was concerned. They were already demonstrating their passion for wing design by the kinds and numbers of contracts they had let to the aircraft industry. But now, as Carstairs told it, I was being asked – apparently as a wing Guru of their choice! – to relinquish immediately my university appointment, enter a Defense laboratory near Rochester, and work on military plane design. "Not," as Carstairs put it, "the nuts and bolts stuff, of course. Essentially just a continuation of your basic wing investigations but maybe with a bit more direct relation to military and strategic aircraft."

"You actually mean, not basic investigations at all but applied things – security-sensitive applied things."

"Well," he sounded put out, "some Department scientists publish a lot of basic things . . ."

"Yes," I said. "But what they publish is trivial. The non-trivial gets classified."

He smiled wryly. "Well, there might be compensations. The position they have in mind would put you in charge of a group of thirty – more than half of them with a Ph.D. There'd be a research budget of about ten million dollars a year at the start. Your personal salary would be about $150,000 per year. There'd be a very good house at low rental, or housing loans if you preferred. Limousines, plane fares and ample travel allowances would be . . ."

I held up my hand. "Mr. Carstairs, I could get pretty good money from industry if I chose, plus more freedom than Defense would ever think of giving. And I wouldn't have to move myself and family to some other place – as you'd want. We like it right here."

"The salary might be hiked up a bit . . ."

I laughed. He flushed. "Apologies," I said. "Montessori was apt to say things like that."

"I'm sorry."

"No. Look. I'm not sneering. It's just that I'm not interested, as I explained to Mr Montessori. And, you know, I'm not a U.S. citizen. Nor is my wife."

"As to that, it could be done soon enough. You've been a credit to the community over the past six years, as far as we know."

I laughed. But I felt myself beginning to frown at the impertinence of the remark, of its casually implied knowledge of our private lives.

"Not interested. And that's final. Please tell your Department so. And not to send someone else next year. Now, I'm sorry, but I have to meet . . ."

Carstairs raised his right hand with its pale, hook-like fingers and pushed it gently towards me, palm first, as if to hold back my words.

"Would you mind just telling me why you're so opposed to coming to Defense and – for that matter – why you left industry?"

"OK. When I was a kid I left Sydney to go to England to study and there I met an obsessed amateur aeroplane designer and builder who was also a wonderful pilot. He was making a plane with the help of another fellow. I helped them in a few ways. The plane he made was the greatest single-passenger aircraft ever produced."

"I understand Vector I was a machine of very advanced design for its time."

"Given the knowledge available in the early thirties, plus the extra knowledge Gibbs White himself was able to obtain from his own researches and his own imagination, and the metals available, the engines to be had, that plane was the best for sheer flying the world's seen up to now."

"Perhaps you're understandably just a mite prejudiced in its favour."

"Well, it flew 550 mph in level flight at 10,000 feet, in 1934. No piston engine plane ever reached that speed again, even 25 years later. It came close to breaking the sound barrier in a dive. Ceiling was 55,000 feet. It could climb 5,500 feet per minute. The diameter of the turning circle of the Messerschmitt Bf 109 at 10,000 feet and 300 mph was 750 feet. At the same speed and altitude Vector I could turn in 500 feet. Vector I wasn't a warplane but could easily have been adapted to be. It would have wiped the sky with any fighter of World War II. With its manoeuverability it would even have beaten the early jets, too."

"So why . . . ?"

"Didn't it? All history now, Carstairs. I feel sure it's in your files. Yes, it'll all be there! Anyway, to finish, that time and that plane were my high point. For me, it came when I was a kid. I knew a great man who managed to make a plane that I remember clearly – in his own words, 'something lovely'. I've learned in recent years I can never approach his powers. It was enough, it has to be enough, that I worked with him. What I've done, what I continue to do, is my rather pleasant way of passing my time and earning my living. If I am above average at what I do, it doesn't mean I'll ever cease to know the difference between myself and a great creator." He began to speak but I stopped him.

"Let me just finish. That plane was built. Every part of it was a part of an integrated functioning whole. It was, to use Gibbs White's own term, conceived and built as a *system.* Engineers and others bandy that term around freely these days. He was thirty years ahead of most of them in thinking of it as a deliberate and constant design concept.

"Most important of all, though, more than all his scientific and technical ability, this man made me know that to build planes, if you are good enough at it, can be like writing music. An end in and of itself. Pure. An adventure of mind and spirit."

"All this is tremendously interesting, Professor Bruce." Carstairs looked taken aback by my outpouring. "But, pardon me, why do you nowadays restrict your own work to the study of wings?"

"Because they are *my* pure thing. Since I'm not good enough to be a great 'whole plane' builder, I build wings."

"But you have designed whole planes; acclaimed in England, I thought . . ."

"I assisted Philip Gibbs White in the testing and designing of a few Parker Falcons just before the war. Yes, they were wonderful little aeroplanes and lineal descendants of his Vector I. There may be one or two of them still flying somewhere around here – probably in California. We designed them as good little runabouts for rich businessmen to indulge themselves with. Sturdy, reliable little machines. And very pretty. But nowadays, they're strictly a bit of fun for connoisseurs of vintage aircraft.

"The thing is that, by endlessly refining, and learning by experience, and resisting the market place, and staying in the lab, I've managed to become rather good at wings. I can go a step in Gibbs White's direction. Only he could do it in his red-haired skull. And he could do the whole bloody plane far better than I can do wings, and in a few years. And all by himself. Anyway, by doing wings pretty well, I'm trying to keep faith with the code of progress in aviation design as best I can, the code I learnt from him, not from his words but by his direct example, silently, every day I was with him."

Carstairs had clearly absorbed this. I guessed that, unlike Montessori, he possibly had some direct experience with aeronautics. There was a genuine gleam of interest in his staring grey eyes as I talked, though his craft demanded, I suppose, a careful blandness.

When he finally spoke it was with more than a trace of warmth, "Very interesting, indeed. The files I've read certainly do no justice to all this as you tell it. Absorbing. Truly. However, I have to tell you that Defense, while greatly respecting independent work such as this, and of course your own work, feel it's desirable for the public good that people like yourself, with a special contribution to make, should be increasingly encouraged to work, at least partially, in Defense projects."

"And if they don't choose to?"

"Well, they can't be coerced, of course. This is a democracy. But if we look at the financing that universities like this one receive for their research, of the sort you do, I think we shall soon start to see a new pattern developing. As the years pass there will be less unattached moneys for such studies as yours, except where university departments join with industry in contract studies, contracts they'll have to win from Government."

"And so, Defense will determine whether any researcher is fit to work on a project. And, since they let the contracts, they'll have the say as to what can be published."

"Yes. That's about it. Of course I could be mistaken . . . And it may be quite a few years yet . . ."

"But you have no fears you will be mistaken."

"Not really. Not in the long run." He managed a thin smile.

"Do you think the universities will accept working for these contracts if they must pay such a price in loss of independence?"

"Professor, I once had some training in physics. Wasn't it Max Planck who, in trying to explain why physicists were eventually won over to accepting quantum theory after many years of opposition, said, 'Final acceptance only required the death of the last of its detractors', or something like that?"

I nodded. "Something like that. So we older fellows who might resist you here and there will anyway finally drop off. And time's on your side."

His answering smile became almost as winning as one of G.W.'s, if you can picture a large pale rodent smiling winningly, as, with the passing years, I have found myself increasingly able to do.

*   *   *

I saw Carstairs out. I was as polite as I could be. I said, "Well, thanks for coming, but I'm afraid nothing you could propose or offer along the lines you've outlined are at all attractive to me." He looked dejected, and I realized he was apt to be scolded by someone or other for his failure. I felt almost sorry for him.

Chapter 48

Anyway, I have always been grateful to William Montessori and to Wilbur Carstairs. If not for the jolting effects of their visitations I would probably have drifted along for years, growing gradually more disenchanted with what I was doing, but with a diminishing will to decide what to do about it. After meeting them things somehow seemed more urgent and I knew I would be impelled to make some choices.

* * *

I had shown G.W.'s recent letter to Janice, who said, "I've never been to Sicily. That would be marvellous. The Greeks had a huge influence on its history and development and many of the Greece-inspired buildings and art are some of the best to be seen. And Crete, too – my God Robert! – we just have to get there one day; their decorations and murals were some of the greatest things of the whole pre-Hellenic period. And there's the restoration of Knossos by Arthur Evans."

"Right," I said, trying to sound casual, but not feeling it.

* * *

During a long weekend, soon after I'd seen Carstairs, Janice and I drove, with the boys, to camp for a day or two at Flattery Rocks on the ocean – a part of the Olympic National Park. We walked around by the water for hours. The boys were in a playful mood, and usually Janice and I would have joined in with them – in fact she did. But that day, for me, it was right just to sit still and look out towards the dark blue of the Pacific, which didn't make me too popular. But it let me focus on what had been unresolved. Not very profound stuff, but needing to be examined for all that.

And I thought back over the years, and of G.W. And what it all added up to.

* * *

The thing was that it added up to very little. Historically speaking, all I could see was the landscape as before. That first great mocking peak of G.W.'s genius, now snow-covered, but still afire with the sunlight. And, between me and it, the unbudgeable fact of a lifetime of the little hills of minor professional successes.

And a lot of things drifted past. Had it been the particular historical and psychological milieu of the times that had aided G.W.'s efforts? Probably not. More likely, as I had already realized, the times had now gone when a single person – even one of genius – could still manage so much.

If one thing had favoured G.W. as a plane-maker, it was his precise identification of the correct time to exert his creative efforts. Somehow he had been able to understand that the work must be done and brought to success just at the point in aviation development when the theory and practice of aerodynamics most closely coincided with his maximum efforts to conceive, plan and build the mightiest aeroplane of the pre-jet era.

It had been my fate to be obsessed with this same type of aviation design opportunity, but in my case many years before it might have been possible for me to demonstrate whatever would have been the best I could achieve. So it all came down to this: I had seen and worked with a person of transcendent abilities at one of those odd historical moments when he had been able to give them the fullest public demonstration. For even a G.W. could not as readily have shone alone in the aviation world that had followed the one he had triumphed in.

I simply had to feel satisfied for having had an adventurous, action-filled life in which I had managed some respectable work in aviation that corresponded with my ability and the times in which I was exercising it, but also, at last, that it was essentially self-defeating – Sisyphean – to go on looking for opportunities and successes of anything like the kind G.W. had.

But then I said to myself, suppose I had been in G.W.'s shoes at the time of his greatest work; could I possibly have achieved anything like what he did – even if I had the greatest imaginable will to do it? And I answered myself at once (indeed I think I even said it aloud): "Don't be more of an idiot than you need to be!"

So now I had finally admitted that no matter how propitious the times might have been, I was deceiving myself to entertain any notion that I could ever have pulled off anything remotely comparable to what he did. And I now knew that my time in aviation had expired.

$$* \quad * \quad *$$

I thought it too abrupt to inform Janice of my feelings and decision all at once, but over a few weeks let out a succession of hints before telling her I was going to take an early retirement, and why.

She was surprised, but not as much as I had anticipated. "Well," she said at last, "I suppose it's safe now to confess it won't destroy me. I've watched you struggle for years, and though I've always known you're very clever and – my God! – determined, I long ago gave up thinking it was realistic for you to be trying somehow to emulate G.W.."

She put her arms around me. "But now, darling," and she gave a little laugh, "what on earth will you do?"

I looked at her for what seemed a long time.

"Yes," I said, "on earth. That's about it. How would it be if we start by taking the kids out of school for a year and joining G.W. in Sicily in the autumn?"

END

ABOUT THE AUTHOR

Alan Weatherley, born and educated in Sydney, Australia, has received awards in Australia and the USA for research and writings in freshwater biology. During a teaching career of thirty-five years he lectured in physiology, evolution, vertebrate biology and ecology. He was Reader in Zoology at the Australian National University, Professor of Fisheries Biology at the University of Tromsö, and is now Professor Emeritus, University of Toronto. Since retirement, he has turned to painting, and writing fiction. His novel *The World That Is* came out in 2002. He and his wife, Robena, are active conservationists. They live in New Brunswick.